STOLEN CHILD

COASTAL FURY BOOK 13

MATT LINCOLN

PROLOGUE

It had been only three days after my gaggle of fans' last trip to my bar to hear one of my stories from my MBLIS career when Mike, the bar's former owner, walked in to pay me a visit.

"Fancy seeing you around here," I grinned at him as he made his way over to where I was wiping down a booth and slid into a seat. "I thought I bought this place off you."

"And look what a dump you've turned it into!" he cried, spreading his arms wide to indicate the whole of the bar, which was stocked full of old nautical memorabilia. "Tacky, if you ask me."

"I didn't," I quipped back as I slung the bar rag over my shoulder, though I knew that my old friend was just ribbing me. "Besides, it's way less tacky than the way it looked when you ran the place."

This was, by all accounts except Mike's own, very true. Back then, my bar was known as "Mike's Tropical Tango Hut," and he'd decked it out in all manner of Hawaiian tiki gear. I'd never liked it, though my MBLIS partner Holm and I had still spent more than a little time there because Mike himself was such good company. A former federal officer himself, Mike always knew what to say to us after a long workday or a particularly tough case.

"C'mon, you wouldn't have spent so much time here if you didn't like it," Mike protested, flashing me a grin.

"Oh no, that couldn't have had anything to do with the company," I laughed, clapping him on the shoulder approvingly. "It had to be all those damned coconuts. That was the real draw."

Mike rolled his eyes, but I could tell he was pleased with the compliment. Even long after my law enforcement career ended, I still loved catching up with the older man. Especially on a slow day like this.

I surveyed the rest of the bar to make sure that no one needed me anywhere else. Just one of my bar girls, Rhoda, was in that day, but it was no matter. I didn't need anyone else. It was a slow, lazy weekday late in the afternoon. There were only two customers in the place, and there had only been a small handful all day long. If the previous night was any indication, the pace would only creep up a bit after five. Maybe a few of the guys from the nearby retirement home would stop in to give us some of their business, or a couple of locals needing a drink after a long day. Nothing more.

But it was alright. Business had been booming on the weekends as of late, more than making up for the slow roll of customers the rest of the week. I had more than enough time to catch up with Mike.

"You good?" I called to Rhoda, who was washing up some dusty old glassware behind the bar since there was nothing else to do after attending to the customers we did have.

"All good here, boss," she called back with a chuckle, surveying the near-empty bar and shaking her head at the notion that I had to even ask the question.

"Alright, then, how have you been?" I asked, sliding into the booth across from Mike.

"Oh, you know, I sit around and read or watch TV, and then I might go to the beach," the old bar owner admitted with a shrug and a half-grin. "Same old, same old."

"Sounds like a dream come true," I laughed, though I knew how many in law enforcement resented the idea of retirement for this very reason, myself included at one point. Mike didn't look too upset about it, though. He'd always planned to retire.

"Sometimes, sometimes," he said with a nod as Rhoda bustled over to us bearing drinks.

"Thanks," I said, nodding gratefully to her. "You didn't have to do that."

"Oh, I have a feeling you're going to be here for a while," she said, nodding in the direction of the door.

I realized that the kids from the local base were making their way inside, and Mike gave me a bemused look as Rhoda ran back to the bar to grab the usual round of drinks for my fans.

"Those kids still hanging on your every word?" he asked with a chuckle.

"Hey, the whole thing was your idea," I reminded him. "Don't go getting jealous on me after all this time."

"Jealous? Me?" Mike asked, pointing at himself with mock incredulity. "Never. If I were telling my old stories from my glory days, they wouldn't be giving you a single second of their time."

"I don't know about that," I said dryly, though I didn't doubt that Mike had a few tales to tell of his own.

"Back so soon?" I asked as the kids meandered over to us. "It was only last weekend that you were here last."

"Yeah, well, someone couldn't wait to hear the next part of your story," Jeff said, glancing over at Charlie and rolling his eyes.

"Hey, you were the one who suggested we come in

the first place," the shorter man protested, punching his friend playfully in the shoulder.

"Come on, kids, sit down," Mike said, gesturing at the booth beside him, and they all piled in as the two of us scooted down to make room for them.

Rhoda appeared not long after with drinks for everyone. All the bar girls knew everyone in this group's order by now.

"Alright, then, where'd you leave off?" Mike asked as he sipped his own drink once everyone was settled.

"I told them the story about Tessa and my trip to Virginia," I explained.

"Ah," he breathed, nodding knowingly. "That's a good one. It really showcases your ability to get into trouble wherever you go, even on vacation."

"Well, in my defense, it was never exactly supposed to be a vacation," I qualified. "Not a typical one, anyway. But your point is taken."

"Don't I remember one of your stories being about some shore leave you and Holm took turning into a James Bond film, basically?" Mac, the lone woman in the group, asked dryly.

"A good point," Mike said approvingly, grinning and arching an eyebrow at me. "What do you say to that, Marston?"

"That one I have to give you," I admitted, cracking a smile myself now. "No qualifiers there."

"Remind me, Virginia's the one where you ran into

that creepy old house to save the kid, right?" Mike asked, narrowing his eyes as if trying to remember.

"Yeah, that's the one," I confirmed with a nod. "That was a pretty wild night. It just never seemed to end."

"You could say that again," the third guy, Ty, murmured with an excited lean across the table. "It was crazy! You found all that old stuff from the *Dragon's Rogue*, including Grendel's journal!"

"That's right," I laughed. "It took a damned long time to comb through that stuff. Then I had to go straight to New Orleans to re-interview those hotel owners who I thought might know our suspects."

The whole affair in Virginia had originally been about getting the journal of the pirate who was last in possession of the ship that once belonged to an ancestor of mine into my possession, in the hopes that its contents would lead me to the *Dragon's Rogue*'s current location.

Things had all gone astray, however, when my photojournalist companion and I realized that the director of the museum that we thought had the journal had been intimidated into silence, and then several goons showed up to take us out. In the end, it turned out that the Hollands, a couple known by MBLIS and the FBI for their drug crime ring, who'd also doubled as nautical enthusiasts, not unlike myself, were behind the attacks.

"You didn't learn anything in New Orleans, though, right?" Mac asked. "That's what you said last time."

"Well, not quite," I said, narrowing my eyes at this. "They didn't know anything directly about our case, but they were able to give us the names of some people who might."

"And?" Ty asked with characteristic eagerness. "Did any of those leads pan out?"

"All will be revealed in time," I said, peering at him over my glass as I took a sip of my drink. I knew this frustrated him, but I found it endearing. Mac seemed to just find it funny.

"That kid was okay, though, right?" Mike asked, pointing at me thoughtfully. "I don't remember you saying anything about a dead kid, anyway. It seems like something you would've mentioned."

"Yeah," I said with a low laugh. "I probably would've. And yeah, he was fine. Shaken, but fine. Stupid kid, running out in the middle of the night trying to catch the bad guys himself without permission."

"Sounds to me like he'd make a good agent one day," Mike argued. "Sounds exactly like you most days of your career."

"Har, har," I said sarcastically, though I had to admit he kind of had a point. "The main difference being that I'm a trained operative ignoring the need for the all-clear from my superiors every once in a while, and this was a little kid disobeying his parents. But he had guts. I'll give him that."

The poor boy had overheard Tessa and me talking to his parents about the strange occurrences at the house next door, which was occupied by the Hollands' lackeys at the time. All he had to hear was the word "pirate" for him to think it was all a game. He was held hostage briefly, but we got him out safe and sound in the end.

"So?" Charlie asked eagerly, looking slightly annoyed that we had to tread through all this old territory just because Mike hadn't heard the story in a while. "What happened next?"

"You all have a one-track mind," I laughed, taking another sip from my drink slowly, just to watch them squirm a little. Even Mac leaned a little closer to the edge of her seat between Mike and Ty. Then, glancing back over at Mike, "You see what you've gotten me into? These kids are in here all the time, it seems, making me tell them stories and drinking my alcohol."

"Face it, Marston, you love this," Mike laughed, and I couldn't deny that, either.

"Yeah, you love us," Jeff teased gently. "Why else would you keep spending all this time with us?"

"Oh, you know me," I joked as Rhoda came to deposit some nuts on our table. "Anything to keep my nose off the old grindstone."

"Anyone who knows you knows that that can't be

further from the truth," the bar girl said, giving me a stern look.

"High praise from one of your employees," Mike pointed out, raising his eyebrows approvingly at her.

It was. I always thought that the bar girls probably liked me well enough, given that there wasn't much turnover for such a transient type of job. I almost never had to hire new help. But it was still nice to get the praise to my face.

"Thanks, Rhoda," I told her, nodding to the nuts but thinking of more than just that.

"Well, go on," she said, hovering near our booth and placing her hands on her hips. "What happened next?"

I laughed again. I'd noticed the bar girls listening in on my stories more and more lately, and they all seemed to know the sequence of events just as well as these kids, even though they all rarely worked on the same night. They must've been filling each other in on my exploits, I realized.

"Alright, alright," I chuckled, setting aside my drink for the time being and glancing up at the small metal ornament hanging on the wall next to an old nautical telescope. "Actually, this case has something to do with a kid, too, though it was even more harrowing if that's possible..."

1

NINA

AGENT NINA GOSSE of the FBI had been working on the Holland case before they pulled her on a "run-of-the-mill" criminal case. When she'd gotten the call from her supervisor, she hadn't exactly been pleased. The Holland case was the biggest one she'd seen in a while, even if MBLIS was the agency on record. Besides, she had been on one of the related cases down in New Orleans before they knew that the Hollands had anything to do with the new drug circulating down there. MBLIS agents had even been on that case, too, which was how she'd met Ethan Marston and Robbie Holm, both of whom had since become friends.

All that went to say that she was more than just grumpy about being sent off to solve some petty crime, or so she thought. Then she'd learned that there was a missing kid involved, and she set all that aside. Cases like this were no laughing matter, and they were more important than some pissing contest about who got the most interesting work or high profile case files.

So this was how she found herself in the parking lot of a dingy old mall in a small colonial town along the coast of North Carolina. The place had its charm, she decided. Well, not the mall, but the surrounding town, at least. It had interesting architecture and a lot of history. *Ethan Marston would love it*, she thought. She found her thoughts drifting to him more than once in a while since their first meeting a few months back.

Nina sighed and headed into the mall. She didn't expect to find much there, but it was where the boy was last seen, so it was a place to start. They were working on a time clock since it had been nearly five hours since his disappearance, and the kid's mom was a government employee at some agency. Transportation, maybe? Nina didn't remember. They were on vacation, staying in some cottage down here before it happened. The police barely existed in a small place like this, too. Between that, the family's higher profile, and the fact that the kid was from across state lines, the FBI had been called.

They didn't know much yet. Just that two men had been seen on security footage stealing the kid away after he wandered outside a shop while his parents were buying lunch at the food court. They'd only turned their backs for a moment, but sometimes that was all it took—still a healthy dose of bad luck.

Nina hadn't met the parents yet. She was told they were hysterical, understandably, and freaking out about what was going to happen to their kid. She reviewed the security footage and opted to let the therapist who the FBI sent with her deal with the family. The people side of the job wasn't exactly Nina's strong suit, after all. Ethan was better at that kind of thing.

Nina groaned as she stepped over some police tape to walk through the large front doors into the food court area of the mall. The food court itself was empty but for several police officers, forensic techs, and a couple of mall security guards. But Nina was more concerned with the area beyond the security guards, a hallway lined by shops.

There was a throng of people there, way more than she would expect for a town with a population of five thousand. Most of them must be tourists, she realized based on their attire, there with the intent of enjoying the beach, some small-town charm, and the warming late spring weather.

But they weren't on the beach now. In Nina's experience, people responded to situations like this in one of two ways. The first was to retreat and isolate themselves, not wanting anything similar to happen to them or their families. The other was to flock to the scene out of some sick but altogether human sense of voyeurism, intent on finding some spectacle in addition to the sunny weather outside.

Clearly, the second impulse had won out for a fair portion of the town's visitors, and no doubt a few locals, too. She did notice that there were no families in what she could only call the audience, though. Those tourists would be hiding away with their children.

"At least some of them are smart," Nina muttered under her breath to herself as she shook her head, stood up a little straighter, and reluctantly made her way toward the crowd and the police officers, who stood near the security guards and seemed unsure what to do with the situation at hand.

"Hey, who are you?" one of the officers, a thirty-ish guy with abnormally large ears, asked, eyeing her with wariness. "No one's supposed to come in that way."

"Sorry," Nina grumbled, pulling out her FBI badge and flashing it at him. "Agent Gosse with the FBI. I was told you knew I was coming."

"Oh, right," the man said, the ears sticking out of either side of his head turning beet red in an instant. "Sorry."

"No worries," she said coolly. "What's going on here?"

She eyed the crowd with some distaste. A teenager tried to hop the caution tape between the food court and the rest of the mall, but it didn't exactly work. One of the security guards tackled him and carted him away in cheap mall handcuffs.

"Look, we tried to shut the place down, but there are just so many of them..." another officer, a balding redheaded man, explained with a pained expression on his face.

Great. These people weren't all that competent, after all. Nina was willing to bet that the biggest crime they'd had here in the past year was some kids smoking pot. Still, there was a silver lining.

"It's alright," she assured him. "Might be for the best. Sometimes these guys come back to scope out the crime scene after the fact."

"I've heard that," the redheaded man said, scratching the back of his head. "Doesn't make much sense to me, though. They have to know that we'll be here."

Nina bit her lip. Yeah, if they didn't know even the basics of criminal psychology here, she was pretty sure that she was in for a ride if she didn't find this kid soon.

"Yeah, but it's not supposed to be logical," she said, letting out a small huff of frustration that she quickly tried to cover up as the other guy's ears grew even redder. "They can't resist. They're either proud of getting away with it—or so they think, anyway—or they're so nervous about getting caught that they go to the crime scene to try to get some sense of control over the police investigation. Same reason kidnappers show up at vigils or even volunteer to help look for the kid they took."

The police officers both stared blankly back at her, looking like a pair of deer caught in the headlights.

"Look, what are your names?" she asked them with a small sigh.

"Uh, I'm Officer Barrow, and this is Officer Kurt," the big-eared man said, gesturing at his colleague. His ears were getting slightly less tomato colored, at least.

"Have you noticed anyone suspicious or out of the ordinary? Or fitting the description from the security tapes?" Nina asked them.

Even if these men weren't used to big cases like this, they were still police officers, and they knew their own community better than anyone. They could still have some valuable input into the community.

"There've been a few weirdos," the redhead, Kurt, said, exchanging a wary look with his partner.

"Weirdos?" Nina repeated, furrowing her brow and taking a step closer to him in anticipation of his answer. "How so?"

"Guys with cameras and stuff from out of town," he clarified, looking uneasily back at the crowd. "I think they're some kind of true crime enthusiasts or something. Is that a thing?"

Nina sighed again. More good news.

"Yeah, it can be," she said, and she wasn't exactly surprised to hear about this. "High-profile cases like this, especially kidnappings and serial murders, can attract a weird crowd. Where did they come from? What were they doing? They got here pretty fast."

It had only been about five or six hours since the kidnapping took place. Nina was mildly surprised that the crazies were already flowing in, though she wasn't shocked. At this point in her career, she'd seen pretty much everything, though she found that whenever she thought that, something ended up surprising her after all—like a weird new zombie drug straight out of a horror film in New Orleans.

"There were a couple of guys from Durham," Barrow said. "They were taking pictures of the crime scene and stuff. Said they had some blog. I told them to beat it, but I wrote down the name of the blog. Here."

Barrow pulled a small notebook out of a pocket on his shirt, flipped to a page about halfway through, and tore it out to hand to Nina. The paper's edges were worn, crinkled, and frayed from being carried around for so long. The notebook itself looked water-damaged. But Nina could read the words, so it did the trick. It was probably nothing but worth passing on to someone to look into if she didn't have the time herself.

"Then there was this other guy. He was pretty old," Kurt continued for his partner. "He was a real weirdo.

He had a whole list of all the stranger kidnappings in the state of North Carolina. Said this was the first one we'd ever seen in Edenton."

"Are we certain that it's a stranger situation?" Nina asked, as her boss hadn't told her anything definitive, just that the parents didn't seem to know the men involved. "Nine times out of ten in these cases, it's someone the child knows or people hired by someone the child knows."

"They seemed like a pretty tight-knit family to me," Barrow said, shaking his head. "I doubt anything like that was going on. Both parents had to take drugs to calm down."

"Interesting," Nina said. That really was unusual, that a stranger would just take a child in plain sight like that. So rare that it was almost a statistical anomaly, which was part of why such crimes gained a cult following of sorts.

"Isn't his mom some kind of government person?" Kurt asked. "Could it be some retaliation for something she did?"

"She works for some random agency," Nina said, shaking her head dismissively. "It's not like she's the mayor or governor or something. She's just a desk worker. I doubt she gets many enemies that way. Besides, I'd expect something a little more sophisticated in a case like that."

"That makes sense," Kurt said, looking a little

defeated.

"What about the guys from the security footage?" she asked. "Have you seen anyone fitting either of their descriptions?"

The two officers exchanged another, almost uncomfortable look.

"We haven't actually been able to look at the footage yet," Barrow admitted, his ears going scarlet again. "We've been pretty tied up here." He gave the crowd behind him a dirty look.

"Okay, but you have their descriptions, right?" Nina asked, an edge returning to her voice. Were these guys serious? No weirdos with Internet blogs were more important than seeing a video of the actual crime taking place.

"Well, yeah, but that was pretty vague," Kurt shrugged. "An average height guy in blue jeans and a t-shirt with brown hair? And another white guy who's just kind of stocky? That could be anybody."

Nina turned her attention back to the crowd with another huff. The officers' usefulness seemed to have passed, though as she surveyed the crowd, she realized that they were right. About a third of the crowd could fit that description.

She, however, had actually seen the security footage. There were dozens of people who fit the vague description that the police officers had provided. There were none that she could see who fit the more specific description seared in her mind, though—a man with a thin, hallowed face and a series of acne scars on his right cheek.

She approached the crowd and began to sift through it quickly in her mind. Her training and long career enabled her to do this quickly and efficiently while not alerting anyone to the fact that they were being scrutinized.

Her short stature, gender, and unimposing persona enabled her to do this effectively. Though she had a sharp personality and a gruff demeanor, people had a tendency to underestimate her until they got to know her. To this crowd, she was only one random, almost invisible person in a sea of police officers, security guards, and forensics techs.

She wasn't able to see everyone in the crowd, given its size, but she was able to sift through the first several rows. No one fit the description of the man in the video.

The security footage also showed that there was another man involved in the abduction of the boy. But he was just a shadowed figure in the distance, the only part of him really visible a gloved hand carrying a gun. A break between his glove and his sleeve showed that he was white. Beyond this, all they knew was that he was of medium height and very muscular.

This was unusual, Nina knew from her career and from what the psychologist had told her on the way there. Normally, these stranger kidnappings were lone-wolf operations. A lone perpetrator, almost always male, would take a child for the purpose of abuse. But two men? Two men indicated that this was some kind of wider operation.

That wasn't necessarily true, Nina knew. It was possible that two lone wolves could pair up to help each other out and make the abduction easier. But it was her fear and her suspicion. The psychologist and her supervisors at the FBI shared her concerns. However, she would expect that if this were part of a wider operation, it would've been more sophisticated. These men were caught on camera, and the one whose face could be seen appeared almost panicked at the moment, as if this wasn't planned. That was more indicative of a lone-wolf situation.

But even if there were two lone wolves, that wouldn't make sense. If they were working together, they had to have planned ahead. The other man was disguised and had a weapon. But the second man wasn't disguised at all.

There were so many contradictions involved that Nina's head was spinning as she tried to sort through it all. It had been spinning for hours, and most especially since she'd viewed the security footage at the police station. None of this made sense. None of it added up. This crime didn't fit any guidebook for how it was supposed to go.

And none of this was good news for that little boy. If the rulebook for working such cases had to be thrown out, how was she supposed to find this kid? Nina worried that even she might be out of her depth on this one as she continued to survey the crowd.

She was so lost in thought that she barely registered a woman yelling at her from just behind the caution tape.

"What?" she asked, shaking her head at the woman, who was leaning forward and hollering something at her.

"Are you a reporter?" the woman, who looked to be middle-aged and was wearing a t-shirt and jeans, asked her, speaking the words slowly and annunciating carefully so that Nina would hear this time.

Nina glanced down at her own attire. A t-shirt and jeans of her own, a uniform that she'd become accustomed to wearing during her months undercover in New Orleans, and had opted to continue wearing when on assignment since it allowed her to blend into the environment. Very few people assumed she was a law enforcement officer when she was dressed like this, let alone an FBI agent. Clearly, it worked, though she doubted she looked like a reporter either. Though since she was behind the caution tape, everyone in the crowd must assume she wasn't an average citizen.

"No. No, I'm not," she said, approaching the

woman. "I'm here looking into what happened here today. Can you tell me why you're here?"

"I'm just wondering what happened to that poor little boy," the woman said, her face falling as if she was disappointed that Nina wasn't who she thought she was. "I was hoping that someone was here to get the word out."

Nina glanced out across the still growing crowd.

"I'm pretty sure that's already been accomplished," she pointed out. "How did you hear about it?"

"Oh, I've been here since this morning," the woman said, jumping at the opportunity to tell her story. "I was in the shoe store when it happened. I just haven't been able to bear to leave. I want to help."

"Shoe store?" Nina repeated, craning her neck to try to see over the crowd. "What shoe store?"

"Oh, over here," the woman said, motioning for Nina to follow her.

Nina ducked under the caution tape and elbowed through the crowd alongside the woman. This didn't prove all that difficult since most people were trying to press forward instead of back. They seemed surprised that the two women were turning around and parted for them, jumping at the opportunity to take over the spaces at the front that they left open behind them.

"I'm Agent Nina Gosse," Nina said, holding out her hand to the woman when they were about halfway through the crowd. "And you are?"

"Matilda Smith," the woman said, scrunching her face at Nina and gazing at her with some skepticism. "Agent? What kind of agent?"

"FBI," she said, and the woman continued to stare blankly back at her. "I like to blend in."

"Right," she said, looking a little shaken by this. "Come on, this way."

She motioned again for Nina to follow her off to the side. The crowd was more spread out now since most of the people were packed toward the front near the food court.

Smith led Nina toward a shoe store, which was boarded up and dark inside. The doors were closed and appeared to be locked.

"Is this where it happened?" Nina asked, remembering that the boy had wandered in front of a store before he was taken, though which shop it was hadn't been clearly visible in the security footage.

"A little further down there, by that tree," Smith said, pointing behind them at a potted plant that Nina wouldn't quite consider a tree several paces away from the store's entrance. She recognized the side of the pot from the background of the security footage.

She walked briskly over to the plant and began to sift through the mulch inside with her hands. Sometimes, perps left things in places like this or in garbage cans that they needed to discard quickly. She knew that the police had already looked through the trash, but she wasn't sure if they'd thought of the tree.

"What... what are you doing?" the woman stammered, giving Nina another skeptical look.

"Looking to see if they left anything here," she explained gruffly, digging her arms as deep into the pot as she could.

She came up empty-handed, however, except for some dirt. She wasn't surprised, considering that the security footage didn't show the perps dropping anything in there, but it was worth a shot considering that the whole plant hadn't made it into the video's frame.

"Okay, then," Smith said slowly, and Nina was pretty sure the woman thought that she was just some crackpot who managed to make it past the caution tape and the security guards.

She pulled out her FBI badge and showed it to her.

"Proof, just in case you think I'm crazy," Nina said, flashing her a lopsided grin.

Smith blinked at the badge and then nodded, seeming to accept this evidence, though she still seemed a bit put off by Nina, who was clearly not what she would've expected. Nina kind of liked this. The way she had a tendency to surprise people was one of her greatest assets.

"Alright, then," she said, shaking her head and giving a shaky laugh.

"So you were in the store when it happened?" Nina asked, urging her to tell her side of the story.

"Oh, yeah, I was checking out," she said, her eyes lighting up at the opportunity to talk about it. "My German Shepherd ate my gym shoes. I needed new ones. He's a good dog, really. He just got left alone for too long that day. My fault, really."

"I'm sure," Nina said dryly, motioning for the woman to move it along.

"Right, so I was buying the shoes, and then I heard someone scream behind me," she continued. "I thought it was a little girl at first, and then I saw that it was a boy, a little younger than I thought. I'd say he was six or seven. That guy in the brown jacket was carrying him."

Nina perked up at this. The more visible man in the video had been wearing a brown jacket.

"You saw him?" she asked, a little sharper than she'd intended. "What did you see? What did he look like?"

"Oh, I didn't get a great look at him," the woman said, scrunching up her face as if trying to remember. "Just that he was white and pretty thin. His cheek looked kind of weird, the one that was facing me."

Nina had to admit, she was impressed. She'd thought this woman an attention-seeker, and those types tended not to give the most reliable eyewitness testimony, instead inflating their own memory and giving wildly detailed descriptions that almost always turned out to be inaccurate.

Matilda Smith, however, had minimized her own reliability as a witness while providing a sufficiently detailed description of the perpetrator that matched what Nina herself had seen on the security tape.

"Thank you," she said honestly, nodding to the woman. "That fits other descriptions. Did you get a look at the other one at all?"

"The other one?" Smith repeated, shaking her head in confusion as her eyes widened. "There was another one?"

"Why don't you tell me what else you remember seeing?" Nina asked in response, not wanting to give the woman any leading answers that could influence her memory or statement at all.

"Well, there were a bunch of people walking around," she said slowly with a nod. "No one intervened. They probably thought the man was the kid's father. That's what I thought at first. I didn't even think that it could be... well, what it turned out to be."

The woman looked uncomfortable naming the crime. This wasn't uncommon in situations such as these. The idea of what could be happening to the child was unmentionable, unspeakable. Nina cringed internally at the thought herself.

"Anything else? When did you realize what had happened?" Nina asked.

"Well, someone mentioned that they saw the man with a gun," Smith said. "Though she said he was wearing black. I thought I might be misremembering, but now I'm wondering if that was the second guy you mentioned."

"Who was this other witness?" Nina asked, pulling a notebook and pencil out of her pocket.

"Oh, I don't know, some lady who worked at the store," the woman said dismissively. "I didn't catch her name. I saw her talking to the police earlier, right before I did."

"Alright, that's good," Nina said, scribbling this down in her notebook. She'd get a full report on the witnesses from the police later on.

"I realized what was going on when the parents showed up," Smith said, her face falling again at the memory. "They weren't that far away. Just a few feet, ordering food. They didn't even realize the boy wasn't next to them anymore. When they realized what had happened, they were both screaming and running around. Then a bunch of us helped them, and the security guards looked for him, but, well, you know..."

"You didn't see the man in the brown jacket again?" Nina asked.

"No," Smith sighed, shaking her head. "I looked everywhere, but he was gone."

"Did you see which direction he went?" Nina

asked, knowing the answer already from the footage but wanting to hear the woman's account for herself.

"Oh, that way," Smith said, pointing to their left, away from the food court. "They would've been stupid to take him past the parents. They must've been watching the family. Targeted him. That was my impression, anyway."

"There's another entrance down this way?" Nina asked, pointing in that direction as well as a chill ran up and down her spine at the thought of these disgusting men creeping on the family for who knew how long. "How far away is it?"

"That's the thing, it's pretty far," the woman said, shaking her head again. "You'd think someone would've stopped them. Do you have footage of them? You must. There are so many shops between here and the other entrance."

"You let us handle that," Nina said, forcing a smile.

They didn't have more footage, though. That was another strange thing. If the entrance was so far away, there should've been more. Smith was right about that. So either these men had a more coordinated plan than Nina had thought and had managed to stop the other security footage, or they had exited the mall somewhere else, taking cover somewhere until the ruckus died down and then slipping out of the food court entrance, or leaving some other way that Nina hadn't thought of yet.

"Hey, look!" Smith hissed in Nina's ear, pointing back toward the crowd.

Nina followed her gaze and immediately saw exactly what Smith did. It was the man from the video, the one in the brown jacket. He'd discarded the jacket, just wearing a plain flannel shirt now, but it was him, alright. The sunken face and pockmarked cheek proved as much.

The man was standing off from the crowd, his hands in the pockets of his jeans, and he seemed to be scrutinizing the crime scene with his eyes narrowed and his expression piercing.

It was exactly as Nina had predicted. He had returned to the scene of the crime, unable to stop himself from checking on the cleanness of his work. He was probably blissfully unaware that he had even been caught on tape in the first place.

"Go," Nina said sharply to Smith. "Run back to the food court. Tell the police what you saw and where. Tell them they need to get all these people out of here now. This place needs to be completely shut down and should've been hours ago."

The woman hesitated, and for a moment, Nina was afraid that she was going to freak out and give away that they had seen the man. But she didn't in the end, returning to herself and running off to go alert the officers and security guards to the presence of the man.

When Smith was safely out of the way, Nina

silently drew her gun and crept toward the man, who had moved a few feet closer to the crowd, each moment seeming to get braver in his curiosity about what was going on behind the caution tape.

As Nina drew closer, for a moment, she thought that he wasn't going to notice her. But at the last moment, he did, and he pulled his own gun out from under his shirt.

"Dammit," Nina cursed under her breath. Then, holding up her own gun and calling out to him, "FBI! Stop now, or I'll shoot."

His eyes widened at her words, and she saw panic there. He had expected the police, even from out of town, but not this. Not the FBI. Nina had seen that look countless times over the years. It usually was followed by a surrender. But every once in a while, as the panic set in, it elicited a fight-or-flight response that truly defied reason.

Unfortunately, this was one of those times, and the man seemed to choose both options at once, running as fast as he could in the opposite direction, away from the food court, and wildly shooting his firearm at Nina at the same time.

As the shot rang out, the crowd was alerted to the man's presence, and pandemonium ensued as everyone screamed and fled, looking around quickly to try to see what was happening.

Nina managed to duck down and get out of the way

of the errant shot, and the bullet ran right into the pot containing the plant she had looked at earlier, causing a series of crashing noises as it broke apart and the small tree fell to the ground with a clunk.

People were all over the place then, obstructing Nina's vision. She looked around wildly, trying to find the man again in the crowd as the shot continued to ring in her ears, and the screams and raging of the panicked people around her vied for her attention.

The crowd's members were running in all directions, not knowing where exactly the shot had come from and who had created it.

Nina leapt into action, pushing around the people frantically trying to find an exit and desperately searching for the pockmarked man in the flannel shirt.

Finally, she caught another glimpse of him, disappearing around a corner not far from the shoe store.

"Move it, move it!" she called to them all.

She ran and screamed out, telling people to get out of the way, but it didn't register, and a large man crashed into her, not having seen her in his pursuit of an exit.

Nina was disoriented from the fall, and her shoulder hurt, so much so that she barely registered the man who had run into her rushing apologies and then standing back with his arms in the air when he saw her gun.

She didn't respond to him, merely getting to her

feet the best she could under the circumstances and hobbling after the escaped perp. She looked everywhere for him around the corner, and the police helped her search the entire mall later on.

But it was no use. He was gone.

2

ETHAN

The MBLIS office was crawling with FBI agents when I arrived one morning several weeks after my return from New Orleans, where I had interviewed the hotel owners who had accepted the bribe of a long lost pirate ship found by the Hollands in return for allowing drug kingpins to take refuge in their properties.

This wasn't surprising, however. It would've been surprising if they weren't there, actually. We'd grown accustomed to sharing our offices in recent weeks, though we still weren't exactly happy about it or used to it.

I elbowed past several agents, grunting good mornings to them that were largely not reciprocated, to make my way over to my desk right next to my partner's, Agent Robbie Holm. Holm was already there, sipping from a to-go cup of coffee and glaring at the other agency's operatives with something resembling disdain.

"Morning," I grunted to him, straightening my jacket from all the jostling amongst the many occupants of what I now considered a far too small office.

"Morning," Holm grunted back, seeming to be in no better mood than I was.

"What's got you all sour?" I asked him as I took my seat and gratefully accepted a second to-go cup of coffee from him that he must've picked up for me on his way there.

"What do you think?" he asked, rolling his eyes in the direction of the FBI agents, who had taken over a cluster of desks near the door, though they rarely seemed to sit down, opting instead to congregate in the entryway in the most annoying manner possible.

"What did they do now?" I sighed, unable to contain my annoyance either.

"They exist," Holm spat, and I sighed again.

The close quarters were really starting to get to everyone, and tensions were rising between the agents from each agency. And they hadn't exactly been great, to begin with, with several of the guys making fun of Holm and spilling coffee on him on their first day in Miami. According to Holm, anyway. I had been in Virginia when that happened, but Diane, our boss, had begrudgingly confirmed that his account of events wasn't exaggerated.

"We're supposed to be working together on the biggest case in all of our lifetimes," I reminded him. "It's incumbent upon us to be the bigger people here. We're hosting them, after all."

I was pretty much verbatim quoting Diane here, with all her pep talks to us over the past several weeks, trying to keep our spirits up and our focus on the task at hand. It certainly sounded when she said these things that she was trying to convince herself as much as she was us, and I felt much the same when I parroted her words back to Holm.

"Oh, not you, too," he scoffed. "I bought you coffee."

"Yeah, yeah, I know," I relented with a shrug. "I'm getting fed up myself."

"I just don't get why they couldn't stay in the police station," Holm complained for the umpteenth time. "There was plenty of room there."

"We couldn't keep infringing on the local police's space after that specific case was closed," I reminded him.

"Ugh, why do you have to keep being the voice of reason?" he asked, though he flashed me a grin.

While I had been in Virginia looking for the journal of a pirate who was last known to be in possession of an old ship I'd been searching for most of my life, following my grandfather before me, things had gotten really interesting at MBLIS in Miami.

Holm and Diane had been attacked late at night in the office by a hitman who had been working for the Hollands, who at that point knew that we were on their tail following a case they were involved with in the Florida Keys.

The hitman got away at first, though Holm and Diane turned out fine, and a manhunt ensued involving MBLIS, the FBI, and the local police. But once the man was found, we couldn't exactly keep using the police station as a base of operations.

This brought us to now, with our small office constantly being invaded by agents who oftentimes seemed determined to crack this case without us.

"We'll get to the bottom of this eventually," I assured Holm, though I was beginning to doubt this myself.

We'd been looking for the Hollands for nearly three months now, and things were not going well. We hadn't had many leads since the couple was spotted going through security at the Atlanta airport, or at least not any that panned out.

As far as we knew, the couple could be anywhere in the world by now. We had reports out to every intelligence agency in the world, and they were both on the FBI's Most Wanted list by then. We got a flood of tips every day, which kept us more than busy, but at a certain point, it was easy to give up hope when all of them turned out to be dead ends.

"Anything new from that list of people that New Orleans couple gave you?" Holm asked hopefully.

I sighed yet again. That list had proved... frustrating. I wasn't sure what I had been expecting, but it wasn't constantly being blown off and ghosted by everyone in the community of nautical enthusiasts in which the Hollands immersed themselves.

"Not yet," I grumbled. "None of them lead to anything so far. We'll see, though. I'm still working on it."

So far, none of the people on the list had been interested in talking to me, beyond explaining that they had no idea the Hollands were like this and had even less of an idea of where they could be now and that they themselves had nothing to do with any of the couple's criminal activity.

I bought this in some cases, but not all. Both the Hollands and the hotel owners from New Orleans proved that there was a seedy underbelly to the nautical community about which I had been blissfully ignorant until recently.

The whole thing was weird and kind of exciting if I were honest with myself. I was used to being the only one who cared about any of this stuff. That there were people out there willing to kill to get some of the stuff that I had already found was kind of validating, in a way, not that I condoned such behavior.

That being said, I was just tired at this point. When my photojournalist friend Tessa Bleu and I had found a bunch of artifacts related to the *Dragon's Rogue* at a beaten-down old house in Virginia, we thought we were close to getting to the ship I had been in search of for so long. Even more exciting was the fact that the Hollands were looking for it, too, so now my personal obsession had become professional. I thought that I could kill two birds with one stone and would be chasing leads left and right until I inevitably found Chester and Ashley Holland and the old pirate ship in one fell swoop.

I should've known that it wouldn't be like that. I knew better after my long career with MBLIS and my long career with the Navy SEALS before that. In reality, cases of this scale required a lot of slogging through paperwork and chasing down what looked to be exciting leads only to meet dead ends left and right and every other direction you could think of.

In a way, I'd been lucky to have so many cleanly wrapped up cases in recent times. I was overdue for something like this. Still, I was starting to get frustrated, and I wasn't the only one.

"Morning, boys," Diane said dryly as she emerged from her office and made her way over to our desks, talking low enough that the FBI agents didn't notice she was there yet.

I flinched. I'd been so deep in thought that I'd barely registered Diane's presence until she was right next to me.

"Scared, Marston?" Holm snickered at me.

"Har, har," I said again, rolling my eyes.

I glanced up at Diane. She had bags under her eyes, much like the ones I saw reflected back at me whenever I looked in a mirror. Holm wasn't looking much better, either, and the FBI agents had already been like that when they arrived. Diane looked worse than usual, though, aging her up a few years. This wasn't exactly a problem, considering she already looked ten to fifteen years younger than she actually was.

"What time did you get home last night?" Holm asked her, clearly noticing the same thing I had.

"Home?" she repeated airily. "What's that?"

"Fair point," Holm chuckled.

I was spending less and less time in my houseboat as of late, though I at least had managed to go home each night. Diane and Holm, along with some other MBLIS agents, hadn't been so lucky, having to sleep at the police station while they were tracking down the man who attacked them. I wasn't a part of that investigation, though.

"You didn't sleep here, did you?" I asked, my brow furrowed in concern.

"Sleep?" she asked in an even drier tone now. "What's that?"

We all laughed, then, just as our colleagues Lamarr Birn and Sylvia Muñoz were walking through the front door.

Birn and Muñoz had been with Holm and me when we first found out about the Hollands down in the Keys. It had been their case, technically, but Birn went and got himself kidnapped early on, and Holm and I had to go down and help Muñoz find him. It had been a harrowing experience, to say the least, missing one of our own. It had happened once before when Holm was in a similar situation. Suffice it to say that it didn't get easier with experience.

The FBI agents barely noticed the other MBLIS agents' arrival, and the two of them elbowed through the masses just as I had to get to their desks right next to mine and Holm's.

"Another day, another headache," Birn grimaced as he plopped down in his seat and glowered over at the FBI agents.

"Honestly, Diane, when are we going to get rid of them?" Muñoz asked, taking her own seat across from Birn. "We work better separately than together."

This was true enough, most of the time, at least.

"We do that, and we lose this case in an instant,"

Diane said, her tone and expression characteristically grim. "They already want it all for themselves. We know as much. But technically, we got there first, and I'm not going to let them forget it."

She gave the FBI agents a dirty look of her own, which was about as critical as our boss was going to get about our new ever-present office mates.

"Hey, they're not all bad," Holm pointed out. "That woman we met down in NOLA, Nina Gosse, wasn't so bad."

My partner winked at me, and I felt my face flush a bit. I had a habit of picking up women on our missions that Holm liked to tease me about, and New Orleans had been no exception.

"You said she contacted you while you were in Virginia, right?" Birn asked me.

"Yeah," I confirmed. "I mean, well, I contacted her first. The FBI's headquartered in Virginia, and I knew she spent some time there after she wrapped things up in New Orleans, so I was wondering if we could get together. But she wasn't in town."

"She hinted about being on this case, though, right?" Holm asked, leaning forward across his desk and whispering, so there was no chance of the FBI agents hearing him. We weren't sure how much Nina had gotten involved, and she'd been cagey about the whole thing, so it was good not to get her in trouble with her superiors for talking to me at all. Holm knew this as well as I did.

"Hinted, yeah," I said slowly, remembering what she had told me. "And something about Lafitte's ship..."

Jean Lafitte was a storied old pirate connected to the New Orleans area whose long lost ship had been a nautical mystery for what seemed like forever. It turned out that the Hollands had found it off the coast of one of the smallest Keys below Florida and sent it off with a drug kingpin from New Orleans as a bribe for the hotel owners' help to get the Haitian zombie drug into circulation in the Big Easy.

That hadn't exactly gone well for the drug lord, who died after a skirmish with me inside that very ship. Holm and I had later found a whole stash of treasure and nautical artifacts inside it. That was technically Nina's case, however, and the FBI had confiscated the ship and all its contents despite my protests. My attempts to use Diane to figure out where it was and what they were doing with it had been fruitless, to put it mildly.

"She didn't elaborate?" Birn asked, leaning forward with his elbows on his knees as he turned to face me expectantly.

"Not exactly," I said. "She was pretty cagey about everything like I told you. And she went quiet a few weeks ago. I haven't heard from her since. She did say in her last message that she thinks we'll be meeting again soon, for whatever that's worth."

"That all but confirms it, then," Diane said, raising her eyebrows. "We have at least one ally at the FBI on this case then, if you manage to not mess it up."

She arched an eyebrow at me and paired it with a pointed look.

"It'll be fine," I assured her. "Nina and I are old friends at this point. Well, not quite old, but still."

"Maybe try reaching out to her again?" Holm suggested, unable to hide his eagerness.

"No," I said quickly, shaking my head. "She's a busy woman, with a lot of things on her plate. If she had something to tell, or at least that she was allowed to tell, she would've sent it by now. She'll get back in touch when she can. Until then, well... I guess we just keep doing what we're doing."

I reached for the first thing on a whole pile of papers atop my desk. Even I had let some of my usual organizational skills slip in recent weeks, though my desk was far clearer than anyone else's at MBLIS still, except for maybe Diane.

I blew a raspberry as I stared at it—a file for a middle-aged woman in Maine who was friends with Chester and Ashley before they disappeared. She'd been dodging my calls.

"That's a happy thought," Birn said sardonically, swiveling back around in his seat and reaching for one of his own papers, though they weren't stacked on his desk like mine were. Rather, they were spilling all over the place across it, even branching out into Muñoz's territory a bit, though she didn't seem to mind.

A phone rang, the sound emanating from Diane's office, and with a huff, she disappeared back inside.

"I don't know what she has to complain about," Muñoz said bitterly after she had gone. "At least she can get away from them by locking herself in there."

This was true enough, though I had more than an inkling that Diane was also sleeping in her office more nights than not, which meant that she was even more overworked than we were. Not good news, considering how uninspiring that work had been lately. This case had predictably turned out to be a marathon instead of a sprint. No one had been on another case in ages.

"Hey, so what about that map you told me about?" Holm said, whispering as he leaned forward again. "The one from the Hawthorne house."

The Hawthorne house was where we found all the artifacts from the *Dragon's Rogue*, along with the carcass of a fake version of the ship the Hollands had intended to use to get me off their trail.

The map was another story, seemingly hand-drawn by the pirate Grendel. My hope was that the marked locations on it along the eastern coast of the United States and its surrounding islands, and even parts of

Canada, would lead me to the *Dragon's Rogue* once and for all.

"What about it?" I asked, hardly paying attention as my eyelids began to droop at the thought of spending another long day going through files and trying to get in touch with people who had no intention of talking to me.

"Well, you kept saying weeks ago that you were going to go to every location and figure out where that ship is," he said, his excitement growing as he spoke.

"It's not that easy, Holm," I sighed, shaking my head and looking up at him from the Maine woman's file. "For one thing, it's a really old map, and the marked locations aren't exactly what I would call exact. I'll need an expert to help me figure out where they are."

"So do that!" Holm cried, though not loud enough that the FBI agents could hear. "Tessa's friend can help you, right?"

He was speaking of George, the old man who Tessa Bleu had enlisted to help me track down Grendel's journal in the first place while I was in New York covertly helping MBLIS deal with some funding issues caused by the mob there.

"Yes, but I'd need to go see him to do that," I sighed. "I already had Percy look at it while I was in New Orleans, too. His expertise is books, though, so he couldn't tell me much. He did confirm I have the real journal now, though."

Percy was a friend of George's who helped me figure out that the first journal sent to me from Virginia was a fake. He was a nice old man, and I'd been glad to see him again and overjoyed that I had the real journal this time, but it disappointed me that he couldn't help with the map.

"What are you two whispering about over there?" Birn asked us with a mock tone and look of suspicion.

"Leaving us out of anything fun?" Muñoz added, calling out to us past her partner.

"More fun than anything we've got going on here these days," Holm shot back with a twinkle in his eye.

"Ah, they're talking about that ship again," Birn said with a knowing nod. "When are you going to let us in on all that action, eh, Marston?"

"What's that supposed to mean?" I asked, turning my torso around in my chair to face him.

"Come on, now, we know the Hollands are after that ship of yours, too," Birn pointed out. "So now it's official business. Diane said as much when she got off the phone with you when you were in Virginia."

"Yeah, I guess so," I said, still not quite catching on to his meaning.

"So, when are we going to get out there and find it?" Birn asked, rubbing his long hands together expectantly. "I call shotgun."

"I... I..." I sputtered, not sure how to respond to this.

"Ah, look, he doesn't want to share," Muñoz teased, shooting a pouty expression my way.

"That's not it," I said defensively, though if I were honest with myself, it was true.

The search for the *Dragon's Rogue* had been passed down to me from my grandfather, and for a long time after he passed, it had become something of a solo endeavor for me in my free time. Then, when the remains of the ship's original owner, an ancestor of mine named Lord Jonathan Finch-Hatton, washed up in a cave off the coast of Miami to be found by an unsuspecting photojournalist, Tessa had become a large part of my search.

Sure, others had gotten involved here and there, most notably Holm being that he was my partner. But by and large, I thought of this as a thing for Tessa and me to share together. I supposed that it was only natural that more people would be brought into the fold now that the *Dragon's Rogue* was connected to a big MBLIS case.

"Come on, now, why don't you talk to Diane about it?" Holm asked, latching onto this idea with predictable enthusiasm. "We could all go out to one of those places on the map and try to track this thing down. Or at least you and me, if she doesn't want to spare us all. She can't say it's not related to the Holland case since they're looking for it, too, and it's not like we're getting anything done here."

"We are getting something done here," I said with an exasperated sigh. "I know it doesn't feel like it, but the more we go through these files and chase down bad leads, the closer we get to the one that's actually going to pan out. Taking half our labor force or more off of that is a big ask."

"Come on. You can't really consider this a valuable use of our time?" Holm complained, gesturing at the lopsided pile of files sitting atop his own desk.

"Of course it is," I shot back. "But I agree it doesn't feel like it. Diane warned us that it would be like this, remember? We have to get it done. This is an FBI's Most Wanted List case now. There are going to be more dead ends than we can count. That's how we work a case like this."

"You can say that again," Birn said sullenly, swiveling back around in his chair to face his own desk and files. "Dead end, after dead end, after dead end…"

"After dead end," Muñoz finished for him sullenly.

"Come on, will you just talk to Diane about it?" Holm pleaded.

"No," I said quickly, with a curtness to my tone that communicated this was the end of the conversation. "Besides, the Hollands are on the run now. They're probably not even thinking about the *Dragon's Rogue* anymore."

The truth was, I'd already talked to Diane about it shortly after I got back from New Orleans, and again a couple of weeks before that day. Both times, she'd emphasized that she needed all hands on deck here in Miami until further notice. She was right, of course. The Hollands probably had put their search for the ship on hold for now, so sending us off to look for it on agency time wouldn't do much to help us find them.

"They could be, though," Holm quipped, unable to help himself. "We don't know that for sure. They could be somewhere on that old map as we speak."

"And if they are, what we're doing here will lead us to them just as well," I replied. "The difference is that if we go, we're missing out on the opportunity to find them if they aren't one of those places, but somewhere else entirely."

Holm opened up his mouth as if to respond, but I cut him off.

"That's it, Holm," I said. "We're needed here. And we have work to do."

3

ETHAN

WE WORKED in silence for a couple of hours until it was the time that most people in Miami were probably waking up to make their way into work. As much as we'd been working late on this case, we'd also been coming in early.

The FBI agents weren't quite so silent, however. They were constantly humming with energy that we didn't seem to have. Holm had joked more than once that they might've sucked it right out of us and taken it for themselves.

Diane said that it was just a different way of operating. The FBI was used to this kind of slog. They thrived on it, even. We were used to catching the bad guys and then moving on to the next case in a clean-cut fashion.

We were also accustomed to always being on the move and catching up on our sleep in between cases.

These guys sat at their desks more often than we did, but they also never seemed to hit a lag in their workload. Apples and oranges, I guessed.

I also got the sense that they liked infringing on our territory. They wanted to be the first ones to catch a big break in this case. It was a weird competition for them, and it was infecting everyone's attitude.

By the time Diane reemerged from her office around eight in the morning, my eyelids were drooping again. I sent several more messages the way of the woman in Maine, as well as half a dozen others on the New Orleans list, and then I pulled out my laptop to sift through their social media accounts.

Most of them were still active since I started contacting them. This told me that they likely weren't involved with the criminal side of the Hollands' operations after all. They would've gone dark if they had been, just like Chester and Ashley themselves.

That didn't mean that they wouldn't have something useful to tell me, even if they didn't understand what it was they knew. Then there were those select few who *had* abandoned their digital footprint in recent weeks. Those interested me even more. That all made the fact that they weren't forthcoming with me all the more annoying.

I'd gone to see several of them personally over the past several weeks if they were in Florida or any of the surrounding states. None of those had been able to tell me much, except for one guy from Tampa, who I hadn't been able to find at all. He was one of the ones who had also gone dark online, so he was at the top of my list of people who were probably involved in the criminal side of things in some way.

What I'd learned from the contacts mostly corroborated what we already knew: that Chester and Ashley Holland were just one of several sets of carefully crafted personas that these two individuals had adopted over the years and that they mostly dabbled in real estate as a cover for their drug operations.

The corroboration was helpful in that it painted a clearer picture. But I was itching for something more immediately interesting, and I knew that everyone else was, too, regardless of the agency from which they came.

This is why when Diane came back out of her office, positioned herself at the front of the room, and clapped her hands loudly to get all of our attention, all chatter and sleepiness in the crowded room died down at once.

"Thanks," she said with characteristic gruffness, nodding to us in thanks. "I'm sorry to interrupt, but I've just gotten off the phone with Interpol."

"Interpol," I heard Muñoz breathe, not exactly quietly, and just like that, the whole room was abuzz again, leaving Diane clearly annoyed that she'd thanked us so soon for being quiet.

"Interpol?" Birn asked, his characteristically booming voice carrying over all the chatter. "As in Europe?"

"Do you know of another Interpol, Agent Birn?" Diane asked coolly, rolling her eyes at him.

"I mean, no, but Europe? We haven't dealt with them before, have we?" he explained.

"Not that I'm aware of, and certainly not in my tenure here," Diane said, casting a wary glance in the direction of the FBI agents. "But that doesn't mean that we aren't more than capable of rising to the challenge."

Birn immediately shut his mouth at this, realizing what he'd done. The last thing we wanted was to remind the FBI that we were a smaller agency with less experience and resources than they had. This was our case, and they were just helping—no reason to give them ammunition to steal it out from under us.

"We did know they could turn up anywhere," I reminded everyone. "This isn't entirely unexpected."

"Did they turn up, though?" one of the FBI agents, a surly guy named Smith who was the one who spilled coffee on Holm when they first arrived, asked. "What did Interpol say?"

"We don't know anything for sure, yet," Diane said cautiously, giving a deferential nod to Smith, which I could tell even from the opposite desk made my partner's blood boil. "We're right not to get ahead of ourselves."

"But what do we know?" Muñoz asked.

"We think they were spotted in Scotland," she said, pursing her lips as this news sent the room abuzz all over again. Then, holding up both her arms and motioning downward with her hands, "Settle down, settle down. This isn't getting us anywhere."

"Scotland?" Holm repeated over the chatter, which was now abating for the third time in as many minutes. "What the hell are they doing in Scotland?"

He shook his head and looked over at me in disbelief. This was interesting. I'd give him that. I knew theoretically that the Hollands could be anywhere, but for some reason, I'd always assumed they would turn up camped out on some island somewhere, not in Europe.

"That's what we don't know yet, though it's not out of the question that they own property there, too, under aliases we haven't uncovered," Diane explained with a shrug.

"More aliases?" Birn asked. "How can there be more aliases? These people have going on twenty identities apiece already!"

"They're sophisticated operatives," an FBI agent named Dobbs pointed out in a suitably pompous tone. "This kind of thing isn't unheard of in our line of work."

Holm rolled his eyes and made a gagging motion in my direction, but I motioned for him to stop. The FBI agents were facing us, after all, given that Diane was standing in front of our desks. We didn't need them hating us even more than they already did.

"This is all of our lines of work," Diane said, giving Dobbs a pointed look, and he shut his mouth. As much as the other agents liked to mess with us, they seemed terrified of Diane. With good reason, too. She was nothing if not intimidating. And she knew her stuff to boot. There was no messing with her, and while she was watching, there was no messing with her agents, either.

"How do we know this isn't just another dead end like everything else we've been working on?" Muñoz asked, and she had a point. I reminded myself not to get too excited about this too quickly. Otherwise, we might be in for a letdown. We were all itching for a big break, but looking for one where it wasn't would just waste valuable time.

"Good question," Diane said, nodding approvingly to her. "Apparently, Interpol's had this lead for a while and is just now bringing it to us since they're pretty sure it's not a dead end at this point."

"Wait, they're not giving us everything when they get it?!" Holm cried in protest. "That's not how it's supposed to work, is it?"

A few of the FBI agents behind us snickered, and I turned around long enough to shoot them a dirty look of my own.

"That's how it works with the tip line here, but not internationally," Diane explained, shaking her head and giving the other agents another look of warning, as well. "They have to sort through their own tips and follow up on them since they're the ones in the area."

"If they gave us everything, we'd be swamped with dead end leads we couldn't even figure out were dead ends because we wouldn't be able to follow up on them," Agent Corey, who was slightly nicer than the other ones by my estimation, explained in a tone that wasn't unkind. "Unless you want to be flying all over the world on a wild goose chase that you have no chance of winning."

Holm looked like he might not actually be opposed to that setup, and knowing him, he probably wasn't, but there was no denying that this wasn't a great strategy for finding the Hollands.

"Got it, thanks," I said, forcing a smile in Corey's direction.

"Are there a lot of international tips, though?" Birn asked, his brow furrowed thoughtfully. "I would imagine that more Americans are paying attention to the news on this case than anywhere else, given that this is where the Hollands are actually from."

"And where they committed crimes," Muñoz added. "With the exception of some islands off the US coast."

"That's true," Diane relented with another curt

nod. "And international agencies certainly aren't getting the volume of incoming tips as we are here. But they're getting a fair amount. Remember, we put out calls about these people to every friendly government and intelligence agency in the world. We knew they could have fled anywhere their money would take them. And they have a lot of money."

"So what did they say?" I asked, impatient to hear exactly what was going on with this lead. My tiredness and annoyance with the FBI and the slow roll of this case had suddenly left me. We might finally be getting somewhere, and my mind was buzzing with all the different possibilities.

"Well, I talked to a guy in Scotland who's been working on this lead for about a week," Diane said, and I noticed that she looked a little more invigorated herself now, and at this point, the persistent bags under her eyes slightly lessened. "A guy in a small town along the coast called in and asked about the Hollands. He'd seen their pictures on the news at a bar one night and recognized them. He sounds like an odd character. He doesn't even own a TV himself."

It sounded like I might like this guy.

"Sounds like a crackpot," Holm said, predictably.

"That's what they thought," Diane said, letting slip a low laugh. "It took them a while to follow up, actually, but the guy kept calling."

"How long's a while?" Birn asked warily, and Diane let out a sigh.

"Too long," she said, shaking her head. "It's been about three weeks. But then again, I don't blame them. They have a lot of other tips and a lot of other cases that are more pressing to them than this one. And he does sound kind of like a crackpot." She nodded to Holm on this last part.

"Three weeks?" Muñoz repeated, letting out an exasperated huff. "The Hollands were in Scotland three weeks ago, and we're just now hearing about it?"

I shared her dismay, but complaining wasn't going to get us anywhere. And I felt for this poor Interpol guy. If this was a small town, he probably had a large geographic region on his plate that stretched far beyond it. He had his own cases, like Diane said, and international cases more pressing to his country than a couple of American drug dealers last seen in Georgia, of all places. I was sure he'd gotten to it as quickly as he could, frustrating as that fact was.

"Let's cut the guy some slack. I'm sure he and his agents did the best he could," I reminded everyone.

"He did," Diane agreed. "And even if he didn't, there's nothing we can do about that now. We need to focus on the task at hand."

"Which is?" Holm asked hopefully.

"Hold on, tell us the whole story first," I said,

holding out my hands to slow everyone down. "How did he figure out that the lead was legitimate?"

"Well, the guy just kept calling, saying he kept seeing Chester and Ashley every day," Diane explained.

"Every day?" Holm repeated, unable to stop himself from cutting her off. "You mean they're still there?"

"They could be," Diane said, nodding slowly. "But let me get to that part. Ethan's right. We'll all need the full story."

"Right, right, sorry," Holm said, holding up his own hands in defeat.

"So, this man is a fisherman by trade, and he says that every time he goes out fishing for the past few weeks, he sees this couple walking along the shore. A man and a woman, about middle-aged, American, and looking like they've had a fair amount of Botox or plastic surgery to pair with a set of bad spray tans."

"Well, that's them. There's no question about that," Birn chuckled.

"I'm sure there are a lot of people who fit that description, though admittedly probably not in a small Scottish fishing town," Diane said with a wry smile. "Anyway, when he saw their pictures on the news, he recognized them instantly."

"Witnesses aren't always right, though," Dobbs

warned. "Especially in cases like this one that are so high profile. People see what they want to see."

"That's what the Interpol guy thought at first, too," Diane said with another nod. "But apparently, they think it's different this time. This man claims to have seen the Hollands so often and so regularly that it can't be ignored."

"So he just sees them on the shore?" I asked. "From how far away?"

"Another good question," Diane said. "At first, pretty far. But then I guess he started seeing them out on the water, too. Not every day at first, but often enough. And then every day, all at the same times and in the same place, like clockwork."

"On the water?" I repeated, perking up even more at this news. "Doing what? In what? A yacht? A sailboat?"

"That's the thing, the guy says it's an ocean liner," Diane said, her brow furrowed now as she said this.

"A what?" Muñoz asked, unable to hide her skepticism.

"I guess this fisherman goes pretty far out," Diane shrugged. "And the Hollands are on some ocean liner with a bunch of other people. He said it seemed like they were looking for something in the water."

Now, this was just too much for me. The Hollands were known nautical enthusiasts, and this sounded straight out of the playbook for how they found

Lafitte's ship in the Keys, painstakingly searching through the water with a team of experts until they found exactly what they were looking for, even though it took months on end.

"That's them," I said definitively. "It has to be. Who else would fit that description, doing that?"

"I agree," Diane said. "That's what made the Interpol agent look into the case some more. The guy started calling about this ocean liner. It was just strange enough to fit the file, and those details haven't been released to the media or the public at all. We're just saying that the Hollands are drug kingpins hiding behind a real estate empire, not that they go digging around the ocean floor for buried treasure in their free time."

"That would inspire a fair amount of sensationalism," Muñoz agreed. "It would just make our jobs harder."

"Agreed," Diane said, crossing her arms. "And it has the added benefit of tipping us off that this fisherman character might just know what he's talking about, though I don't see how we could've foreseen that."

"Has he ever talked to them or anything?" I asked, unable to keep the nervous excitement out of my voice. "Has he gotten a good look at what they're doing or any idea what they're looking for?"

It had never occurred to me that the *Dragon's Rogue* might not actually be anywhere near the

Americas anymore. Could it have ended up right back home in European waters? There would be a kind of symmetry to that, I decided, as well as some irony considering how much time the Hollands and I had spent sorting through the waters closer to our homes.

"He says he tried to talk to them a couple of times, but they're not very talkative," Diane said, and I thought I just might explode from my anticipation, my mind reeling with all this new information. "He asked them what they were doing in Scotland once when they were still sticking to the beach, and they just said they were taking an extended holiday. Then out in the water, he asked if they were fishing, and they said 'something like that,' but didn't elaborate."

"They have to be looking for one of Marston's pirate ships. They've just got to be," Holm said, and I kind of wished he hadn't. The FBI liked ribbing me for that stuff even more than my own colleagues did.

No one said anything now, though, not even so much as a snicker, and I realized that the FBI agents were just as excited as we were to be finally getting a breakthrough in this case. Maybe they had been getting more frustrated with the slow pace of things than they had let on originally.

"That was my first thought, too," Diane said, glancing over at me apprehensively. "Anyway, as I was saying, the Scottish fisherman didn't talk to them at all after he saw the FBI report on the news. He steered clear of them after that. Still saw them, though."

I noticed that Diane brushed over the talk of the pirate ships. This struck me as intentional, and I narrowed my eyes at her.

"What's going on?" I asked her. "What aren't you telling us?"

She swiveled to me, hands on her hips, and heaved a sigh.

"You don't miss much, do you, Marston?" she asked, cocking an eyebrow at me. "Look, I'm not holding anything out on you. I've told you everything I know. It's just that... I know you're going to want to work this."

I blinked at her, not comprehending what she was saying.

"Uh, yeah, duh," Holm said, voicing my own thoughts. "Of course we're going to work this. Man, I haven't been to Europe since the Navy. Don't think I've ever been to Scotland, though."

"That's what I'm trying to tell you," Diane said, looking as if the words pained her to say. "No one's going anywhere, at least not yet."

I thought my jaw might drop all the way to the floor, and just like that, the room was abuzz again. Everyone was talking, not just whispering this time, and Diane's efforts to silence us were proving unsuccessful in this round.

"You've got to be kidding me!" I cried, gaping at her. "You can't drop that bomb of a lead on us and then pull the rug out from under us like that!"

She shook her head at me, uncomprehending. Everyone was too loud, and she couldn't hear me.

"You've got to be kidding me!" I screamed again, louder this time, and it carried over all the noise now.

"Look, look, I knew this wasn't going to be popular," Diane said, motioning for us all to calm down and listen some more, and the chatter dropped back down to a mere buzz, enough for her voice to carry over it. "But it's not up to me. This might not even be our case for the time being."

"What?" Holm cried, sounding even more aghast than I had. "What the hell is that supposed to mean?"

"It's Interpol," Dobbs said bitterly, shaking his head. "They're claiming jurisdiction, aren't they?"

"They are now," Diane sighed. "I'll fight it, but Scotland is understandably concerned. They've had mob problems for God knows how long, and they don't want to add a major international drug operation on top of it all."

"I... I..." I stammered, not sure what to say. "Surely they can't think cutting us out will help matters."

"No, they don't," Diane said, shaking her head. "They understand that our agencies have done a lot of the legwork here, and when push comes to shove, the Hollands—or whatever their real names are—will most likely be extradited to the United States to stand trial."

"Most likely?" Muñoz interjected. "You mean there's a chance that they won't be?"

"You've got to be kidding me," I said again, staring at Holm and shaking my head. He looked back at me with the same shocked expression on his face that was no doubt on mine.

"Look, it depends on what Scotland finds out about what the Hollands are doing there if it's the Hollands at all," Diane explained.

"There's no way it's not them!" Birn argued. "You heard that description and what they're doing. There's just no damned way!"

"I don't disagree," Diane said, pursing her lips. "But either way, if Scotland wants to try the Hollands for some major transgression there before extraditing them here, that would be their right. It just depends on where all the chips fall with this one, and we just can't see that far ahead yet, no matter how much we'd like to."

Her mouth was set in a thin line now, and I could tell that she didn't like this any more than we did. That was some consolation, at least. I knew she would be fighting for us all the way through this mess.

"Look, you have to just send us out there to observe," I argue, trying to sound measured and understanding, though it was difficult. "Just Holm and me. Or even just me. We could help them work the case, track these people down. We've been working this for the better part of the year! Our insight and experience could be invaluable to them."

"I don't disagree with that, either," Diane assured me, giving me a small smile. "But don't underestimate Interpol. Those guys know their stuff. If they really need us, they'll call for us. Until then, we just have to sit tight and keep following other leads as they come up."

"Other leads?" Muñoz repeated, true to form and aghast. "What other leads? We know where they are now, don't we?"

"Not for certain yet," Diane said patiently. "We can't abandon other leads just because we have a good one. Great one, even. Additionally, there's more to be learned about these people. Prioritize your work on the Hollands' background for now. The more we know about them, the better."

"Come on," I argued, at a loss as I shook my head at her. "You've got to at least try to get us over there. We'll be a help to them, even if they don't believe it yet."

"Believe me. I tried," Diane said wanly. "But they're not having it, not yet. They're wary of too many people crowding around the case and freaking the Hollands out. And they do have a point. For all we know, they could still be keeping tabs on us."

This was a valid enough concern, I had to admit.

The second Holm and I got on a plane to Scotland, someone might tip off the Hollands. Still, I wanted to go so badly. It was killing me to be so close, yet still so far, from catching these people and maybe even finding the *Dragon's Rogue*.

"Don't worry," Diane told me kindly, no doubt seeing my conflicted emotions on my face. "We'll still be involved, and there'll be hell to pay if they try to steal the whole case from us. I promise you that. In the meantime, we still have work to do."

4

ETHAN

Tensions were predictably high in the office after Diane told us about her call with the guy from Interpol. No one was happy with what we'd just been told, and I was starting to feel more claustrophobic than ever, between all the stacks of files, the phones ringing off the hook with new tips, almost all of them no doubt dead ends, and the FBI agents all chattering amongst themselves in disdainful tones about what was going on.

"I knew this was going to go sour," I heard Agent Smith mutter bitterly after Diane had returned to take refuge in her office. "We never should've let them take the lead on this case."

"It's not like we had a say," another particularly unfriendly man named Forrester added. "None of us wanted to come here in the first place."

"Well, we should've fought harder," Smith said, giving Dobbs and Corey a pointed look as if he didn't think they had quite risen to the occasion.

"Hey, I fought just fine," another guy named Hunt said. "So did he." He gestured to his partner, a plain-looking guy with a permanent scowl named Barnes.

Barnes nodded in agreement and turned his unpleasant expression on Dobbs and Corey.

Holm and I exchanged a bemused look. They were really talking about this right in front of us, emboldened by the bad news and Diane's newfound absence and distraction.

"Shut up," Dobbs hissed, glancing over at us quickly and averting his eyes the second he saw that I was watching him. "They can hear you."

"We're supposed to play nice, remember?" Corey added.

I heard a snickering sound behind me and knew that Muñoz must have been listening, too. She was no doubt wondering how these guys possibly thought they'd been playing nice up until this point.

From the second the FBI agents had arrived, they'd been relentless in their disdain for us. It had started out more brazen, with the coffee spilling and constant jabs at Holm, Birn, and Muñoz during the manhunt for the Hollands' hitman. Once I arrived on the scene, things grew more subtle, however, in response to more than a few good talkings-to from Diane.

There were whispers, and snickers, and the pedantic explaining of things everyone at MBLIS had known since the early days of our law enforcement training. All while Diane wasn't looking, of course, though I doubted that much escaped her notice even when she was tucked away in her office.

It was annoying, to say the least. But until now, they hadn't expressed their hatred for the very idea of working with us in the first place, at least not in front of our faces.

"Oi! If you have something to say, why don't you come over here and say it?" Holm called over to them, and his eyes narrowed in a blistering glare that was altogether rare coming from him.

"Shut up!" I hissed to him. As much as I hated this, I didn't exactly want to get into it with the FBI agents. Well, really, I didn't want to get into it with Diane, who would get into it with us if we caused a scene.

"You think we should just let them sit there and blame us for this?" Holm asked, throwing his arms up in the air in exasperation.

"Do you want Diane breathing down our necks for the next God knows how long?" I shot back.

My partner seemed to consider this briefly, dropping his arms and shooting a wary look in the direction of Diane's closed office door.

He didn't have time to make a decision, though.

"Come on, what are you, Robbie, scared?" Smith

sneered, notably using Holm's first name even though the two of them weren't anywhere close to being on a first-name basis. "Scared of your girl boss just like you are a little coffee?"

"Holden!" Corey cried, giving his partner an astonished look. "This isn't like you. A little healthy competition between agencies, sure, but this is too much. If you're not careful, I'll get you pulled off this case."

I glanced back at Birn and Muñoz, who both looked just as surprised by this response as Holm and I were. For Smith's own partner to threaten him like that, he must've been really out of line. Indeed, he'd gone much further than he had any other time since the other agents arrived in Miami.

"What did you just say?" Smith asked, turning his ire on Corey now.

"He's right, man, you went too far," Forrester said begrudgingly. "We all know Diane's better at this job than a lot of people in the FBI."

"You don't really believe that, do you?" Smith asked him, open-mouthed. "If we'd kept this in-house, we would've caught them by now. And Interpol wouldn't be acting like they could walk all over us, now, would they? We all know that hardly anyone over there probably even knows what MBLIS is."

"They damned well know that the Hollands are on our Most Wanted List, though," Forrester argued. "And Interpol plays by its own rules. You should know that."

"Yeah, they took that human trafficking case from us a while back," Dobbs pointed out helpfully. "At least they haven't completely stolen it yet. They're just seeing what they can do without us while they gather information."

"*Us*?" Hunt asked with emphasis. "What us? She made it clear enough that if she were to send someone, it would be them." He gestured vaguely in Holm's and my direction with a glower at Diane's office door.

"Exactly," Smith agreed, clearly glad to have some backup from amongst his own ranks. "And you can't say that wouldn't be a mistake, can you, Doug?" He narrowed his eyes at Forrester as if challenging him to dare to disagree.

"Well, they are the ones most well-acquainted with the case," the other man pointed out, practically wincing as he said it because he knew what Smith's reaction was going to be.

"Please, they stumbled onto this case," he scoffed, true to form. "You can't seriously think that this agency has the training and resources necessary to take on something this big effectively?"

"No, which is why we're working together," Forrester said, his tone more measured than I would've been able to manage. Judging by Holm's nondescript grumbles across from me, he had a few choice words of his own that he was avoiding voicing, to his credit.

"Then why do we have to work together at all?"

Smith asked as if explaining something very simple to a small child. "It's just pageantry. We don't want to be seen as taking a smaller agency's case, so we're throwing them a bone. But then we all get shafted since they're slowing us down."

At this point, I thought it was high time that I stood up for myself and my agency, though I was sure I wouldn't be quite as vulgar about it as Holm. At least I hoped I wouldn't be.

"Come on, you can't be serious," I shot back, piercing my gaze on the lot of them. "Most of us are former Naval intelligence officers. Muñoz was a pilot. Holm and I were SEALS. And we may not have the big shiny cases or the public reputation that you do, but we do good, solid work here at MBLIS. And we found the Hollands where you failed to God knows how many times."

"Hey, you all dropped the ball, too," Dobbs pointed out. "They were in your territory just as much as they were in ours. But your point's taken."

"You really think there's anything you guys can do that we can't?" Smith said, scowling right at me. "Not a chance. We'd run circles around you in this case if Interpol let us work it."

"I'd like to see you try," Birn chuckled. "We both need each other here. That's why we're working together. Besides, why would MBLIS exist if some other agency could do our jobs? It wouldn't make any sense."

"If you're expecting the government to make sense, I've got some bad news for you, buddy," Smith pointed out, and most times, I would say it was hard to argue with that point.

"Look, what makes you think you can do our jobs?" I asked, sidestepping his point and going back to a previous one.

"Why couldn't I?" he asked with a shrug. "I was in the Marines. I've got all the skills you have, plus my FBI training. And all the resources of the FBI."

"*You* have *all* the resources of the FBI?" Muñoz asked, arching a skeptical eyebrow at him, a satisfying lopsided smirk of her own etched across the right side of her face.

Smith blinked and just glowered at her before doubling down on one of his other points.

"You know what I mean," he said with a small laugh that I guess was meant to taunt her more but just made her raise her eyebrows even higher. "Anyway, I asked you first. What can you do that we can't?"

"Uh, we know all about the sea," Muñoz said, in a tone that said this should be obvious. "And who sails it, and why, and what benefit they get from it. We know all about the criminal politics on the water, and on the islands, and alongside the shore. We've built relationships in these communities, and we have knowledge that goes a long way when we get there. You're just a bureaucrat in a suit with an attitude problem."

Alright, maybe we should've shut Muñoz up along with Holm. But that was fun to watch. As she spoke, Smith's face fell until he looked just as sullen as Hunt, and there was a long period of silence after that in which we could've heard a pin drop.

I gave Muñoz an approving look, though I didn't love that she'd insulted Smith, most likely escalating tensions between our two groups even further. That said, he'd asked for it. There was no denying that. It was satisfying to watch.

"I think that settles matters," Corey said at long last, nodding slowly. "We all need each other. Each of us has something of value to add. Otherwise, we wouldn't be here, and we'd all do well to try to work together better."

Holm grumbled something about *him* not needing to work together better, and *Smith* being the cause of all this, and then something else about coffee, but I couldn't make much of it out. This was probably for the best, since if I couldn't hear him properly, no one else could, either.

"That's right," I told Corey with a grateful nod, after giving Holm the side-eye in a warning. "We need each other. We need your resources and knowledge of international affairs and agencies, and you need our expertise and knowledge of the case itself. I get that things are getting pretty claustrophobic around here—and I know we're all feeling it, so don't try to convince me otherwise..."

Everyone nodded and mumbled in agreement.

"Well, there's something we can agree on, at least," Forrester chuckled, and we all laughed.

"Right, so we just have to get through this thing," I continued. "It's going to be close quarters for a while, and I know none of us are happy about all this mess with Interpol and Scotland. We all want to be headed out there as we speak. But that's not happening, so as Diane said, we just need to sit tight and see this thing through. If we work together, we're more likely to break this thing."

"If we ever even get the chance to work it," Holm grumbled. "Interpol could solve the case on their own, for all we know."

My stomach dropped a bit at this suggestion. I didn't like that thought at all, and I hadn't really considered it before. It just seemed like a foregone conclusion to me that after going through all this trouble with the Hollands, Holm and I would be there when push came to shove and we finally caught the couple.

That might not be the case anymore, though. We were in a whole different ballgame now.

"Come now, that's no way to talk," Birn said brightly, standing up and grinning at us all. "This is just a bump in the road and not a bad one at that. We have a real lead! Let's enjoy that, even if we're not the ones following up on it just yet. In the meantime, I have to get the hell out of this place for a little while, or I'll lose my mind. Anyone up for a late breakfast?"

5

ETHAN

Holm, myself, and Muñoz all ended up joining Birn for that breakfast, leaving the FBI agents alone in the office with Diane.

"Do we really want to leave them alone in there?" Holm grumbled for about the tenth time as Birn pulled us into a seedy diner parking lot.

"Oh, will you stop it already," Muñoz groaned from the front seat. "Just chill out. It's fine. What do you think they're going to do, burn the place down? Stage a hostile takeover of our office? Give me a break. Honestly, Holm, even for you."

That shut him up, and I chuckled and shook my head as we climbed out of the backseat and followed Birn and Muñoz into the diner.

I'd had a quick bowl of instant oatmeal before going into work, but with my tiresome schedule lately and the lack of flavor and heartiness that accompanied that meal, I was looking forward to getting a real sit down for once, as well as being away from the FBI agents and getting to steal a moment with just my MBLIS colleagues.

I'd never been to this particular diner before. It was an unassuming place, tucked away on the outskirts of town, away from all the major tourist spots. If I were honest, it looked pretty dingy to me, but my already-grumbling stomach and I kept an open mind.

"What is this place?" Holm asked as Birn and Muñoz climbed into a booth next to a long window facing the parking lot. My partner and I sat down opposite them.

"We come here all the time," Birn said, gesturing between himself and Muñoz. "My cousin Buddy owns the place."

"Really?" I asked, intrigued. I hadn't heard Birn mention a cousin before who was here in town.

"It's the best-kept secret in Miami!" Birn beamed, gazing down at the laminated menu in front of him. "You should feel lucky we decided to share it with you. But I figured we all needed a pick-me-up after the morning we've had."

"Morning," Muñoz scoffed, peering down at her own menu. "It's only 8:30."

"Ugh, don't remind me," Holm groaned, dropping his head into his hands.

I turned my attention to my menu. It was one sheet, front and back, and it looked to offer a staple of regular diner favorites. It didn't look like anything special to me, but the more I looked at it, the more my stomach grumbled, and I was having trouble deciding what to get because I wanted everything.

Thankfully, a tall, jovial-looking man with a potbelly sporting a dirty white apron came out of the back kitchen and made a beeline right for our table to rescue me from my indecision.

"Lamarr, Sylvia, you didn't tell me you were gonna make it in today!" the man bellowed, clapping Birn on the shoulder and beaming at him. "And you brought friends!" His voice was warm, and it carried.

"This is my cousin, Buddy," Birn said, grinning just as broadly as the other man as he reached up with his long arm and clapped him on the back while remaining seated. "Buddy, these are Ethan and Robbie. They're MBLIS agents, too."

"Taking a break from the old grind, I see," Buddy said, nodding approvingly to Holm and me and shooting us a wink. "Well, I'm all for it. What can I get ya?"

Everyone was looking at me since I was in the end seat.

"Uh, I'm having trouble deciding," I said, clearing my throat. "Why don't you bring me whatever you recommend?"

"Oh, you won't regret that," Buddy assured me with a jovial laugh to match his demeanor. I handed over my menu.

"I'll have the chocolate chip pancakes," Holm said predictably, as he always had a sweet tooth that needed abating.

"I'll have my usual," Muñoz said.

"Me, too," Birn offered, and I wondered how often they came in here.

"We're in a few times a week, at least," Muñoz said, reading my mind as Buddy meandered back to the kitchen, making small talk with the other customers as he went, shaking hands and patting shoulders every which way.

"He seems happy," I remarked, watching him.

"He's the happiest guy I know," Birn confirmed with a nod and a laugh. "I know you wouldn't understand it, Marston, but some people love the simple life. I have half a mind to retire and join the business with him."

"Oh?" I asked, arching an eyebrow at him. This was the first I'd heard of this.

"Well, you know, getting abducted and held prisoner by a bunch of drug dealers on a remote island makes you do some thinking," he chuckled, though there was a somberness in his eyes that told me he was serious.

"I would imagine so," I said thoughtfully, glancing

back at Buddy as he engaged in a lively conversation with one of his waitresses.

"Just don't go running out on us yet," Holm said, serious as well. "We need everyone we can get right now, and I don't want to be even more outnumbered by those FBI guys."

"Come now, enough complaining," I said, shooting him a look. "All it feels like we do lately is complain."

"With good reason," Holm argued.

"Fair enough," I relented with a shrug.

"Don't worry, old friend, I'm not even close to being finished yet," Birn said, an excited glint in his eye as he leaned forward on the table, crossing his arms there. "Speaking of which, what do we all think about this whole Scotland business? Pretty cool, huh?"

"Which part? The one where Interpol's stealing our case, or the one where they didn't even bother to tell us until at least a week after the fact?" Muñoz asked coolly.

"Come on. I thought I said no complaining!" I cried as the waitress that Buddy had been talking to rushed over to dole out coffee. Birn nodded to her in thanks.

I wasn't sure I needed any more caffeine after the stressful morning I'd already had in this still young day, but judging by the fatigue I'd been experiencing lately, I figured that I would be a fool not to accept it. So I began sipping on my cup, vowing to nurse it slowly enough that my blood pressure wouldn't spike too much higher than it had already.

"Okay, okay," Muñoz said, holding up her hands in defeat. "No more, I promise."

"Thank you," I said definitively, nodding to her.

"Now, what about Scotland?" Birn asked, just as eagerly as before. "The good parts, I mean. The parts where we have a good lead, and we might actually be close to breaking this thing."

Holm opened his mouth as if to comment on the fact that we might not actually be the ones to break it, but he shut it again with one sharp look from me.

I was frankly done with all the bitterness after this morning. We'd been simmering in it for weeks now, all of us: FBI, MBLIS, Diane herself, it didn't matter. We didn't need any more negativity. It had lost its usefulness ages ago, and I was honestly glad that we'd finally had it out with the FBI agents, in a way. Now we could at least try to get to work putting it all behind us and focus on the task at hand. Or tasks. There were many of them. More than I could even count, probably.

"I think it's exciting!" Muñoz said, setting aside her coffee and leaning forward on the table just like Birn. "I mean, think about it. We could actually have a case in Europe soon. That'd really be something."

"Ever been?" I asked her.

"Yeah, I was stationed in Germany for a while in the military," she said thoughtfully. "Haven't been to

Scotland, though. That would be fun. I love their accents."

"Weird thought, people like the Hollands camping out in a tiny Scottish fishing town," I chuckled with a nod. "I can't think of many other places I'd expect them to end up less."

I tried to imagine the leathery-skinned Hollands with their puffy cheeks and spray tans trying to blend in with the local crowd, and the whole thing just seemed even more ridiculous.

"Maybe that's why they're there," Birn suggested with a shrug, taking another sip from his coffee cup. "It's the last place they think we'll look for them or that they'll be noticed."

"They'd stick out like a sore thumb, though," Muñoz said, resting her chin in her hand, her elbow propped up on the table. "They had to have known that someone would notice them, recognize them from the reports."

"I don't know. They seem to have gotten unlucky to me," Holm reasoned, setting his own coffee back on the coaster. "I mean, how many news reports about them even reach all the way out there? Diane said it was a small town and that the fisherman guy doesn't even own a TV. He saw the report in a bar of all places. Maybe he's not that much of a crackpot, and that's just the culture there. Everyone could be pretty disconnected from the rest of the world, in a remote place with an older population."

"True, and they could be sticking to a remote location even within a remote location," Birn added with a nod. "For all we know, they never leave wherever they're staying except to go out on the water. And they probably own where they're staying, knowing them. They don't have to deal with neighbors or landlords or hotel owners or anything like that. I bet the water's pretty calm, too. The fisherman could be the only person who even had a chance of noticing them."

I had to admit that this all did make sense, but it didn't quite sit right with me.

"No," I said, shaking my head. "They'll have to have food or something brought to them, at the very least. They don't seem like the types to live off the land. And if they were just trying to lie low, why go out on the water at all? There's no reason to risk it. There are other places they could've gone to escape detection more effectively."

"I'm still with Marston," Muñoz said, nodding to me. "What you say makes sense, but it doesn't quite add up. The fisherman said that they're out there looking for something. What is it, then? There has to be a reason they're there other than just hiding out now that we know about them."

Just then, Buddy and the waitress returned bearing plates galore. What felt like a hundred different gloriously greasy smells wafted my way, and my stomach grumbled so hard that I was afraid the others could hear it. They must not have, though, since Holm didn't bother to tease me about it.

Buddy deposited three plates in front of me.

"I recommend everything, so I brought you a sampling of some of my favorite dishes," he explained, beaming down at me. "Make sure to let me know what you think. Enjoy your meals, folks. I'll be back to check on you later."

He winked at me as he sped off, leaving me to try to decide what to sample first: the steaming hot buttermilk pancakes, the cheesy scrambled eggs tossed with healthy (or delightfully unhealthy) gobs of sausage and bacon, or the biscuits slathered in gravy.

"You got the works, Marston!" Birn exclaimed, looking longingly at my plates, which paled in comparison to his lone, though hefty, omelet dripping with what looked to be several kinds of cheese. "You guys are going to be crashing this place forever now. I made a mistake showing it to you."

He didn't look too perturbed by this thought, however, digging right into his own meal.

I could practically hear Holm licking his chops as he descended on his own plate, a stack of pancakes that stretched about a mile high, all drowning in chocolate. Muñoz, not to be left out, had two pieces of fat French toast next to a couple of runny fried eggs and sausage links.

I had a feeling we were all going to be crashing hard into a food coma in not too long and took a hefty gulp from my coffee mug. I would need that caffeine, after all. My blood pressure was already going to spike anyway with all this food.

It was worth it, though. It turns out that Birn wasn't lying or biased when he called his cousin's diner the best in the city. It really was, and I wasn't more than a few bites into each of my samplings when I decided there was no way Holm and I weren't coming back at least as much as Birn and Muñoz.

We ate in silence for quite some time, enough for the waitress to come back to check on us and refill our coffee mugs. The food was just too good to waste time talking instead of eating.

"What about the Hollands, though?" Holm managed when he was about halfway through his plate, the human vacuum cleaner that he was. "What do we think they're looking for out there?"

"You've got some, well…" I gestured all around my own face as I gazed at my partner's, which was pretty much covered in chocolate at that point.

"Whoops, sorry," Holm said, grabbing his napkin and dabbing a bit at his face, though it didn't help much. "Did I get it?"

"Sure," I chuckled, realizing that he was probably a

lost cause at that point, given that he still had half his plate left.

"Well, do we think it's that ship of yours, Marston?" Muñoz asked, ignoring Holm and me. "We know they're looking for it, right?"

My pulse quickened at the mere mention of the *Dragon's Rogue*.

"I don't know," I said honestly, shaking my head. "The ship was originally built and commissioned in Europe, but I've been operating under the assumption all this time that it's somewhere in the Americas' waters, based on its last known location, and that stuff with the *Searcher's Chance*. I suppose it's a possibility, though."

"These people are like, obsessed with this stuff though, right?" Birn asked. "Like you, but even more. It could be anything, then, right? There are other long lost pirate ships out there. If I've learned anything working with you, it's that."

"I wouldn't say that anyone's more obsessed than him," Holm said, jutting a chocolate-covered thumb in my general direction.

"Alright, alright," I said, rolling my eyes. "Point taken. But what he means is that they look for more than one ship, while I've only ever really intentionally looked for the *Dragon's Rogue* and maybe the *Searcher's Chance*. The rest of it all just kind of fell in my lap."

"Yeah, because only you would have buried treasure falling right into your lap," Holm said, rolling his eyes.

"Hey, you were with me when we found Lafitte's ship," I pointed out.

"Please," he scoffed. "There's no way I would've even ended up on that mission unless I was with you."

"So you're saying I'm a better agent than you," I teased.

"No, I'm saying you're a weirder one," he corrected, and I had to give him that one as we all laughed.

"Birn's point is, this could be any artifact that they're looking for, right?" Muñoz asked. "Or do they only work on one project at once? This is the part of their file you've been working on, Marston."

Everyone looked to me for confirmation, and I nodded.

"Yeah, I mean, they have to, right?" I asked. "We know that they found Lafitte's ship sometime in the last year, then pawned it off on Clifton Beck, that gang leader from New Orleans, for some reason that really doesn't make any sense yet. At the same time, they had that thug Joey working on the whole *Dragon's Rogue* and Grendel's journal thing in Virginia."

"Wait, why doesn't that make sense?" Muñoz asked, holding up a finger to stop me. "I thought they did that as a way of helping out with the whole Haitian zombie drug thing you guys were working on."

"Yeah, but why did they want it in circulation in

New Orleans?" I asked. "It wasn't their drug. They weren't making any money off of it, as far as we know, and we've looked deep into it. If they were directly involved, we would know it by now. And why'd they leave all that treasure on board for the gangbangers to just take instead of keeping it for themselves? None of it adds up."

"Weren't they tailing you in Haiti, too?" Birn asked.

"Someone was," I confirmed with another nod, wiping some syrup off my own lip. "That's how they knew I was looking for the *Dragon's Rogue* in the first place."

"This is gonna sound crazy, but hear me out," Muñoz said, and I nodded yet again. "Do you think that maybe they left Lafitte's ship there for you to find?"

I paused with my fork halfway to my mouth, gravy dripping off the biscuit and down onto one of the pancakes.

"I... I hadn't thought of that," I managed, blinking at her.

I really hadn't, though now that she mentioned it, I wasn't at all sure why. The Hollands had sent me the fake journal, after all, and they'd been constructing a fake *Dragon's Rogue* for me to find, too. So why not Lafitte's ship? Was it even the real deal? Could it be a fake, too? I hadn't had much time to look at it or any of its contents before the FBI hauled it away. An expert like George, or maybe even Percy, would be able to tell for sure.

"You think that was a fake like the other one?" Holm asked in a hushed tone, reading my mind. I looked over and saw that he'd all but abandoned what was left of his own meal, as well.

"I... I don't know," I stammered, my mind and heart still racing in tandem at the possibility. "The FBI took everything, and Diane hasn't been able to find anything out about it since."

"I mean, it's our case now, though, right?" Birn asked with a shrug. "That turned out to be a Holland case, even though we didn't know it before."

"Yeah, but Diane said they're still cagey about it all," I explained. This had been a sore spot over the last several weeks between Diane and me. I wouldn't shut up about it, and she wouldn't stop telling me that the FBI would get around to it when they got around to it. They just needed to finish their own evaluation of the artifacts first. When they did, we would be the first to know their findings.

"Cagey?!" Holm explained. "I swear, this is our case. They'll do anything to keep this stuff from us. Don't they care about actually catching the bad guys?"

"Of course they do," Muñoz scolded. "And not all FBI agents are like Smith. Didn't we just all have it out about this an hour ago? Aren't you done yet?"

She had a point. Complaining about the FBI's

involvement with this case wasn't going to get us anywhere.

"Hey, isn't that woman agent you worked with in NOLA on that case?" Birn asked. "I mean, she was down there with you, there when you found the ship. It'd make sense if she was in on the whole thing."

"And you said she was cagey about the Holland case, too, when you talked to her last," Holm said excitedly, pointing his fork at me and sending droplets of chocolate all over the table between us. "I bet he's right. She must be working on that!"

"I don't know," I said cautiously, shaking my head and not wanting to get my own hopes up. "I know they sent her back to teach some classes at the academy while she wound down from her undercover work."

"But she's not doing that anymore, right?" Holm asked, his eagerness unabated. "Otherwise, why would she be all weird about talking to you about it?"

"I don't know," I said again, a little sharper this time. "And I'll let you know what she says as soon as I hear from her, just like I promised earlier. Until then, there's no use worrying about it."

I said this just as much to convince myself as I did them. I wasn't sure what to make of all this speculating. Muñoz's new theory was going to stick with me for a while, and I knew that. And I couldn't exactly afford to get distracted right now, not if Holm and I were going to prove that they needed us in Scotland.

"Well, if the ship is a fake, the question remains as to why," Muñoz said, determined not to drop the subject as she narrowed her eyes and furrowed her brow, lost deep in thought.

"I thought you just said why," Holm pointed out, flicking his still-chocolaty fork in her direction now. "Because they wanted to mess with Marston after finding out he was looking for the *Dragon's Rogue* in Haiti."

"Yes, that's the why, but *how*," Muñoz clarified. "That still doesn't make sense to me."

Holm looked just as confused as he was before she said this, but I knew exactly what she meant.

"The question is, how was Lafitte's ship supposed to mess with me?" I asked as an explanation for Holm and Birn, who also looked a little lost. "I wasn't looking for it like the *Dragon's Rogue*, was I? The reason for the fake journal and the fake *Dragon's Rogue* was to get me to give up looking or even to think I found the ship when I really didn't. None of that holds in this situation."

"I guess you're right," Birn said, now adopting the same thoughtful look that was etched across his partner's face.

"Yeah, I guess that makes sense," Holm said with a sigh, setting down his fork at long last. "Or doesn't, I mean."

"And the treasure wouldn't make sense either," I

added. "And all the artifacts. Could all of those have been fake, too?"

"It didn't look fake," Holm said almost defensively as if he didn't even want to think about that possibility.

"Neither did Grendel's journal," I pointed out. "I never would've been able to tell if it weren't for that old book repairman Percy's help. And even he said that most appraisers wouldn't be able to tell, it was that good of a forgery."

"Well then, we need to tell the FBI that," Birn said quickly. "Do they know?"

"Yeah, they know everything about my search for the *Dragon's Rogue* now," I said with a nod, staring down at the plate in front of me.

This was a sore spot for me, for some reason. It was bad enough having everyone at MBLIS now directly involved in my search, but the FBI, too? This was supposed to be a thing between myself and my grandfather, and now between Tessa and me. For some reason that I couldn't quite explain, that bothered me. I didn't want all these strangers all up in my business like that, and I did consider the *Dragon's Rogue* to be my business, in a way.

"I wonder if they've considered all this," Muñoz mused, sipping on her coffee as she spoke, holding the cup between both of her hands. "They may not have since they're not as close to the case."

"Which is why we should have the damned ship!"

Holm exclaimed. "And why we should be on a plane to Scotland right now. We're the ones most familiar with the case, so we should be the ones who are working it."

I didn't disagree, but if Holm continued to go on like this, we were never going to get anything done, and he would probably alienate just about everyone at the other agencies who were supposed to be on our side in the process.

"Look, we just need to bide our time, like Diane said," I sighed, hating myself as I said the words. "We can still help. All it takes is a phone call for us to make our suspicions known. I'll talk to Diane about it and have her make sure the FBI knows all about the possibility that Lafitte's ship could be a fake."

"A phone call?" Holm scoffed, bugging his eyes out at me. "You can't be serious. You know as well as I do that we'd be way more help actually there than we could ever be over the phone."

"Yes, but that's not the point," I said, shaking my head. "It's just the way it is. Throwing a tantrum about it isn't going to fix anything."

"And just sitting around and letting other agencies steal the biggest case we've ever gotten?" Holm asked me, incredulous. "That's your plan?"

"No, my plan is to keep doing good work and to keep pestering Diane about things until she pulls through," I said, in as patient a tone as I could manage.

"And she will pull through. She always does. She has our back. It's just a matter of time."

I looked at each of my brunch companions in turn. They all knew I was right, that there was nothing more that we could really do. It just sucked. I could see it on their faces, and I agreed with them.

We all went back to eating, though I could tell that most of us had lost our appetite, not that I had much left to begin with given how much food Buddy had given me. Even Holm was just picking at what remained of his pancakes now.

"I guess that would explain why they sent the ship to New Orleans, to begin with," Holm mused after giving up on the rest of his meal and pushing his plate away from him. "They must've known we would've ended up there since that's where the Haitian zombie drug was going."

"They were looking for the ship for a long time before that, though," I pointed out, falling on the part of this timetable that troubled me. "And Clifton Beck—well, there were conflicting reports in our interviews about when exactly he was in the Keys. I guess it could've been after they found out about us, but the timetable would be tight. We do know that the ship didn't end up in NOLA until after we were on the case, though."

A Little Torch Key bartender's account of events would place Beck in the Keys a couple of weeks before

Holm and I were in Haiti. But other accounts presented a slightly hazier picture.

"They could've known about you even before that, though, right?" Birn asked. "I mean, these people are everywhere, and we have a lot of drug cases."

"Yeah, I guess so," I admitted, a chill running up and down my spine at this thought. "They've known someone in law enforcement was looking for the *Dragon's Rogue* for years now. I guess word spread about me through the nautical community. Though their thug, Joey, said that they didn't know about me specifically until Haiti."

"I don't like any of this," Holm said, leaning back against the booth and rubbing his stomach uncomfortably. "I feel like I'm going to throw up. I hate the idea of these people following us around on our cases."

"You sure it's just that, and not the fact that you mowed down nearly five pancakes covered in chocolate, syrup, and powdered sugar?" I asked, cocking an eyebrow at his plate, and everyone but Holm laughed.

"You could maybe say that it's a combination of factors," he admitted, cracking a half-grin and chuckling along with us, then.

"Everything going alright here, guys?" Buddy asked, walking over to our table.

"It was all excellent, thank you," I said, smiling up at him. "We'll be back for sure. Often."

"I knew I shouldn't have shown you our secret

spot," Birn complained, shaking his head at me, though he was still smiling.

"I'll be right back with your check," Buddy told his cousin, and the jovial man meandered back over to the front counter to chat with another one of his waitresses.

"He seems happy," I remarked, nodding in the diner owner's direction.

"He is," Birn confirmed. "I told you, retirement is where it's at. But not complete retirement. Everybody's gotta have a second act, even you, Marston."

"Wait, he's retired?" I asked, still watching Buddy.

"Former Marine," Birn grinned. "Don't tease him for it, though. I know we're all Navy guys here."

Buddy didn't take long to come back over, and he handed a single check to Birn. I reached for my wallet.

"Don't even think about it," Buddy said, clapping me on the shoulder and gesturing with his other hand at Holm and me. "Yours were on the house. Just make sure to come back and see me some time, okay? And catch all those bad guys for us."

6

ETHAN

I LEFT Buddy and his staff an enormous tip as thanks, and Holm did the same. One thing was for sure: that diner wasn't just Birn and Muñoz's secret anymore. They'd have to put up with us showing up there at least as much as they did when we weren't in the office.

After eating, we drove around for a little while, letting the food settle and our minds wander, before heading back into the office, dreading the piles upon piles of files and paperwork still left for us to go through.

I couldn't speak for the others, but I dreaded our FBI companions a little less now than I had that morning before going into work for the first time that day. We'd duked it out, but it seemed like we may have finally come to some kind of understanding. At least we were all united against the common enemy of Interpol now.

When we got back into the office, Diane was still locked away at her private desk. I could hear her muttering something on the phone but couldn't make out any distinct words.

"Took you long enough," Agent Smith called to us when we walked back in, but he was smiling instead of smirking now. I thought that maybe I was right, and things were turning up on that front, at least. I figured we were due for a break somewhere.

"Where'd you go?" Dobbs asked.

"Wouldn't you like to know?" Birn grinned at him and gave all the FBI agents a mischievous wink, which elicited several confused looks and cocked heads.

"What's that supposed to mean?" Smith asked, but no one answered him. I got the sense that while he was okay with sharing with his fellow MBLIS agents, there was no way that Birn was going to stick a bunch of FBI agents on his cousin's diner. I couldn't blame him.

"What'd we miss?" I asked the other agents as Birn and Muñoz exchanged a mischievous look.

"Not much," Forrester said with a shrug. "Just more paperwork. Diane was yelling on the phone with Interpol some more. That was kind of fun."

"Oh?" Holm asked, raising his eyebrows. "I can't believe we missed that."

It was always fun to watch Diane rage at people on

the phone. She'd been a real force to be reckoned with when MBLIS was having funding difficulties, but I wondered what had happened to playing nice with Interpol. That plan seemed to have gone down the drain.

"Did you get any idea what it was about?" I asked. "I mean, she said she was going to play it cool with them for a while, didn't she?"

"An hour is a while for Diane," Holm pointed out, and I chuckled and had to admit that he wasn't wrong about that.

"She didn't say," Corey said, shaking his head. "Something about Scotland, obviously. Hunt listened through the door. Maybe he remembers better."

Somehow, I didn't like the image of the FBI agents listening in on Diane's private conversations. It wasn't like Holm and I weren't guilty of doing the same before, but we worked for her. These guys... well, sometimes it was hard to tell when they were operating in good faith, is all.

"I think it just escalated," the usually silent Hunt said with a shrug. "She was trying to convince them to let Marston fly to Scotland, but I guess they didn't respond well. She kept getting madder about it, and then there was a lot of yelling. I could even hear the guy on the other line. He was talking so loud. Couldn't tell what he was saying, though."

I exchanged a knowing look with Holm.

"Told you she'd have our backs," I said, and I felt a swell of pride that we were Diane's agents and warmth toward her for going to bat for us even when it might not be in her own best interest.

"Yeah, but if she carries on like this, she might find herself without a job," Muñoz remarked, her eyes wide with worry. "It's one thing yelling at Sheldon the ridiculous pencil pusher, but Interpol? That might come back to bite her in the ass."

"It might bite us even more not to be in Scotland when they break this case," Holm pointed out, and Muñoz gave him a grudging nod of agreement.

"How long has she been talking to Interpol?" I asked the FBI agents.

"Oh, that was a while ago," Dobbs said with a wave of his hand. "I think this is something else. She came out and saw you guys had gone, and we told her you went to lunch or breakfast or whatever, but then she got another call. No yelling on this one, though."

I exchanged another look with Holm. Could there be another break in the Holland case? If so, wouldn't she be yelling some more about getting us out there?

"How long ago was that?" Birn asked.

"About forty-five minutes, I'd say," Dobbs said, checking his watch to be sure. "We're dying to find out what it's all about."

"Hopefully, we do get sent out there now," Holm said hopefully, voicing some of my own thoughts.

"Man, wouldn't it be great to be a part of that investigation..."

I agreed, but I didn't think we could get that lucky, not so soon.

"Could be another case," Muñoz offered. "I know we haven't been taking many with the Hollands being our top priority, but we're due for some emergency to come up, aren't we?"

She wasn't wrong. There was a certain point at which pawning cases off to other agencies and local law enforcement wouldn't work anymore. Something too big and too important would come along to distract us from breaking the Holland case, eventually.

"Man, that would suck," Holm muttered, shaking his head at the thought. "To get pulled off on some other case while Interpol's breaking the Holland case without us?"

"We don't know they're breaking it," I pointed out. "And I, for one, would prefer to be doing something other than sitting around here all day. I'd take a new case."

I knew it wasn't going to happen, though. We all did. In order for us to get called out on another case right now, something really high profile would have to happen. Like, national news, "someone had better get out here quick before things get ugly" kind of high profile.

I sat down at my desk across from Holm and began

to rummage through my stack of files again. I abandoned them quickly and checked my tablet to see whether the Maine lady had responded to any of my inquiries. Nope, still nothing. Predictable.

It was another half hour of this before Diane exited her office, her hair looking slightly disheveled and her eyes blinking more than they should.

"Oh, good," she said, her voice slightly weak when she saw us. "You're back. Robbie, Ethan, can I see you in my office, please?"

Holm and I exchanged a look. Usually, Diane just told the group what was going on. It had to be something important for us to be pulled aside like this.

I was all too happy to abandon my fruitless search for anything useful to do, so I cast aside the Maine lady's file and my tablet and followed Holm into Diane's office, the eyes of Birn, Muñoz, and all the FBI agents searing into my back as I did so.

I shut the door to Diane's office behind me when I entered. There was only one chair across from her desk, and Holm was already sitting in it, so I propped myself against the closed door and surveyed the room.

I hadn't been in Diane's office for a while, and it was mostly as I remembered, except that her usual pristine desk was covered in disheveled files much like our own were outside. Piles were spilling over, individual pages were sticking out every which way, and she generally just seemed to have lost control of the whole endeavor.

This, more than anything, I took to be a sign of just how crazy and out of sorts things had been at MBLIS in recent weeks. I'd never seen Diane so stressed, and this was the biggest sign of it. While she usually appeared pretty well put together, except for the now ever-present bags under her eyes, this was indicative of what was actually going on.

"Uh, do you need any help to clean this up?" I asked her, trying to be helpful. "If you want, I could—"

"No, Marston, I'm fine," she snapped, giving me a look that told me to shut up right now or else.

"Right, sorry," I muttered, silently vowing never to bring the matter up again.

"What's going on?" Holm asked excitedly, leaning forward with his elbows on the arms of his chair as all hints of fatigue left his own face, replaced by the eagerness that I was trying to prevent myself from feeling, as well. "Did Interpol come to their senses? Are we going to Scotland?"

Diane sighed, and I could see on her face that this wasn't the case. She probably would've announced it to the group if it was, and I knew then that I was right not to get my own hopes up.

"No," she said, pursing her lips. "I'm afraid that it's nothing like that."

Holm's face fell just as quickly as it had risen, his body slumping back into the chair in defeat.

"Seriously?" he asked as if he couldn't believe his ears. "You've got to be kidding me."

"You can't be surprised?" I said, shaking my head at him. "It's only been a couple of hours. Something big would have to happen for them to change their minds so quickly."

I glanced over at Diane again as I said this, and I realized that there was a glimmer of hope left in me that something big *had* actually happened. I searched her face for any sign that there was news about the Hollands, that the Interpol guy had caught them red-handed, even that this case was done and over with and Scotland was stealing our perps right out from under us. But her face was unreadable, aside from the tiredness that was still there.

"No, nothing like that," she said, shaking her head weakly.

"What, then?" I asked, a sense of foreboding building in my stomach.

"Dammit, the lead fell through!" Holm exclaimed, throwing his arms up in the air in frustration. "The fisherman guy was full of it, and it wasn't the Hollands after all. We're back to square one. That's it, isn't it?"

My eyes widened, and I stared at Diane, searching for any hint that he was right.

"No, it's not that either," she snapped, giving him a

fierce look. "And it would serve you well not to go jumping to conclusions so often, Agent Holm."

"Right, sorry," he muttered, just like I had moments before, staring down at his knees.

Everyone in that office knew that more often than not, Holm's gut served him and MBLIS well. But I shared her exasperation at that moment. I just wanted her to get to the point, and Holm was slowing things down.

"Look, it doesn't have anything to do with the Hollands at all," Diane said, wincing as she said the words as if she was anticipating us to respond poorly to this. "I'm going to have to send you two out on another assignment."

Holm's jaw dropped open, and he just gaped at her, for once at a loss for words. I was not, however.

"What? A new case?" I asked, floored.

Muñoz had been right after all. There was another case for us to work, and that meant that it had to be big. Big enough for Diane to look even more tired than she was already and for Holm and me to get sent away from Miami when they needed us here more than ever.

"Yes," she said, pursing her lips. "And it's a big one."

"Come on, why can't Birn and Muñoz go?" Holm complained. "We're the ones who've been working the Holland case since the beginning. We shouldn't be sent off when we're in the middle of it."

I didn't disagree, but I was also eager to hear what

this new case was. It had to be big for Diane to pull us right now. I hadn't been lying when I said that I would prefer a real case to looking through files all day, though I did wish it had come at another time, and not on the day when there was finally some movement with the Hollands, even if it was on the other side of the ocean.

"That would've been my first choice, as well, but the two of you were requested personally by the FBI," Diane said, wincing again as she said it. She didn't like this any more than Holm, I realized. She didn't want us to leave her alone with the FBI agents in the middle of the Holland case, but this was more important than what she wanted.

"The FBI?" I repeated. "But it doesn't have to do with the Hollands? How does that work?"

"Annoying coincidence," Diane sighed. "More than annoying. It's dangerous and upsetting. A government employee's child has been abducted."

There was silence in the room then. We all knew that none of our concerns about the Hollands, about the FBI, about Interpol, or anything else mattered when it came to a kid.

"Was it a stranger kidnapping?" I asked at long last, my stomach sinking all the way to the floor.

"Looks that way," Diane confirmed.

"When?" Holm asked, leaning forward again in his

chair now, his eyes no longer excited but still highly attentive.

"Early this morning," she said. "At a mall in North Carolina. The FBI was originally put on the case because the family is from out of state, and the mother works for the CDC. The whole thing's a mess."

"So how does MBLIS come into it?" I asked, shaking my head in confusion. North Carolina was a coastal state, sure, but the perp would have to be foreign, or the kid would have to be taken out of the country somehow for this to fall under our jurisdiction.

"That's what I've just been on the phone about," Diane explained. "A Coast Guard ship thinks they spotted the kid and the perps who took him out on the ocean, headed into international waters."

"Wait, did you just say perps?" Holm asked, his face turning white. "As in more than one?"

"That's right," Diane said with a nod. "It's kind of a weird case. I don't know the full details yet, but there are indications that it was a lone-wolf situation, but also that it was more coordinated, and it can't be both."

I pressed my back against the door, mulling this over. That didn't make a lot of sense. But then again, they wouldn't call us if it wasn't a tough case. Not right now, anyway.

"I'm guessing it's all over the news?" I asked.

"All over it," Diane confirmed darkly with a curt

nod. "Local, national, you name it, this kid's face is on it, which is one good thing, at least. It'll make it easier to find him in theory, anyway."

"There's no indication of who these people are that took him?" Holm asked. "Or why? Do we have descriptions?"

"We have some security footage from the mall," Diane explained. "Got a good look at one of the perps, a profile from the side. The other guy was dressed up in a ski mask and gloves and the whole deal. Had a gun, too."

"That... doesn't make any sense," I said, furrowing my brow at this. "That sounds like..."

"Both a lone-wolf and an organized operation?" Diane finished for me. "Yeah, exactly. Even more puzzling is that the first guy showed back up at the mall while an FBI agent was looking around. There was a shootout, a lot of commotion in a crowded area, and he got away again. No sign of the kid, though. Then, about an hour later, there was the sighting on the water."

"Is the agent alright?" Holm asked, and Diane nodded again.

"Yes, you'll meet him—or her, I actually don't know, I guess—when you get there," she said. "And you'll be glad to hear you're done with commercial flights. That's all been cleared up after your recent successes."

"Well, there's some good news, at least," I muttered, thinking about how Holm and I had endured a screaming child for hours on our flight to New Orleans.

"Why did the FBI request us, though?" Holm asked, more curious than complaining now. "Why can't Birn and Muñoz just go?"

Diane shrugged.

"I don't know," she said. "The guy just told me that they know about you two now, and they like your work. Your reputations precede you, I suppose."

"Well, that's no surprise," Holm grinned, leaning back in his chair with his hands interlocked behind his head now, a look of gloating etched across his face.

"What, now you're happy about it?" I asked, arching an eyebrow at him.

"Hey, who am I to deny the people what they want?" he asked with a shrug.

"The people?" I repeated, blinking at him. "What people? One guy at the FBI who has Diane's number?"

"Come on, let me enjoy the moment at least, Marston, sheesh," he said, waving a hand at me as if to shut me up.

I simply ignored him and turned my attention back to Diane.

"When do we leave?" I asked her.

"As soon as you're ready," she said. "You know how these cases are. You're on a ticking clock."

7

ETHAN

When we exited Diane's office, leaving her behind, no one was working, and everyone was staring at us expectantly.

I exchanged a look with Holm. Diane probably didn't want to tell us about this mission in front of everyone because it would prompt all kinds of complaining that we'd be gone during the Holland case, as well as complaining from Birn and Muñoz that they hadn't been sent instead, considering how bored they were.

"Well?" Muñoz asked, bugging her eyes out at us. "What was that all about?"

Holm didn't say anything, so I figured this just had to be on me.

"We caught a case," I said shortly, swiftly walking over to my desk and beginning to gather up my things amongst all the piles of files and other documents about the Hollands and their associates.

"What case?" Birn asked. His tone was a weird combination of whining and disbelieving, like he was suspicious of what we were saying.

"I guess it's all over the news," I said without turning to face him. "Missing kid."

"The one in North Carolina?" Agent Forrester asked, incredulous. "That's an FBI case. My buddies back in Virginia have been talking about it in the Slack all day."

"Huh?" I asked, shaking my head uncomprehendingly at him.

"It's a group chat thing," Muñoz smirked. "We don't use it."

"Surprise, surprise," Smith muttered sardonically.

"Okay, whatever, well, it is an FBI case, but they asked us to come help," I said, as Holm began to pack up his own things to get ready to go.

"Do you know who the agent is on the case?" Holm asked, turning to face the other agents. "They requested us personally, for some reason."

"No idea," Forrester said with a shrug. "We just know it's a big deal. Hey, how come it's your case now? You're not going to steal this one out from under us, too, are you?"

I blinked at him, registering what he was saying. I realized that until the whole mess in the Florida Keys, technically, the Holland case had been under the FBI's purview because of everything Nina Gosse had gone through in New Orleans. They just didn't know that the Hollands had anything to do with it yet.

It was weird, thinking that the FBI thought of us as the ones sweeping in on their territory here. No wonder they'd been sour since they arrived. Not only were we stealing a case from them, but they were being forced to work on it for us, on our turf, no less.

I felt a bit better about the whole thing with this realization. At least we weren't the only ones who saw ourselves as being antagonized here.

"It is an FBI case. We're just going to help them out," I explained. I almost added "like with New Orleans," but figured that would just hit on another sore spot with the FBI agents.

"I guess the Coast Guard spotted the kid and one of the perps heading into international waters," Holm added. "So they called us in."

"You?" Birn asked, an almost hurt look on his face, and I silently cursed Diane for making us break the news to them all by ourselves. "Why you? Shouldn't you be working *this* case?"

"We wish," Holm muttered bitterly, and I rolled my eyes. Of course, the people who wanted to go on this mission were staying behind, and the ones who wanted to stay behind were going. I would expect nothing less, given how things were going for us lately.

"I don't know why, but we don't really get a say in it, do we?" I said, in a tone that I hoped had some finality in it. "Besides, that's not what matters. Who's going, which agency's case it is. A little kid is missing, having God knows what done to him, and somebody needs to find him. Who cares who?"

Everyone was quiet after this until Muñoz gave me a deferential nod.

"Of course, Marston's right," she said. "It doesn't really matter. We're all itching to get somewhere with this case or another one, but we shouldn't lose sight of our priorities. Go ahead, get that kid back to his parents. We'll try not to break this case without you."

She gave me a wry grin at this, and I chuckled, though I secretly prayed that they wouldn't. As much as I wanted more movement on the Holland case, I also didn't want to miss out. Although maybe that meant that I needed to get my priorities straight, too.

"Ready to go?" I asked Holm, and he nodded.

We both waved on our way out the door.

"Bring us back a postcard," Birn called after us.

I dropped Holm off at his place briefly, and I ran home to my houseboat to pack some clothes and other items before heading to the airport to board our flight, a private MBLIS plane.

Thankfully, there were no screaming children to greet us this time around, given that this plane wasn't open to the public. I sipped on seltzer water, my tablet propped up on the small desk between Holm and me as we floated through the clouds toward North Carolina.

"Whatcha looking at?" Holm asked me, diverting his attention from where he had been peering out the window at the bright blue early summer sky beneath us.

"News reports about this whole thing," I said, shaking my head as I scrolled through an article about the parents going on the news, pleading for anyone with any information to come forward and bring their son back to them.

I scanned the photographs for any sign of an FBI agent. I only saw one person who might fit the bill: a woman in a skirt, blouse, and suit jacket who always seemed to be standing right next to the parents. The police detectives always had guns at their sides to identify them, and they stood a little further away, but this woman could be hiding her weapon somewhere and disguising herself in plain clothes.

It was possible, however, that the FBI agent involved wasn't anywhere near the parents but was out there somewhere hunting down the perps. It was a tough call. The parents were an important part of dealing with a situation like this, and panicked parents could also make matters worse inadvertently by offering an enormous reward or revealing details about the investigation on television. There was a fine line between working the case and preventing further damage from within.

"What do they say?" Holm asked, leaning forward and trying to peer over at my tablet's screen. "What are we dealing with here?"

"It is a weird case," I said, shaking my head again as I clicked on an article about the perps. Or rather, perp. It seemed that only a description of one was released to the media.

"How so?" Holm asked, craning his neck to try to see, so I shifted the tablet to give him a better view.

"See this here?" I asked, pointing at the blurry, cropped security footage picture of a man with acne scars on his cheek, dark hair, and a hazel-colored jacket. "This is the picture of the perp that's been circulating in the media. The guy looks like a lone wolf, right?"

"Sure does," Holm agreed, scowling at the picture. "I'd like to clock him a new one. I'll tell you that."

The guy did look like a creep, even without the information we had about him, I decided. But that was beside the point.

"Me, too, but that's not what I mean," I said quickly. "This is the only picture that keeps appearing in any of the articles. There's only the mention of this one guy, but nothing about the other perp. Diane said there were two, right?"

"Yeah, she did," Holm confirmed with a nod, his

brow now furrowed in confusion as he followed my reasoning. "She said that he was all geared up in a ski mask and stuff, right?"

"That's right," I said, nodding. "But there's no mention of that in any of the official reports from the police or the FBI. Nothing. Some witnesses who were interviewed by the media said something about a man with a gun, but people seem to be chalking that up to eyewitness testimony being shaky at best."

"Now they come around," Holm huffed. "Usually, they'll run with anything on a story like this."

"I know, that's what's so weird," I said. "The police and the FBI must be keeping the second perp quiet for some reason. It would make sense, in a way, if they think this is more organized than a lone-wolf operation. People are already panicking. It'd be so much worse if they thought there was some kind of child sex trafficking operation going on."

"God, do you think there is?" Holm asked, his eyes widening.

I knew my partner was smart enough to know that this was a possibility, but it wasn't exactly fun to think about. My stomach churned just at the thought, and I began to regret eating all that rich food at the diner earlier.

"That's what we're going to need to find out," I said quietly. "Another reason they probably didn't release any of this to the media is to avoid tipping any organization off that we may know about them. We have the upper hand in that way, for now, though until we find that kid, we're going to be racing against the clock. That's the most important thing here."

"Usually, these aren't stranger situations," Holm said, biting his lip and shaking his head. "Usually, it's someone known to the kid who took him. But in those news conference photos, it looks like they're operating under the assumption that the parents had nothing to do with it, and they don't know anyone who could've done this."

"Both things could be true," I mused, leaning back in my chair and running a hand across my face as I pondered this. "It's not unheard of for law enforcement to treat it as a kind of Schrodinger's cat situation, and getting the parents in front of the cameras can reveal a lot about their own psychology. Even so, the parents were with him when it happened, and all reports say they were distraught. I doubt they're involved, but given the statistics, you're right that we should keep an open mind about it."

"Could be only one parent knew about it, so the other had a genuine reaction," Holm suggested. "I heard about a case like that overseas a few years back."

"Yeah, that was a nasty one," I said, wincing again at the memory. "The mother had her own kid killed, and the father didn't know a thing about it. It took so long for the authorities to crack the case because he just kept going on publicity tours, quit his job even, trying to find his kid, and they never considered the possibility that one of the parents could've done it because his reaction was so genuine. But it was her all along."

"An open mind, then," Holm said with a curt nod, leaning back in his own seat and looking more than a little green. "We just need to figure out what happened to this kid."

"I know," I said, gazing out the window some more. "We're going straight to the police station when we arrive. We'll see if we can meet with the parents and talk with the FBI agent and detectives on the case. We'll have a better idea of where we stand then. In the meantime, the Coast Guard's out looking for the kid, and so are the police and state troopers on land."

"I kind of want to join the search myself," Holm said, his tone troubled. "Directly, I mean."

"We will," I assured him. "But we have to get our bearings first. The last thing we want is to waste time looking in all the wrong places when a little investigating would've pointed us in the right direction."

8

ETHAN

Holm and I were met at the gate by a young officer who looked like an all-American kid, if a bit bedraggled, with his golden blond hair tousled beneath his cap and a worried, anxious look in his eyes.

"Agents Marston and Holm?" he asked us as he rushed over, taking our bags despite our protestations.

"The one and only," Holm grinned. "Or two, I guess. And you are?"

He held out his hand to the young man, who shook it and then mine, shifting my light suitcase to his other hand briefly.

"Officer Ryan Hollister, sir," he said. "Man, are we glad to have you here."

"That bad, huh?" I asked, worry percolating in the pit of my stomach as we followed the young man out into a private parking lot near our gate, where his police car was waiting for us by the door with its hazard lights on.

"We've never seen anything like this here, sir," he said, shaking his head. His eyes were about the size of a couple of golf balls. "And the media's everywhere, and the parents are freaking out, of course. You could say we're a bit out of our comfort zone on this one."

He placed our luggage on an empty seat and opened the passenger and backseat doors for us, and I climbed in the front while Holm settled in the back next to our luggage.

"There's no harm in admitting that," I assured him as he got behind the steering wheel. "Most departments three times your size would be out of their depth, but that's why we're here."

"The FBI been any help?" Holm asked.

"Oh yeah, they sent two people," Officer Hollister said brightly as he pulled us out of the parking lot and onto a nearby interstate, headed in the direction of his small town not far from there. "I've only really talked to the psychologist, though. The other agent, the one who was at the mall, she hasn't been in the station much. Lots of tracking down the bad guys, I guess."

I noticed that the young officer looked a little envious at this. Maybe he had aspirations for becoming a detective.

"Ah, yeah, she ran into the guy in the mall, right?"

Holm asked, leaning forward as Hollister pulled into the left lane.

"Yeah, that was rough," the kid sighed, shaking his head and peering back at Holm in the rearview mirror. "She nearly caught him, but some idiot in the crowd got in the way, I guess, ran right into her, and knocked her over. When the perp shot at her, everyone freaked out."

"Why was there such a big crowd?" I asked. "They didn't shut the mall down after the kid was taken?"

"Tried, but there weren't enough of them and too many people who wanted in," Hollister sighed. "It was mostly mall security at that point and a couple of officers. Everyone else was out looking for the kid or back at the station with the parents."

"Makes sense, I guess," Holm grumbled. "The security part, I mean, not the crowd. I don't get why anyone would want to be near a crime scene like that."

"It's like watching a car crash," I sighed, shaking my head. "All morbid curiosity and no common sense. Probably would've caught the guy if it weren't for the crowd, though he may not have been there in the first place if it weren't for them giving him a chance to blend in, so I guess it's all a wash at the end of the day."

"That's one way to look at it," Holm said, and I got the sense that he had another way. I didn't exactly disagree.

"How are the parents?" I asked Hollister. "Is the FBI

psychologist getting through to them?"

Sometimes parents were the opposite of helpful in these situations, even if they didn't have anything to do with the kidnapping itself. They were distraught, or enraged, or trying to run the investigation themselves, questioning everything the police and assembled experts said or did. Any reaction was understandable in my mind, given the situation, but the FBI was right to send an expert to deal with them. That was probably the woman I had seen in the picture, I realized, always hovering near the mother and father of the missing boy.

"They're understandably upset," Hollister said, pursing his lips. "I can't even imagine... if something like that happened to my daughter, I'd be screaming bloody murder."

I glanced over at him in surprise.

"Think I'm too young to have a kid?" he chuckled, arching an eyebrow at me. "Don't worry. You're not the only one. At least I'll still be young when she goes off to college. Any kids of your own?"

"No," I said. "A little busy with my career, I'm afraid."

"Same here," Holm added.

"That's alright," Hollister said brightly. "At least you probably get to sleep through the night more often than not."

We drove on in silence for some time until we

arrived at our little coastal destination. I could see the water off in the distance, and I lowered my window to take in the familiar salty air. There was nothing like that smell.

Hollister took his car through the streets of the tiny town, and we passed several shops in a small downtown area and some quaint residential areas with cozy little houses to match the aesthetic of the town itself.

It was very quiet, quieter than I expected even, especially for the afternoon on a hazy early summer day.

"Most of the people pack up and leave?" Holm asked, no doubt thinking the same as me.

"Seems like it," Hollister remarked. "If they didn't leave when the first news hit, they did after the shooting at the mall. That seemed to scare everyone into some common sense, at least."

I did see a number of police cars as we rolled through the town, though, no doubt belonging to officers searching for the missing boy. Even though the Coast Guard believed they spotted him and one of his abductors at sea, it was always possible that it was a mistake, or that the boy was already back on land for some reason. There was no reason to abandon the search on land until we knew for certain where he could be.

Finally, we pulled into a police station, likely the only one in town.

"Here we are," Hollister said, parking near the front door. "Back to the old grindstone. I'm sure my boss will want to have a word with you before you question the parents or any other witnesses. The FBI agent might be back by now, too."

"Of course," I said, nodding to him. "Thank you for picking us up. Hopefully, we'll run into you again soon."

"You can count on it," the young man grinned as he followed us out of the car and opened the door for us. "The chief's office is right back there. He should be waiting for you. I let him know when you arrived."

Hollister pointed us in the right direction, and we thanked him again and headed on our way.

Eyes followed us as we made our way through the main desk area. There were a number of officers and detectives there, some of them surely in from neighboring towns, clustered around a whiteboard detailing the case.

I didn't notice the woman from the pictures who I assumed to be the FBI psychologist anywhere, nor the parents, or anyone who might be the FBI agent. They all had badges that looked more like policemen's than that of a federal agent's.

We didn't stop to talk, and no one talked to us, though I felt a pervasive nervous energy in the room, perhaps accentuated by the cups of coffee and energy drinks that were strewn all over the place. No one was probably going to sleep until this kid was found. Not for long, at least.

The door to the chief's office was ajar, but I knocked anyway.

"Come in," a gruff voice called, and Holm and I walked through, closing the door behind us.

Inside, we found a weary-looking man who I would place in his early sixties sitting behind a massive desk piled high with files, not unlike Diane's at that very moment. The man appeared to have been picking one of his eyebrows, and the remaining hairs were sticking up in the opposite direction they should've. He was slumped over and looked like he was in need of a good night's sleep and maybe a Xanax, even though it was still afternoon.

"I'm Agent Ethan Marston, and this is my partner, Robbie Holm, from MBLIS," I said, nodding to the man behind the desk. "We're here to help out with the missing child case."

"Of course you are," he sighed, waving a hand to indicate that we should sit in the two wooden seats across from him. "I'm Chief Raskin. Welcome, we're glad to have you."

He sounded just as exhausted as he looked.

"We're glad to be here," I said, taking my seat, closely followed by Holm. "Why don't you update us on what you have so far?"

"I'm afraid not much since the FBI called you in,"

he said, and I noticed the hint of a Southern twang in his raspy voice. "We've been looking and looking, but he's not anywhere in this town, or if he is, he's hiding real good."

"We were told there were two perps seen in the initial video, but only one showed back up at the mall later, and only one is mentioned in media reports," Holm said, and Raskin nodded.

"Yeah, the FBI took the lead on that one," he said. "Thought it would be best not to tip 'em off that we know about the other perp since he was all bundled up and only a couple of witnesses got a decent look at him. We've kept those witnesses quiet for now, but it's only a matter of time until the reporters get to 'em, I'd say."

I thought that Raskin looked a bit more world-weary than I would've expected for a department of this size.

"You always worked here?" I asked him.

"Oh, no, sir," he said, shaking his head. "Not at all. I used to be a detective up in Durham. I got one or two cases like this in my tenure, though never this high profile. Thought this job would be less stressful, but... well, the world has a way of laughing at you, doesn't it?"

"Yes, it does," I agreed with a chuckle. "Only the one perp was at the mall, then? We know that for sure?"

"We've scoured all the tapes for any sign of the other guy," Raskin said with a shrug. "Can't say they're great tapes, but I feel like we would've noticed him in that getup. Though he could've been dressed normally, then, and we never would've known the difference since we never got a look at his face."

I nodded, considering this. It was possible that both had been there the second time, then.

"No sign of the boy, though?" Holm asked.

"Oh, no," Raskin said, shaking his head for emphasis. "No way. That I'm sure of. If that kid was there, someone would've noticed him. His face is everywhere, and the crowd at the mall knew it. It's why they were there in the first place."

"Only one guy was seen on the boat, though?" I asked. "Do we know which one?"

"The Coast Guard guy picked the man with the face out of a photo lineup," Raskin said, indicating a spot on his cheek that told me he was talking about the man with the acne scars. "So we're guessing it's him. We didn't get a good description of the boat itself, though. It could've been the other guy was hiding in a cabin somewhere."

"He had to have gone out there between the scuffle at the mall and when the Coast Guard saw him, then," Holm mused, and I nodded.

"Alright, then, if there isn't anything else, I think it's high time we spoke with the parents," I said.

9

ETHAN

I'D BEEN DREADING this part since we'd caught the case. I didn't want to have to look these parents in the eye and deal with their grief and pain, let alone question them about whether they could've had anything to do with their son's disappearance.

We'd have to do that subtly. For obvious reasons, parents didn't tend to respond well to that kind of questioning.

Raskin led Holm and me down a small hallway lined with interrogation rooms until we got to a waiting area at the back with a couch, a couple of comfy chairs, and a vending machine. A man and a woman I recognized as the boy's parents from the news sat on the couch. The father was crying, and the woman had her arm around him. Another woman, who I also recognized from the news, leaned close to them in one of the chairs, her hands folded and resting gently on the edge of a coffee table between them. She was murmuring something to them.

Raskin cleared his throat when we were there, clearly embarrassed about interrupting.

"Sorry," he muttered, staring down at his shoes. "The MBLIS agents are here."

"Thank you, Eddie," the woman told him, murmuring something else to the parents and then rising to greet Holm and me with her hand extended. "I'm Doctor Osborne. You can call me Ellie. I'm a psychologist with the FBI."

She was who I'd imagined then when I saw the photographs.

"Ethan Marston, glad to meet you," I said, taking her hand. "And this is my partner, Robbie Holm."

She nodded to Holm and shook his hand, too.

"Why don't we take a step out and chat for a few minutes?" she suggested, and I nodded.

"Y-you're leaving?" the mother sputtered, looking like she might burst into tears just like her husband at this news.

"Just for a few minutes," Osborne assured them. "I need to talk with these agents about your case."

That seemed to calm the woman, who no doubt wanted everyone to get on with what needed to be done so we could find her son sooner, even if it made her uncomfortable. She nodded and gave me a weak smile as Holm and I followed Osborne toward one of the interrogation rooms.

"I'll just sit with 'em a minute," Raskin said, looking like he would prefer to do anything else at that moment.

"Thank you," Osborne said gratefully, and he walked over to take her place in the chair next to the coffee table.

In the interrogation room, Osborne shut and locked the door behind us and then sat down. Holm and I took our seats across from her.

"Sorry about that," she said. "They've developed an attachment to me. It's not uncommon in situations like these."

"Do you work a lot of these cases?" I asked.

She was a stern-looking woman, probably in her early fifties, with streaks of gray running through her long hair, which was pulled back in a very tight ponytail.

"A fair number," she said with a curt nod. "Well, considering how many there are, that is, and there aren't all that many. I'd say I've worked about a dozen in my time. This is the most high profile one, though. That girl in Colorado came close, though."

I vaguely remembered that case, enough to know that they'd found the kid. That gave me hope.

"Why don't you tell us about the parents?" Holm suggested, folding his hands in his lap.

"The average American family, I'd say," Osborne mused, her brow furrowed together in thought. "The mother works for the CDC in Atlanta, as I'm sure you've heard. Pretty high up, too. The father's in advertising. No other children. Two dogs. No cats. Live in the suburbs. Cookie-cutter in a lot of ways, I like to call it."

"Anything beneath the surface?" I asked.

"Oh, there always is," she said, giving me a small, knowing smile. "I just haven't found it yet. But then again, I'm sure you know that everyone's more complicated than they seem, given your line of work."

"A bit pessimistic," Holm pointed out, and I had to agree.

"You misunderstand me," she said, shaking her head. "It's not that I think every family has some dark secret. It's just that no one's as average as they seem. I just haven't figured out what's different about these people yet, though. In between the media coverage and keeping them somewhat composed—and sometimes medicated—over the past few hours, I haven't had time for much else."

"I think I understand that," I said, nodding slowly. "Do you suspect them?"

Osborne sighed and pursed her lips as if trying to decide how to respond to this.

"I don't know," she said at long last. "You know the details of the case, Agent Marston. It's an odd one. Usually, it's someone known to the child, but it's hard to work this whole thing out. I'm relatively confident that neither parent recognized the unmasked perpetrator, but we all know there were two men who took him."

"Yes," I said, thinking this over. "That could explain why one of them had his face covered. He could be someone they know, or who the child knows."

"Agreed, though if he's the only one who knew him, and not the parents, it probably would've been more of a benefit to be unmasked to lure him in," Osborne added.

"Could've been to avoid detection," Holm shrugged.

"But the other one didn't seem so concerned about that," the woman said, shaking her head slowly. "It is an odd case. None of it quite adds up the way you expect it to."

"I suppose that's why we're here," I said, giving her a small smile. "In the meantime, I think I'd like to talk to the parents myself if you don't mind."

"Of course," Osborne said, nodding her head gratefully to me.

"Has anyone else spoken to them much?" Holm asked.

"Not in detail," she admitted, shaking her head as she rose to reopen the door to the interrogation room for us. "They've been very busy trying to find the child, and I'm more than competent."

"I'm certain that you are," Holm said quickly, looking alarmed that he might have inadvertently called Dr. Osborne's expertise into question. "I didn't mean to..."

"Don't worry, I didn't take it that way," she said, giving him a thin smile, which I imagined was the best she could manage on a good day. "I was just reiterating the point."

Together, we all made our way back to the sitting area, which was silent but for the father's continued sobs. The mother was also crying now. Chief Raskin looked even more uncomfortable than he had when we left him.

"Don't worry, Eddie," Osborne told him, resting a long, thin hand on his shoulder gently. "We can take it from here."

"Uh, thanks," Raskin said, seeming surprised to see us, like he hadn't noticed our return, though he looked more relieved than ever that we had. "I'll just be in my office if anybody needs me."

"Thank you," I told him, and he scurried off as quickly as he could, leaving us alone with the parents.

Osborne settled back into the chair once occupied by the chief, and I sat down in another across from the boy's mother. Holm crossed over to a bench against the wall, closer to the father's side of the couch.

"Hello, I'm Ethan, and this is my partner, Robbie," I said as gently as I could, speaking directly to the mother, who looked right at me with tears streaming down her face. The father still had his head in his hands, though his shoulders shook less now. "What are your names?"

I knew from the police and media reports, of course, but it was better to ease witnesses into difficult conversations like this.

"You're with that other agency?" the father asked, raising his head weakly. "The one the FBI called?"

"MBLIS, yes," I confirmed, and the mother nodded knowingly. She must have been familiar with most government agencies, I realized, because of her job.

"I'm Annabelle Watson, and this is my husband, Curt," the mother said, rubbing her partner's back. "Our son's Mikey. Well, Michael, but we call him Mikey. You know that, though, of course."

She shut her eyes tight as if trying not to visualize what might be happening to her little boy at that moment, and I had to force the thought away myself.

"Why don't you tell us what happened?" I asked her gently.

"I know you've probably told the story a thousand times already today, but if you could just indulge us one more time, we'd appreciate it," Holm added when the woman hesitated to respond.

The woman reopened her eyes and nodded, and so did her husband.

"We... we went to the mall early this morning, the

second it opened," she explained. "Mikey forgot his toothbrush and his bathing suit, so we needed to get him a new one. He insisted on packing himself, you see. He wanted to be a big boy. He wouldn't even let me check to see that he had anything. I figured I might as well encourage some independence. We both work, you see."

She choked up again, and I nodded to her to make sure she knew that I didn't think it was her fault.

"I understand," I assured her.

"Well," she continued, gulping down her tears. "By the time we were done at the department store, he was crying because he was so hungry, and we hadn't had breakfast yet."

"Most of the places in the food court were still closed," Curt added. "But there was a pretzel stand open, and so I went to get him one of those. He wanted the fancy one, covered in cinnamon and sugar and all of that. He likes those."

The man gave a watery smile at the memory.

"What happened next?" I urged gently, hating myself as I did so.

"Well, the stand only took cash, and I didn't have enough coins," Curt said, his voice shaking. "Mikey was looking at some gumball machines, and I called Annabelle over to see if she had any quarters or another dollar bill."

It was the father's turn to shut his eyes tightly now,

not wanting to go on. His wife looked at me apologetically.

"That's when it happened," she said, her voice as small as that of a mouse. "When I turned my back, just for a minute, to give Curt some coins. When I turned back around, Mikey wasn't by the gumball machines anymore. He was all the way down the hall by one of the stores, and then he was screaming, and that man was holding him..."

She grimaced and shivered, not wanting to go on herself now.

"I'm so sorry," Holm said softly. That was all there was to say when it came to something like this.

"Thank you," Annabelle murmured, interlinking her arm with her husband's own and placing her other hand on his knee.

"Did you only see the one man?" I asked.

"No," she said, shaking her head. "Well, Curt only saw the one. I saw both of them. The other man was hard to see at first... he just kind of blended into the wall, with his dark clothes. Then I saw his gun."

"Was it drawn?" I asked.

"I don't know," she said, shaking her head. "I'm sorry, I don't remember."

"That's okay," I assured her. "I'd rather you tell us that than make something up because you think it's what we want to hear."

"That's what she said," Annabelle said with a small smile, nodding in Osborne's direction.

"Glad we're on the same page," I said, smiling back at her, though I never doubted it. "Why don't you tell me what you remember, Curt?"

"I-it's all a blur," he stammered, shaking his head. "I'm sure Annabelle can tell you better. She's always had a better memory than me."

"Why don't you just tell us what you do remember?" Holm prompted gently. "It doesn't have to be much."

"Well, I... I just remember paying the pretzel guy," he began with a deep breath. "Or trying to pay the pretzel guy, at least, but Annabelle screamed and grabbed my arm, and I dropped all the coins. I bent over to pick them up without thinking. It was just instinctive."

"It's alright," I assured him, just as I had his wife. "You didn't do anything wrong."

"Well, once I registered that she was yelling, I turned around, and I just saw this guy in a tan jacket carrying Mikey off. I didn't notice anything else. I just saw red and ran after them."

"We both did," Annabelle added. "But by the time we got to the store they were in front of, they were gone, and I couldn't hear Mikey screaming anymore. Some lady from the store helped us, then. I don't remember much else until the security guards showed up."

"It's all a blur for me, too," Curt said, shaking his head and gulping down another sob. "I just remember someone in a mall uniform giving me some water, and then the police came and were talking about a security tape. Have you seen it?"

He looked between Holm and me hopefully.

"Yes, we've seen it," I said, nodding. "It tells us some, but not a lot." I wanted to temper their expectations. It was important to keep hope, but also important to be realistic.

"Dr. Osborne said that the other FBI agent ran into the man in the jacket again at the mall," Annabelle said excitedly, looking at me with wide eyes as if she was willing me to tell her that we'd caught the man.

"Yes, we haven't been able to find him, though," I said quietly. "Did Dr. Osborne tell you about the Coast Guard?"

There was a long silence.

"Yes," Curt said quietly at long last. "But you don't... you don't really think that they could be taking him... to some other country or something like that?"

It clearly took an effort for him to get the words out.

"We don't know," Holm said honestly. "But that's why we're here. To find out, and to bring him back if we have to."

"Have you done this before?" Annabelle asked. "Gone into other countries to rescue people?"

"Yes," I assured her. "Many times. It's our job."

She nodded, seeming reassured at least a little by this. Curt seemed to calm slightly, as well, when he saw his wife's reaction.

"Why don't you tell us a bit about yourselves and about Mikey?" I asked, wanting to get a better sense of their family life.

"Well, Mikey's seven," Annabelle said, giving me a watery smile. "He just finished the second grade, and he was so excited. We came on this vacation the second he got out of school. His favorite subject's reading."

"I don't think he's going to be a scientist like his mom," Curt chuckled. "Maybe a college professor or something like that."

"What about the two of you?" I asked. "Would you both say that you have a good relationship with Mikey?"

"Oh yes," Annabelle said, predictably, as no parent was going to admit to the alternative, especially with a child this age. "We both work, as I said, but we make sure to take time off whenever we can and to see him off in the morning and spend every night with him after we get home."

"No late nights at the office?" Holm asked her.

"Well, I won't say never," she admitted with a weak laugh. "But only a couple times a month for me. And

Curt never does, never. He's always home with Mikey. With my line of work, it's hard to get out of it sometimes, though. You'll understand."

Her eyes were almost pleading as she looked at me. I knew from experience to double the figure she'd given me, but four or five nights out of the month wasn't even close to bad if you asked me.

"Better than most," I told her.

"Do you have children?" she asked.

That was the second time someone had asked me that that day.

"No," I said, shaking my head. "Never had the time."

"Oh," she said, looking a little disappointed.

"Look, I promise that we're going to do everything we can to find Mikey," I said, leaning forward and placing a hand over hers gently. This seemed to cheer her up again.

"You work for the CDC, right?" Holm asked Annabelle before turning to Curt. "And you're in advertising?"

"Yes," they both said.

"Do you think that anyone from either of your jobs could have a problem with you or even an interest in Mikey?" Holm asked. "A disgruntled client, maybe? A former employee?"

"Oh, no, nothing like that," Annabelle said dismissively. "I work in a lab all day! Unless you think some virus is going to grow feet and come after me for experimenting on it."

She laughed nervously at this as if trying and failing to lighten the mood for herself all at once.

"And I'm just an ideas guy," Curt said apologetically with a shrug. "No one works for me, except maybe a summer intern now and then. I just sit around and come up with ideas for commercials for gum and stuff."

"Alright, this is helpful, thank you," Holm said, giving them an encouraging smile.

"Is it?" Annabelle asked, giving another uncomfortable laugh. "I feel like we haven't really been able to tell you anything."

"Ruling things out is just as important as new information," my partner told her with a nod.

"What about Mikey?" I asked. "Are there any family friends that he's particularly close with?"

"I mean, I don't think so..." Annabelle said, startled by the question, her eyes widening as she realized what I was suggesting. "You don't really think that someone we know..."

"Anything is possible," Dr. Osborne said, breaking her silence. "We talked about this earlier, Annabelle. Most of these situations are not stranger abductions, even though those are sensationalized in the media. Usually, it's someone known to the child, and even someone you trust deeply."

"Certain types have a way of worming themselves into people's lives before they even realize it," Holm explained.

"I... I don't think any of our friends would..." Annabelle said, sounding almost out of breath at the idea.

"Our friends are just work friends," Curt explained. "We both went to college up in New England. All of our old friends are still there. We have people over a couple of times a month, but none of them have kids yet, and I've never seen anyone take an interest in Mikey."

"This is helpful, thank you," I said. "What about extended family? Is anyone close by? Aunts, uncles, grandparents? Anyone close to Mikey, or who might have a difference of opinion about how you're raising him?"

"We live away from family, too," Curt said, and his tone was a bit strained then as he shifted uncomfortably on the couch. "What do you mean about opinions about how we're raising him?"

"Sometimes grandparents have certain ways they think the grandkids should be raised, and they get all up in arms about it," Holm explained, narrowing his eyes at the man. "Families are weird. I'm sure you get that."

I studied both Curt and Annabelle closely. They both seemed tenser, more uncomfortable than they had before, if that was even possible under the circumstances.

"Sometimes, you don't even realize how angry these family members are until they show up and take the kid," I added, studying their reaction, watching them grow even tenser with each word I spoke. "The parents might not even realize how much tension is there until the police are already involved."

"Annabelle, maybe we should..." Curt said as he turned to face his wife, his voice trailing off as if he was afraid to finish his thought.

"What? What is it?" I asked, a little sharper than I'd intended.

I exchanged a look with Dr. Osborne, who was leaning forward in her chair with her elbows on her knees now, full of interest. Clearly, she had no idea what they were talking about, either.

"It's extremely important that you're forthcoming with us, Curt, Annabelle," Osborne said, looking at each of the parents in turn with an almost scolding gaze. "I thought I made that very clear."

"It's just... I..." Annabelle stammered, seeming to be at a loss as to what to do.

"Annabelle," I said slowly, my tone warning. "This is a very serious situation. If you don't tell us everything, you might never see your son again."

This had the desired effect, and the woman burst

into tears as her husband wrapped both his arms around her, taking his turn comforting her.

"We... we understand," he managed. "It's just that... well, we're worried we might never see him again, anyway."

I blinked at him, taken aback.

"Huh?" Holm asked, echoing my own thoughts. "How does that work?"

"Well, it's just that... well, I'm Mikey's father, it's just... not technically," Curt admitted, which didn't do a lot to clear things up.

"What do you mean you're not *technically* his father?" Dr. Osborne asked, her tone just as stern as her face now.

"Well, Curt and I met in college," Annabelle said, raising her face from her hands now to reveal that her cheeks were all red and splotchy, and the whites of her eyes matched them. "We'd been good friends for a long time. Then, in graduate school, I got pregnant with Mikey, and the father—another student in my program—didn't want anything to do with it. He quit the program, and I was alone. Then Curt and I reconnected after I got my Ph.D., and Mikey was still a baby then."

"I'm the only father he's ever known," Curt said, his jaw set firmly. "I don't know what this guy's thinking."

"The biological father turned back up," Holm said.

It wasn't a question. That was the only logical conclusion to this story.

"God knows why," Curt spat. "Never a word in seven years, and then all of a sudden he shows back up, expecting everyone to be all gung-ho to let him take our kid."

"Well, people grow and change," Holm reasoned.

"Not that much," Curt said bitterly.

I would probably feel bitter, too, if that happened to me… if some other man showed up and tried to take my kid away. I could see the other guy's side, too, though. Maybe he wasn't ready before, but now he was. That was allowed. It was one of those situations where no one was exactly wrong, but everybody usually lost.

"Why didn't you tell us about all this before?" Dr. Osborne asked, her tone almost accusatory. "This could've saved us a lot of time."

"Jackson wouldn't do anything like that," Annabelle said defensively. "I hate him for doing this to me—to us, really. He was always a bit immature and flighty, but he wouldn't hurt a fly. He's just a quiet science nerd like me. He didn't take Mikey. There's no way."

"What do you think?" I asked Curt, as the man didn't look quite as certain as his wife.

"I don't know him as well as she does," he said, averting his eyes from mine.

"Tell me what you think anyway," I said.

He opened his mouth and then closed it again, as if afraid to respond. Finally, he spoke.

"I didn't think so, not until you said all that about families in these situations," Curt admitted. "And I never liked the guy. Never. He walked out on his kid. *My* kid. So now, I don't know anymore."

"Is he suing for custody?" Dr. Osborne asked.

"Yes," Annabelle said, her voice small again as she nodded weakly. "He transferred to another program after he left ours, I guess, and he got his Ph.D. and now works as a research scientist out in California. He has a lot of money, and he's getting married soon, and he wanted to take Mikey with him out there for the summer. We wouldn't allow it."

"Has he met Mikey?" I asked.

"No," she said shortly, shaking her head. "We wouldn't allow that, either."

I sighed. It didn't sound like anyone had really handled this situation well, to put it mildly.

"Can you write down his full name and address for us?" Holm asked, pulling a notebook and pencil out of his jacket and passing it over to Curt.

The man nodded and began scribbling away.

"You didn't answer my question before," Dr. Osborne said. "Why didn't you tell us about this?"

"Well, Jackson's suing for full custody of Mikey!" Annabelle cried as if this should make everything obvious to us now. "How are we supposed to win if the judge finds out Mikey got stolen away from us right under our noses while we should have been watching him?!"

She broke down in sobs now and buried her head in her hands again while her husband tried to soothe her.

"You can't have honestly thought that someone wasn't going to find out anyway," Holm said, shaking his head in disbelief.

"I don't know," Annabelle wailed, and Curt just hung his head.

Holm and I exchanged a bewildered expression. No matter how long I did this job, something always managed to come along and surprise me. The sheer stupidity of it all really was staggering. Surely they had to know that this Jackson character would be a prime suspect in their son's kidnapping. But then again, after what they'd been through, I doubted they had much time or wherewithal to think or reason much at all, and I couldn't really blame them for that. I remembered being told that they'd even been sedated earlier since they were so distraught.

We took all the biological father's details from Curt and Annabelle, and Dr. Osborne comforted them some more, which was interesting to watch since she didn't strike me as the nurturing type. In the end, she just ended up giving them each some pills and telling them to get some rest and that we'd talk to them some more later.

Then the three of us reconvened in the nearest interrogation room, leaving an officer with the parents in case they came up with any more spontaneous revelations to share about their home life.

"You see that a lot?" Holm asked as soon as the interrogation room door closed behind us, jutting his thumb back in the direction of Curt and Annabelle.

"More often than you'd think," Osborne sighed, sinking back into the chair nearest to the door as Holm and I made our way around to the other side of the interrogation table. "Though even I have to say that this is a bit extreme."

"Families often withhold important details in these scenarios?" I asked, arching an eyebrow at this. "You'd think they'd say anything that might help them get their kid back."

"It's not that simple," Osborne said, shaking her head. "Of course, they want their child returned to them, more than anything. But there's also often a lot of shame about losing a kid like this, especially in plain sight, when the parents were supposed to be watching them. I doubt any of it's conscious, but it's not exactly surprising that sometimes they'll withhold important details to make themselves look better, or seem like a more rock-solid family, and rationalize it away as if those details couldn't actually be important to the investigation."

"I assume we're all in agreement that this Jackson character should be the focus of our investigation?" Holm asked, squinting down at the crumpled sheet of paper Curt had given him. "Hell, the kid could be halfway to California by now."

"Not if the Coast Guard actually saw what they think they saw," I said thoughtfully. "Unless they're planning to sail all the way around Mexico to get there."

"I doubt they'll be heading to California at all if the biological father did take the boy," Osborne remarked. "He'll have to know we'll come after him, eventually. Going back home won't do him any good. He'll want to hide out somewhere, even adopt new identities, if this was planned at all."

"You think it might not have been planned?" Holm asked.

"These are often impulse abductions," Osborne said with a nod. "Say the bio father shows up and tries to meet his son again, only to find them gone. A neighbor tells them where they went, and he goes after them. Maybe he takes a friend with him or hires someone to make it seem like a stranger abduction. So sort of planned, but still on impulse."

"I imagine that this all could explain some discrepancies in the case," I said, nodding slowly. "This

Jackson fellow could be the man in the mask, and the other guy could be a friend or a hired gun. We'll have to check and see if he has any weapons registered to him in California, or even in Georgia if the whole thing really was that impulsive. Then see if the weapon matches the one on the video if he has one. I suppose he could've bought it illegally, though."

"These are all important considerations," Osborne said with a deferential nod to me. "I'll keep working on the parents, and if we get ahold of Jackson, I'll want to talk to him, too, straightaway. Until then, I think it's probably best if you discuss the other details of the case with my colleague."

10

ETHAN

Holm and I went to update the detectives and police officers before doing anything else. They were predictably not pleased with what Curt and Annabelle had withheld from us all until now.

"You've got to be kiddin' me!" Raskin exclaimed, shaking his head when we informed him and his men and women what we'd learned out by the whiteboard bearing all the details of the case. "This was vital time wasted when we could've been looking for the kid's real dad."

"Curt is his real dad," I pointed out. "He just has two."

"Three parents," Raskin sighed, placing his hands on his hips. "Aren't two bad enough?"

I chuckled, thinking that he might be right, in a

way. If the bio father ended up not being the perp... well, I didn't even want to go down that road yet. That would complicate things even more for everyone. There would be another terrified parent to deal with, and we'd be back to square one.

I shook my head to clear it. No, I thought it had to be the biological father. It was too perfect of a setup. A custody case, an overly protective mother and stepfather, a jilted father just potentially desperate enough to pull a stunt like this. As worried as Curt and Annabelle were about their custody case, and understandably so, I could never see a judge taking the boy away from the only loving parents he'd ever known full time.

After updating the police, Holm and I, realizing that the FBI agent wasn't back from her survey of the town yet, decided to go look for a hotel while we had a few free moments. There was no telling when that would come next.

As we were making our way through the parking lot, a car pulled in, and I caught a glimpse of a familiar shock of spiky black hair as the short, skinny woman inside crawled out of the driver's seat.

"Nina?" I called out to her, stunned.

"Hey, Marston, Holm, you made it!" Nina Gosse called back to us as she beamed and waved, making her way to where we stood by the station's front doors.

"W-what are you doing here?" I stammered, unable to connect the dots, given my surprise.

"What do you mean what am I doing here?" she laughed, shaking her head at me as she pulled me in for a hug and then shook Holm's hand. "I'm updating the chief about my afternoon, and then I was hoping to run into you guys. I guess I got the second one done first, though."

She winked at me, and I couldn't keep a grin from spreading across my face.

"Are you the agent on this case?" I asked her, though even as I said it, I knew that there wasn't any other reason that she would be here.

"Who else do you think called you lazy bums in to work this case with me?" she asked, punching me playfully in the shoulder.

"Hey, who're you calling lazy?" Holm asked, hands on his hips, with a fake indignant tone.

"You just get here?" she asked me, ignoring the question.

"About an hour or two ago," I said. "We've been talking to everyone on the case, and we had an... um, interesting conversation with the boy's parents."

"Uh oh, that doesn't sound good," she said, narrowing her eyes at me. "What's going on?"

I checked my watch. It was getting on to be around time for an early dinner, considering that we'd skipped lunch. I realized I hadn't eaten anything since the diner that morning.

"We actually need to update you on a few things," I

said. "Maybe we can go grab a bite to eat and talk over the case."

"Sounds like a great plan," she said with a nod. "I can deal with Raskin later. You boys have a car with you?"

"No, an officer drove us here in his patrol car from the airport," I explained, shaking my head.

"Alrighty then, I'll drive," Nina said, hopping back into her car and gesturing for us to climb in alongside her.

Holm made as if to take the passenger seat but then elbowed me playfully in the ribs and headed toward the backseat door.

"You just can't go one mission without a little romance, can you, Marston?" he whispered in my ear, and I felt both of my ears go beet red as I ignored him and climbed into the car next to Nina.

It was good to see the FBI agent again, and not just because I'd been wondering what was going on with her end of the Holland case if she really was working on it. We'd connected in New Orleans, and I'd wanted to take the time to see her again ever since. I was hoping we could meet up and discuss the Hollands while I was in Virginia near the FBI headquarters, but this was the next best thing.

Besides, other than Holm and myself, Nina was probably the best agent I knew. I couldn't think of anyone I would want to work with more on such a high stakes case. If anyone could bring Mikey home to his parents—no matter how many of them he ended up having when all was said and done—it was her.

"I noticed a little seafood place downtown earlier," Nina said as she pulled us out of the parking lot. "You like that, right, guys? It'll be just like old times down in NOLA. Well, maybe not quite. No one has food that good."

"Sounds great," I said, smiling over at her, and I tried to ignore Holm's snickering in the back as Nina took us out onto the open road.

The downtown was almost as dead now as it had been earlier that day when Officer Hollister had taken us through there on the way to the station. There were only a handful of cars on the whole collection of streets in the area.

"Was it like this when you got here?" I asked Nina, gesturing at the empty streets.

"No way," she said, shaking her head. "This place was packed earlier, and so was the mall. You know how it is, a big case like this hits the news, and all the crazies flock in. One guy even had this weird true-crime blog where he tracks every missing kid case in the region."

"That sounds... kind of fishy," Holm pointed out, and I had to agree. Why would someone take such an interest in child abduction cases?

"That's what I thought," Nina said with a nod. "I'm

going to look through it later when I get a chance, see if I can find anything useful. He didn't fit the description of either of our perps, though, so I let him go. He could've just been a crackpot. Get all kinds of those with serial killer cases, so why not this, too?"

"I guess so," I chuckled, shaking my head in wonder. It took all sorts, I supposed.

Nina pulled in front of a small restaurant stuck between a gift shop and a comic book store. There was a dancing crab on the front door. There was one other car nearby, and I only saw a single table that was occupied through the broad front window.

"Had lunch here earlier," Nina said as she unbuckled her seatbelt. "Owner said he wasn't going to shut down, even if no one showed up, so I told him I'd probably come back, make sure he had somebody to serve, at least."

Sure enough, when we all walked into the restaurant, a cheerful-looking middle-aged man behind the bar looked up and waved.

"Back so soon, Agent Gosse?" he asked as we approached him. "And you brought friends, too. I appreciate the business."

"Well, if you've still got some of those fresh crab legs, I'll be coming back as long as I'm here," Nina assured him, flashing the man a half-grin.

"Come now, how about a window seat?" the man

asked, leading us up a step to a table right in another window off to the side of the restaurant. We could see the thin outline of the ocean in the distance from there.

"This is perfect, thank you," I said, nodding to him as I sat down next to the window. Nina took a seat across from me, and Holm sat facing the window between us.

The man quickly returned with glasses of water and menus for all of us. We all ended up ordering the crab legs, on Nina's recommendation, and a steaming pile of buttery lobster biscuits soon appeared in the middle of the table to tide us over until the main course arrived.

"We're eating well today, eh, Marston?" Holm asked, chomping down on one of the biscuits before Nina or I had a chance to get a crack at the basket.

"Sure are," I chuckled, still a little full from our big meal that morning at Birn's cousin's diner, though I reached for the biscuit basket just the same.

The biscuit was as buttery as it appeared, and it melted in my mouth.

"So what've you been up to?" Holm asked when he was done licking his buttery fingers, arching an eyebrow at Nina. "Marston says you might be working the Holland case without us?"

"Well, I was working something," Nina said cagily,

though she avoided the question. "Then I got called out here when all the commotion happened this morning."

Holm narrowed his eyes at her and opened his mouth as if to press the issue on the Holland case, but I spoke before he got the chance.

"We heard you had an altercation with one of the suspects at the mall this morning?" I asked, though I wasn't about to drop the Holland issue entirely. I'd talk to Nina about it before the night was done, but I wanted to get the most pressing business out of the way first, and that was Mikey's case.

"Sure did," Nina said sullenly. "Some idiot ran into me, though, and I couldn't catch the guy. Typical of him to show up. Lots of these lone-wolf types can't bear to stay away from the crime scene. They're too proud of what they've done or nervous about not knowing how the police are working the scene or both. The problem is, the video makes it seem like there was some other guy with him, so none of it's quite adding up."

I exchanged a knowing look with Holm, and then together, we launched into a retelling of everything we'd learned in our conversation with the boy's parents. By the time we were done, the biscuits were gone, and there were steaming crab legs sitting untouched in front of each one of us.

"You've got to be kidding me," Nina managed, and I thought I could almost see the steam of anger coming out of her ears. "These parents, I swear. It's like half the time they don't even want their kids back."

"You worked a lot of these cases?" Holm asked her.

"A few," she sighed. "And it's always the same. Well, this is the worst example of it, but still, it's always the same."

"You mean you've had something like this happen before?" I asked, a little surprised even though Dr. Osborne had told us that it isn't uncommon for parents to withhold information in an investigation like this.

"Yeah, I worked one in Ohio a while back where the mom neglected to inform us about an old boyfriend who thought she wasn't taking good enough care of her kid. It turned out when he left her, he took the boy with him, and she expected us to not need this information. The whole thing was a mess."

"Sounds like the boyfriend might've had a point," Holm muttered, reaching out and grabbing one of the crab legs but not moving to crack it open with one of the mallets the restaurant owner had provided.

"He did," Nina sighed. "Wasn't his kid, though. And anyway, I had a better impression of these parents. I didn't really talk to them myself—that's not my strong suit—but Osborne seemed to think they were decent parents."

"I think they are," I said. "That's what's so strange about it to me. They seem like good, attentive parents who love their kid. So why do this? Why withhold information like this? It just doesn't make any sense."

"Osborne would say it's not supposed to," Nina pointed out. "That it's not conscious, or something like that. That the fear and pain make people do stupid things."

"Yeah, she said something like that to us," Holm muttered, and Nina nodded in his direction.

"Well, there we go," she said. "I don't know. Maybe we're wrong, though. Maybe they did engineer this whole thing."

"What?" I asked, shaking my head in confusion. "How do you figure that?"

"People do weird things during custody cases," she explained, grabbing a crab leg of her own and beginning to beat at it with the mallet. "It wouldn't be the first time a parent staged a kidnapping just to get the upper hand."

"Wouldn't that be this Jackson guy's plan, though?" Holm asked. "To make the legal guardians look bad in front of the judge?"

"Could be," Nina said with a nod. "And I agree that's probably our best theory. But we can't rule these parents out yet, either. Desperate people do wacky things. They might've thought that Jackson had something on them, something about their relationship, or their jobs, anything really, and panicked and thought that getting Mikey out of here and starting a new life with him somewhere was their only way out. As I said, it wouldn't be the first time. Most of these cases end up being something like that, strange as it may seem."

"They didn't say anything about something bad like that," Holm mused. "Though I suppose that doesn't mean much, at the end of the day."

"Yeah, I don't know how quick I'll be to trust them after this," I agreed. "They could easily be hiding something else if they were hiding this."

"At least we have a decent place to start now," Nina said. "I assume you have the detectives trying to track down this Jackson guy?"

"Yeah, they were already able to find him on the Internet," I said, thinking back to our meeting with the police after we spoke with the parents—well, two of them, anyway. "He works at some research university in Southern California. They're trying to get ahold of him now. They'll call me when they have something, though I wouldn't be surprised if it takes a while."

"What makes you say that?" Holm asked.

"Because my money's on Jackson having the kid," I explained. "And I doubt he's going to be picking up the phone anytime soon if he does."

"Fair point," Holm relented. "So, what about this whole Coast Guard thing? What do you make of it?"

Nina sighed again and cracked open another crab leg.

"I'm not sure," she said, shaking her head. "I'm the one who took the call. The guy seemed sure that he saw Mikey, and the man whose face we plastered all over the news, the one I saw at the mall. He was certain of it. But that doesn't necessarily mean anything. People get a glimpse of something all the time and then convince themselves it's more than it actually was, especially in a stressful situation like this."

"You still called us," I pointed out.

"Of course I called you," she scoffed, grinning at me. "You think I'd pass up an opportunity to work with you two again? It was the perfect set up."

"So you have doubts that the kid's actually at sea?" Holm asked.

"Of course I have doubts, I always have doubts," Nina shrugged. "Wouldn't be doing my job if I didn't. The thing that really sticks out to me is that at the mall, the guy wasn't wearing that brown jacket from the video anymore. I figured he must've seen himself on the news and tossed it. It would be the smart thing to do. But the Coast Guard guy said he was wearing the jacket when he saw him, and that was after the mall."

"Which makes you think that he just might've seen a man vaguely matching that description and a little boy out on the boat and then jumped to conclusions when he saw the newscast back onshore," I finished for her, nodding knowingly. "That would make sense."

I thought back to that morning when Diane had told us about the Scottish fisherman who spotted the Hollands in a similar manner off the coast of Scotland. Interpol had ignored him for weeks, thinking much the same as Nina and I had just said, that he had extrapolated more to what he saw than was actually there once the news reports about Chester and Ashley were fresh in his mind. This was a better reason than any not to discount any eyewitness accounts just because they might sound implausible at first glance.

"What are you thinking about?" Nina asked me, noticing that I was deep in thought.

I exchanged a look with Holm and made a decision. Nina was with us in New Orleans. The Holland case was, in a way, as much hers as it was ours. I doubted anyone would care if we shared this new information with her. For all we knew, she already knew it and was working the case with another team of FBI agents somewhere other than Miami.

So I launched into another explanation, this one of the whole Scotland and Interpol situation that had eaten up so much of our morning before catching this case.

Nina gave no indication that she knew what we were telling her already, but she didn't stop us from relaying the information, either. In fact, she seemed even more engrossed by this story than by the one about Mikey's parents keeping their custody case from us.

"I think I follow your meaning," she said quietly when I was finished, nodding slowly. "You think it would be wrong to ignore the Coast Guard account lest we end up in the same position as Interpol with your other case. Don't worry, then. I brought you here for a reason. I won't be ignoring it. And the Coast Guard's out scouring the water for them as we speak."

"Good," I said, nodding to her, and noticing that she called the Holland case mine and Holm's, and not *her* other case, too. "So, I know that I probably shouldn't ask…"

My voice trailed off as I watched for her reaction. I could tell she knew exactly what I wanted to ask. She was too smart not to, and she gave me a wink for good measure.

"No, you probably shouldn't, Marston," she said with a small smile. "And I shouldn't tell."

She lingered on that sentence, meeting my eyes. So she did know something, I decided. She had to. Otherwise, she wouldn't be saying there was anything to keep from us.

"Come on, this is an MBLIS case, isn't it?" Holm complained, clearly catching on to the same thing I had. "Our agencies are supposed to be working together, aren't they?"

"They are," Nina said, nodding again and seeming to mull this over. "But not every agent knows every detail of a case this big. There are lots of different facets to consider."

"It has to do with Lafitte's ship, doesn't it?" I asked, unable to contain myself any longer. "The FBI still has jurisdiction over that, technically. I know because I keep asking Diane about it. Come on. It could really help our investigation to have some answers about it."

"I know it would," Nina said, pursing her lips. "Which is why you haven't heard anything yet, I'm afraid."

I thought about this for a second.

"You mean you think you might have something, but you don't know for sure yet, and you don't want to tell us until you do?" I asked.

I had to admit that this made some measure of sense. Nina and her team—whatever it was they were working on—wouldn't want to sidetrack us when we should be looking for the Hollands and pursuing our own leads. Still, it was tantalizing to know that there was something going on that we weren't exactly privy to yet.

"You could say that," Nina said quietly. "They've been keeping us updated on what you're doing, though. I left this morning before the news from Scotland must've come in. I'm sorry, I can imagine how frustrating it is to have someone else working this case when you should be there yourselves."

"Kind of like finding out that someone else is working your case and not giving you all the details," Holm said bitterly, and I shot him a look. I was sure that Nina was telling us all that she could. I hated this just as much as he did, but it was what it was, and antagonizing her wasn't going to help matters any.

"Holm—" I started to say, making to scold him, but Nina held up a hand to stop me.

"It's okay," she said, hunching over her plate. "I understand. I'm almost as frustrated as you are, believe it or not, not being able to talk about things yet. But we'll get there, I promise. I just wish we didn't have this nightmare of a case to take us all off the rest of our workload."

"Finding this kid is the top priority," I said. "Then, we can worry about the rest of it."

Nina and Holm both nodded in agreement, and I finally turned my attention to my crab legs. Nina and Holm were both close to being done with theirs, but I'd talked so much that I'd almost forgotten mine. Luckily, they were delicious even after the wait, dipped in butter and sprinkled with cracked pepper and creole seasoning.

"You guys got a place to stay yet?" Nina asked us after a long period of silence in which we just enjoyed our meals and the view of the water in the distance, a brief reprieve during a particularly stressful case.

We both shook our heads.

"We were just about to do that when we ran into you," I explained. "Though I doubt we'll spend much time there. Probably just catch an hour or two every now and then in the station until we crack this one."

"Fair enough, but the FBI's putting me up in an inn not far from here," she said. "Osborne, too, though I doubt she'll spend much time there, either. You two might as well stay at the same place, in case anything happens. I double-checked that there's still space this morning before I called for you, and now that most people are clearing out of town, I'm sure it won't be a problem."

"We'd appreciate that," Holm said, nodding to her.

"We can head back to the station, then get you guys checked in whenever we leave for the night," Nina suggested.

Left unsaid was the phrase *if we leave at all*. In a case like this, the clock was always ticking, and come morning, Mikey would've been missing for a whole twenty-four hours, without much sign of him since. That was bad, and it was just going to keep getting worse with each hour that ticked by without a new lead.

"Sounds like a plan," I said, forcing a smile. It was

important to keep up morale, as much for my own sake as for everyone else's.

Our best hope was that the Coast Guard would catch another sign of the boy or the perps tonight, or that the biological father would turn up with some information. Until then, all we could do was keep looking.

11

NINA

It was good to see Marston and Holm again, even if Nina couldn't be as forthcoming as she would like to about Lafitte's ship.

In truth, she'd been arguing for weeks with her supervisor about bringing the MBLIS agents into the fold on what they were doing in Virginia. Her pleas fell on deaf ears, however. He just kept saying that they had to wait until they knew for sure what they were dealing with.

Well, Nina thought that they'd know for sure faster with Marston's help. He knew more about this stuff than pretty much anyone, after all. Regardless, she didn't want to get kicked off the case entirely. Then where would she be? So, for now, she just had to keep her mouth shut, as much as it pained her.

None of that mattered now, however. Her only

concern was finding Mikey, the image of his wailing, terrified little face from the security footage seared into her brain, there every time she closed her eyes.

When they got back to the police station after their meal, she had to resist the urge to march straight back to that lounge area and rip those parents a new one for holding out such important information on them for so long. Osborne, seeming to anticipate this urge in her colleague, ran out to greet them as soon as she heard that the agents had returned.

"Now, don't freak out," she warned, and Nina glowered back at her.

"I have half a mind to—" she started to say, her fists clenching at her side.

She and Osborne were standing near the door leading back to the interrogation rooms and that lounge area while Marston and Holm were chattering with the detectives over by the whiteboard, trying to find out if anything new had happened since they left the station.

It hadn't, of course. If anything came up, all three of their phones would've been ringing off the hook. But hope sprang eternal.

"I know you do," Osborne said sternly. "But it won't help anything. You know that."

Nina growled and clenched and unclenched her fists some more. The good doctor was right, of course. They'd worked together on that case in Ohio where that mother didn't tell them about the boyfriend, and Nina had completely lost it then when Osborne wasn't looking. The mother had stopped cooperating with them entirely after that. And it was all Nina's fault. She didn't want that to happen again, for Mikey's sake as much as her own.

"Alright, alright," she sighed, shaking her head to clear it and then wiggling out her arms, trying to release some of the tension. "But please tell me you at least made it clear that they could've killed their son, pulling a stunt like that."

"Not in so many words, but they know," Osborne assured her, her expression turning dour now. "I just hope they're not holding anything else back now."

"Do you think they could be?" Nina asked, her brow furrowing in concern.

"Who knows?" Osborne muttered, shaking her head. "I had a feeling there was something they weren't saying before, but I was thinking something along the lines of them not being home as much as they said or sending him to daycare when they said they didn't. Sometimes parents are weird about stuff like that and hold back the information. I never thought it was something like this, though. I didn't get the feeling from them I got with that God awful woman in Ohio."

Osborne had been invaluable on that case, Nina remembered. It was the first one they'd worked together, and Osborne had been suspicious of the mother the whole time. She never really thought it was a stranger abduction.

That the psychologist's intuition wasn't serving her as well on this case troubled Nina. This whole thing seemed muddled. Both planned and unplanned, first a stranger case and now a custody battle. None of it was sitting right with her.

"What's your gut tell you?" Nina asked the other woman.

"My gut tells me that we don't know enough yet," Osborne admitted, her mouth set in a thin line.

"Great," Nina sighed, her voice dripping with sarcasm, though she appreciated the psychologist's honesty. That they didn't know enough was important information, in and of itself.

"I'd better get back to them," Osborne said, pointing behind her toward the lounge area. "They're going to wake up any second now that I'm gone, I imagine. That would be my luck."

"Had to drug 'em again?" Nina asked, though she already knew the answer. No parents in this situation would sleep this early in the evening on the day their child was abducted otherwise.

"Unfortunately," Osborne said with a curt nod. "They got very distraught when I... made things clear to them."

"Well, that's good at least," Nina shrugged. "That might mean they weren't behind this after all."

"That's my hunch, but I was wrong earlier, so I'm not making any more predictions," the doctor promised. "As for whether it was the biological father or a true stranger abduction, I wouldn't know where to begin answering that question."

"That'll be up to us, then," Nina said, nodding to the other woman in gratitude and then making her way back over to the MBLIS agents while Osborne returned to the parents' side.

Predictably, there wasn't any more news about Mikey, not from the Coast Guard and not about the biological father. The police hadn't been able to reach Jackson at his residence in San Diego, and when they contacted law enforcement out there, a detective had found that the man was gone, his breakfast left half-eaten on the kitchen counter. The man's fiancée was nowhere to be found, either, though they didn't have her name yet. Jackson didn't seem to use social media at all.

This troubled Nina and she didn't seem to be the only one.

"If he was behind all this, why would he leave behind half his breakfast this morning?" Holm asked as he, Marston, and Nina all congregated at a desk in the corner after debriefing with the detectives.

"We also have to take into account the time difference," Marston pointed out. "By the time Jackson was eating breakfast, Mikey was probably taken already, unless he got up to eat in the middle of the night."

"Fair point," Nina said, pointing the ball of a pen at him thoughtfully. "So if it was his food, he wasn't here in North Carolina when everything went down."

"Do we know how old the food was?" Holm asked.

"They said it looked relatively fresh," Marston shrugged. "And it's still afternoon out there. I suppose it's possible that it could've been from yesterday, but then there was that neighbor who saw him leave in a hurry this morning."

"Oh yeah, I almost forgot about that," Nina said. She'd been lost in thought during some of the detectives' updates, worrying about Mikey and where he could be now, let alone what could be happening to him.

Marston's phone buzzed, and he picked it up.

"Oh good," he said as he read through a text message. "That's Diane. She got in touch with all our contacts on islands along the coast. They're going to be on the lookout for Mikey and the guys in the video."

"Good, that's good," Nina said, nodding slowly. "I'm wondering if maybe we should release the footage of the second guy to the media, just in case."

"Let's give it 'till morning," Marston suggested, scrunching up his face as if he disliked all the possible options here. "We don't want them to know we know about the second guy, and we don't want even more public panic and sensationalism than we've already got. If we don't have a new lead by morning, we can still release it then."

"Good thinking," Nina said, gladder than ever that she'd called in the MBLIS agents to help her and Osborne. "It'll be easier to get coverage in the morning, anyway. Most people will be asleep by now."

The three agents stayed at the police station late into the night, waiting on any word that Jackson or his fiancée had been located or that the Coast Guard saw Mikey and his abductor again. But no news came, and around two in the morning, Nina thought that it might be time to call it a night.

"Come on," she said, standing up from her adopted desk and motioning for Holm and Marston to follow her, both of whom looked like they were in the midst of falling asleep if they hadn't already. "We won't be any good to anyone as zombies tomorrow. Let's go get you guys checked in at the inn."

Both agents nodded weakly and rose to follow her. Nina waved goodbye to the others who remained in the station. A new slate of officers and detectives had come in about an hour earlier to replace the others, while the lead detective on the case grabbed some shut-eye in the back, having agreed to stay the whole night there, and the rest went home to get some well-needed rest.

"Heh, zombies," Holm chuckled weakly as they

made their way out to the parking lot. "You know, because of our New Orleans mission."

"Yes, I can't say I needed that one explained to me," Nina quipped, giving him a wry smile.

Back at the inn, Nina and Marston had to check Holm in for him as he leaned against the wall with his eyes closed, practically snoring already. Marston then helped him upstairs to his room not far from Nina's and deposited him fully-clothed on his bed.

"Thanks for all your help today," Nina told him as he shut the door gently behind him, leaving Holm alone in his room. "I'm glad you're here."

"I'm glad we're here, too," he said, giving her a wide if sleepy smile.

"Are you sure about that?" she asked. "Because I got the sense from Holm that you two weren't too happy to be pulled off the Holland case, even for a little while."

"He was less happy about it than I was," Marston admitted as he followed her slowly down the hall toward where her own room, and his, were located. "I, for one, was glad to leave all that paperwork behind for a living breathing case. If just for a little while."

He winked at her, and Nina felt a familiar, not altogether unwelcome, jolt in the pit of her stomach.

"Anyway," he continued. "A missing kid trumps everything. Even Holm gets that, though he might not like it."

"I'm glad to hear it," she murmured, stopping in front of her door. "Well, this is me."

"I'm down here," Marston said, gesturing at a room two doors down from her. She nodded vaguely and swallowed a yawn.

"I'll see you bright and early in the morning, then," she said, already wincing at the thought of having to wake up in only a few short hours.

"Sleep well," he said, ever the gentleman as he nodded to her and took a reluctant step toward his room.

"You know..." she called after him. "You could..."

The next thing she knew, she was in his arms, and their lips met. She'd forgotten how warm he was, how inviting.

Finally, he broke away from her, and she reached behind her to scan her hotel key against the lock.

"I thought you'd never ask," he said, grinning down at her.

"Yeah, it kind of took me long enough, didn't it?" she laughed, reaching up to take his face in her hands and kiss him again as she leaned her elbow down on the doorknob.

Suddenly, she wasn't quite so tired anymore, and a few hours felt like a good long time.

12

ETHAN

We managed to get a couple of hours of sleep, at least, though when Nina's phone started screeching at five o'clock in the morning on the bedside table, I had to suppress the urge to groan, roll over, and plaster a pillow over my head.

We ended up getting up in the end, though, and crawling back into the police station at what I imagined must've been a snail's pace.

Dr. Osborne was waiting for us in the front desk area. Several very sleepy detectives and officers were still congregated by where Nina, Holm, and I had left them mere hours before.

"Sorry to call you in so early," Osborne said, crossing over to us the second we stepped through the front doors.

"It's alright," Holm yawned, running a sleepy hand across his face. "Nature of the case, and all."

"What happened?" I asked, hoping that there was some kind of lead that had materialized to justify pulling us out of bed just three hours after we got there.

"Jackson showed up," she said simply, and I blinked at her.

"What do you mean showed up?" I asked. "He just came here of his own volition?"

"Seems like it," the psychologist confirmed with a nod. "He wasn't here, and then he was. None of the detectives seemed to be able to find him. We're lucky he came when he did."

"Well, if he just showed up here, that has to mean he didn't have anything to do with it, right?" Holm asked. "I mean, what perp would walk right into a police station if he wasn't turning himself in? Wait, he wasn't turning himself in, was he?"

"No, he wasn't," Osborne said, shaking her head. "Which makes me think that you might be right, and he didn't take Mikey after all."

Her mouth was set in a thin line as if she didn't like this at all. I could see why. If Jackson didn't take the boy, that meant that someone else did. Someone who could be far more of a danger to Mikey in the short and long term.

"It's not unheard of for perps to needle themselves

into an investigation in a case like this, though," Nina considered. "It's unusual for a familial abduction case, but not unheard of. We shouldn't rule anything out just yet."

"Agreed," Osborne said, nodding to her. "I haven't gotten a chance to talk to him much yet, so I don't have a great read on him at this point. He's waiting in an interrogation room for you."

"What did he say when he got here?" Holm asked.

"I wasn't out here, but the detectives said he just walked into the station and started demanding to hear all the details about the investigation," Osborne said. "He's kind of a nervous Nelly, though, so he lost his confidence pretty quick. By the time they came and got me, he was stuttering everything he said. Still kept asking about the boy and the investigation, though."

I sighed. This didn't tell us much. Sure, these could be the words and actions of a concerned father, but they could also be those of a nervous, regretful perp.

"Have the parents seen him yet?" I asked. "The other parents, I mean."

"No," Osborne said, shaking her head. "I thought it would upset them more, and I didn't want to put them together until we'd questioned him first. I'd like to question the parents some more, too. Perhaps one of you could join me?"

There was a period of silence as all three of us said

nothing. Everyone wanted to get the first crack at Jackson.

"Fine, I'll do it," Holm said at last, though he didn't exactly sound happy about it. "I wouldn't want to break up the party."

He winked at Nina and me and then began to follow Osborne down the hall past the interrogation rooms and toward the lounge area, where I assumed the parents were still waiting.

"He's in the third room on the left," Osborne called back to us.

"Thanks," Nina said, waving to her in thanks.

"Alright, let's do this thing," I said, stopping in front of the appropriate room, which had a one-way window on it revealing a nervous-looking man in his thirties, tapping his foot expectantly on the floor and fidgeting with the zipper of his thin blue jacket.

Nina and I entered the room and took our seats across from the man at the interrogation table. He jumped at the sound of the door, and his eyes followed us all the way there. Neither of us spoke until we were seated.

"Jackson Moore?" Nina asked him, and he nodded vigorously to match his knee bobbing up and down from all the nervous tapping. "I'm Agent Nina Gosse with the FBI, and this is my colleague Ethan Marston with MBLIS. We're here to ask you a few questions."

"Wh-where's my son?" the man stammered, looking between us expectantly.

Nina and I exchanged a look.

"Well, that's what we're trying to find out, Jackson," Nina told him, folding her hands in front of her on the table and peering right at him.

"Y-you don't know where he is?" Jackson asked, his eyes widening and his hands spreading flat against the table, hard so that I could see the whites of his knuckles.

"No, we don't," I said, studying him closely. "That's what we're doing here."

"Well, what are you doing talking to me for? Go find him!" Jackson cried, spreading his arms wide and motioning for us to leave him there and go look for Mikey.

Nina and I exchanged a look. A perp trying to learn about the investigation probably wouldn't make that suggestion, instead wanting us to stay behind and unwittingly reveal details of the investigation to him, wasting our energy not looking for the missing boy at the same time. That said, it was possible that Jackson was still the perp and just panicking about having to talk to us. More than possible, judging by his nervous body language.

"We have people who are doing that, and they're not going to stop anytime soon," Nina assured him.

"For the time being, why don't the three of us have a little chat?"

"About what?" Jackson asked, looking between us wildly. Then, something resembling realization seemed to dawn on him. "Wait, you don't think it was me, do you?"

"Well, it is often a family member or acquaintance who takes a child in these situations," I explained carefully, exchanging another look with Nina and seeing that she also had an inkling that this man might just be genuine. "And there is a custody disagreement taking place, according to the boy's parents—"

"I'm his parent!" Jackson cried. "And I'm no acquaintance. I've never even met my son. They wouldn't let me."

I sighed and ran a hand across my face. It was far too early in the morning, and I was operating on far too little sleep to mediate such a complicated family drama. But I supposed that this was what I signed up for, in a way, working a case like this one.

"Alright, alright," Nina said, shushing him. "Let's just calm down for a minute here. Why don't we start at the beginning? Mikey's mother says that you weren't exactly happy when she got pregnant and didn't want anything to do with your son. What changed?"

"Th-that's not true!" Jackson stuttered, his pale face turning beet red in an instant. "I mean, I'll admit I was scared, and I ran at first... But then she blocked my number, and she changed apartments, and no one would help me get in touch with her!"

"You mean you came back?" I asked, taken aback.

"Well, I'll admit that it wasn't right away, and I-I didn't look as hard as I should've," Jackson said, hanging his head so I could only see the tips of his bright red ears. "And when I didn't find her, I was kind of relieved. I thought I got a chance to start over, so I transferred programs and moved out to California when I got this job. But the whole time, it was just eating at me, so about a year ago, I tried to get in touch with Annabelle. Found her on the CDC website."

This struck me as a slightly more plausible story. In this century, if Jackson really wanted to find his son, he would've been able to. He just needed some time to come around to really wanting to, and by the time he had, Annabelle had left him behind. It was a tale as old as time, and an unfortunate one, really.

"We're told you have a fiancée? Did she have anything to do with any of this?" Nina asked. It was a smart question. Sometimes big life events spurred these changes of heart.

"Oh, no, I contacted Annabelle a year ago," Jackson said, shaking his head and looking in our direction again. "Jeannette and I really only got together about six months ago. We've been friends for years, so things moved quickly."

"Alright, and where is she now?" Nina asked. "We've been trying to get in touch with her."

"Sh-she's in Germany for a research conference," Jackson stammered, seeming surprised again at this. "Has been for a week and won't be home until next Saturday. W-what do you want to talk to Jeannette for?"

"Well, we've been trying to get in touch with you," I said. "Pretty much constantly since we found out about you yesterday afternoon. But when the police showed up at your house, you were gone, and no one could find your fiancée, either."

Jackson's eyes widened at this, as he no doubt realized how bad this must've looked.

"Oh, no, no, no, no, no," he said, shaking his head wildly and moving his whole body along with it. "No, no, no, no, no, you can't think that I had anything to do with this, that Jeannette—"

I cut him off, holding up a hand to silence him.

"Don't worry. If you didn't have anything to do with this, we'll figure that out," I said. "There's no reason to panic if you didn't do anything wrong."

"No reason to panic!" he cried. "My son's missing, and you're wasting time trying to track me down instead of finding him!"

I exchanged yet another look with Nina. It was looking less and less like this nervous little man had anything to do with his son's disappearance, and as good of news as that was for him, he was right that it wasn't great for Mikey.

"We promise that there are people out looking for your son right now," Nina reiterated. "They're doing the best that they can."

"You're the best that they can!" he exclaimed, looking wildly between us again. "You're an FBI agent, and he's a what-cha-call-it agent, and that other lady said she was with the FBI, too. So what are you all doing here? You need to go find my son."

"Jackson, we need to rule you out first," I said sternly but kindly. "And the quicker we can do that, the quicker we can get out doing what you want us to be doing. Do you understand that?"

He looked right at me for a long while, his whole body tense and constricted, hunched over the table.

"Okay," he said finally, letting some of that tension go as his shoulders slumped. "Okay, then."

"Alright, so let's jump ahead to all this custody business," Nina suggested. "Why wouldn't Annabelle let you see Mikey?"

"She said he already had a dad, and that I lost my chance," Jackson said, blinking away what must have been tears. "And I apologized for that, I really did, but I think I deserve a second chance. I'm not trying to replace anybody, but he's my son, too. And then, after a few months, when she still wouldn't let me see him, I talked to a lawyer. I didn't want to do anything so drastic, but I felt like I didn't have another option."

I had to admit that I felt for the guy. I could see both sides, so surely they should've been able to work out some kind of arrangement that worked for everyone involved.

"Why don't we jump ahead to yesterday?" I suggested. "If you didn't know that we were looking for you, how come you're here? Why did you leave San Diego?"

"Well, I was eating breakfast, and I saw Mikey on the news!" Jackson cried, becoming agitated at the memory. "And then I saw Annabelle and her husband, and I watched long enough to see where they were, and then I hopped on the first flight out."

That would explain why Jackson's breakfast was left sitting there half-eaten, his door unlocked. If I saw my kid on some police report on the news, I'd probably forget myself, too.

A sinking feeling was beginning to form in the pit of my stomach. It was looking less and less like Jackson had anything to do with Mikey's disappearance. And that was bad news for Mikey.

"Do you own a gun, Jackson?" Nina asked.

"Wh-what?" he stammered, taken aback.

"A gun," she repeated. "Do you own one?"

"N-no, I wouldn't even know how to use a gun,"

Jackson said, and he sounded honest to me. "I'd probably end up shooting myself by accident."

He laughed nervously, though the humor didn't reach his eyes. By the look of him, with his pale skin, anxious demeanor, and haphazard clothing, I thought he was probably right about that. I doubted Jackson saw much of the world outside of a lab.

"Do you mind if we check on that?" Nina asked him. We would anyway, of course, but whether he gave permission revealed something in and of itself.

"Um, yeah, yeah, do whatever you want," Jackson said, looking a little surprised again. "Just—just don't waste too much time on me, okay? You need to find Mikey. You need to find him."

"We're doing the best that we can," I assured him. "We promise."

"But you can't promise that you'll get him back," Jackson said, and it wasn't a question. He may be nervous, but he was clearly an intelligent guy.

"No," I said quietly. "We can't promise that, I'm afraid. We wouldn't be honest if we did."

"And you don't want to give us false hope, I understand," Jackson said, nodding and sniffling and looking down at his hands. "I understand."

"Agent Marston, can I talk to you in the hall?" Nina asked, glancing over at me.

I nodded and followed her back out the door, leaving Jackson still sitting there behind the one-way window, where we could see him, but he could no longer see us.

The hall was empty but for the two of us.

"I'm starting to think that this guy didn't do it," Nina murmured when the door was safely shut behind us.

"Yeah," I said, swallowing hard as that sinking feeling in my stomach grew more profound. "Me neither."

"Which means..." her voice trailed off as if she didn't want to speak the words.

I nodded. She didn't have to tell me what this meant. This was in all likelihood a real stranger abduction, and now we were back to square one in our investigation, whereas Mikey had lost nearly another day. This wasn't good.

"We should probably have him talk to the parents," I said with a sigh because I didn't actually want to force this family drama. "See how they interact. Then we can probably rule this possibility out for the most part and have the police in San Diego look into Jackson's movements in the past few days and rule him out definitively."

"Yes, I think that would be best," Nina said, nodding slowly and checking the time on her phone. "Let's go tell the police now."

So we left Jackson waiting for us and headed back out into the main room of the station, where Chief

Raskin had returned, looking even wearier and his eyes even more bloodshot than they had been the previous day.

"Howdy, agents," he said, saluting us when he saw us, a fresh cup of coffee in his hands. "What've you got for us?"

So we relayed our conversation with Jackson to him and our suspicions that, in all likelihood, this was a stranger abduction after all.

"Well, I'll be damned," Chief Raskin sighed when we were finished, running a weary hand across his face in a now-familiar gesture. "Kind of feels like starting over, doesn't it?"

"Yeah. Yeah, it does," I said, not able to find a way to sugar coat it.

"But it's not, really," Nina said quickly. "We have a better idea of what we're dealing with, or at least what we're not dealing with. We can put our contacts in San Diego on the case of ruling out Jackson entirely, and we can focus all of our energy on the stranger abduction angle now. The first order of business is trying to find this boat the Coast Guard supposedly saw and getting a better description of it. I'd say it's more likely than not that they really saw the kid, now. We know a stranger probably took him, so the international angle is more likely."

"Yes, I suppose so," Raskin said, nodding slowly. "Well, we'll get right on the San Diego thing for you.

I'll make a few calls. I'll try to see about the boat, too. The only description we've got is pretty loose, though. There are a million white motorboats out there. Without a make and model, it'll be hard to know where it came from. There's one boat shop down by the water. We already checked to see if anyone rented anything out yesterday, but there was nothing in the owner's log. Everyone cleared out pretty early after this whole mess went down."

"Thank you," I said, nodding to him and making a mental note about the boat shop. "We just need to chat with the parents—all three of them—one more time, and then we'll join the search ourselves."

Raskin and his officers and detectives nodded to us in return, and Nina and I headed back to retrieve Jackson from the interrogation room. He looked like he was about to burst when we found him.

"Is there any word?" he asked, practically leaping out of his chair when he heard the door open. "You were gone a while, is there anything new?"

"We're still looking," I assured him, which was, no doubt, not the non-answer he wanted, but he nodded and grumbled something resembling thanks to me, anyway. I decided I didn't dislike him so much after all.

"We think it might be time for us all to have a talk with Annabelle and Curt," Nina said, and Jackson visibly winced.

"I don't think they'll want to talk to me," he said

quietly. He left unsaid that he probably didn't want to talk to them, either.

"Well, you're all this boy's parents, so you're going to have to figure out how to get through this thing together," I pointed out, and the man just hung his head and nodded as Nina opened the door for him.

Holm and Dr. Osborne were talking to Curt and Annabelle, who were still sitting on the couch when we found them. I noticed that they looked a little more put together today, at least, though that wasn't saying much.

This was short-lived, however, as the second they caught sight of Jackson, they both jumped up from where they were sitting and started screaming at him.

"What's he doing here?!" Curt roared, pointing violently in the other man's direction.

"Where is he? Where did you take him?" Annabelle cried, tears suddenly streaming down her previously clear cheeks.

Apparently, Annabelle had changed her tune since the previous day, when she'd been adamant that Jackson couldn't have had anything to do with Mikey's disappearance. It was more likely than not hope, for the same reason that Nina and I had hoped that Jackson had the boy. It would be simpler that way, and we would be closer to finding him.

Osborne and Holm both looked back at us questioningly for good measure.

"Alright, alright," Nina said, more than a twinge of annoyance in her voice, and I saw why she let Osborne handle the parents on her own before. "Everybody just calm down."

"We're in the process of officially clearing Jackson," I explained, and Holm's shoulders slumped while I watched the corner of Osborne's mouth twinge downward. They knew it was better for Mikey if Jackson had him, too.

Of course, none of the parents were completely in the clear yet. As far as I was concerned, all three of them were suspects until we knew what happened for sure. Someone else Mikey knew could've taken him, too, which was why the Atlanta police were interviewing everyone he knew from school and daycare.

"So... so it wasn't Jackson who took him?" Annabelle asked, her whole body sagging at the notion.

"How could you think that I would do something like that!" Jackson challenged her, his pale face suddenly beet red for the second time in an hour. "He's my kid!"

"He's not your son. I'm his father!" Curt cried, taking a step in the other man's direction.

I moved between them, holding out my arms in either direction.

"He's both your sons," I said as calmly as I could. "I think everybody just needs to get nice and clear about that. And all this fighting and going back and forth isn't going to help us find him any faster."

All three parents hung their heads, then.

"Hey, uh, what's going on, boss?" Holm asked, rising from his seat and crossing over to mutter into my ear.

I quickly pulled him and Dr. Osborne aside while Nina begrudgingly watched the three parents, who were now pacing in opposite corners of the lounge area from each other. I explained everything we'd learned from Jackson.

"God, we have to find this kid," Holm said, shaking his head as his expression darkened. That sinking feeling in the pit of my stomach was pulling me practically all the way to the ground then, and I nodded.

"Yeah," I agreed. "We really do."

Time was running shorter every second.

We returned to the main lounge area, where the parents were still on opposite ends of the room, glowering at each other, while Nina stood tenuously in the middle, looking like she wanted to be pretty much anywhere else.

"Alright, now this is a small police station," Osborne announced to them. "So we can't exactly keep you three separated this whole time. Now's as good a time as any to learn to get along, if not for your own sakes, for Mikey's."

At the mention of the missing boy's name, something shifted on each parent's face, and they glanced uneasily at one another. Then, almost in unison, they nodded somewhat reluctantly, though agreement was agreement as far as I was concerned. I'd take the win.

"Good," I said, nodding to each of them in turn. "Now, can you all stay here and talk to Dr. Osborne? I'm sure they can get you anything you'd like here. You can even get a hotel room, though you'll understand that someone will have to remain with you at all times. We can't rule anything out yet."

"We understand," Annabelle murmured, her eyes swimming.

"Why can't we help look?" Curt asked, a twinge of anger in his voice. "We want to help find our boy."

"We appreciate that, but these people are armed and dangerous," Nina reminded him. "You could end up doing more harm than good."

"People? As in plural?" Jackson asked, his tone and expression frantic, and I realized that he only knew what was in the police reports.

I sighed, not wanting to get into this all again right then. I was itching to get out looking for Mikey myself.

"Don't worry, I'll get them all updated," Osborne assured me, sensing my reticence.

"Thank you," I said, nodding to her in thanks. "You all stay here. We're going to go find your son."

13

ETHAN

We joined the police search after that and spent the rest of the morning combing through every corner of the town and the surrounding area, looking for anywhere that the perps and Mikey could be hiding. We spoke to shop owners in town, as well as homeowners in the residential areas. None of them knew anything, though all of them expressed support for our investigation and concern for the missing boy. More than a few of them also hinted that they'd love to hear more details about our search to fuel the local—and now, even national—gossip mill, but we always rebuffed these requests by thanking them for their time and going on our way.

In the end, we had to determine that the perps and Mikey were likely no longer there, either skipping out to sea as the Coast Guard report suggested, or driving or even flying off to some other corner of the world that we had yet to reach in our search.

"Damn, it's getting hot," Holm said when it was getting to be around lunchtime, running a hand through his hair. It glistened in the sun, a thin coat of sweat atop his head.

"Maybe we should break for a spell," Nina suggested. "We've been at it for hours, and we have to eat sometime. We can get back to it in not too long."

Holm and I both nodded at this, and we climbed back into her sweetly air-conditioned rental car and headed back to the seafood place downtown, where we each ordered a healthy portion of the house chowder to go along with those buttery biscuits.

The owner brought it all to us quickly, saying the soup was already brewing.

"This one's on the house," he told us when he brought it all out, along with another basket of the biscuits. "You just find that boy, you hear?"

We ate as quickly as we could, once the food had arrived. That sinking feeling that had been in the pit of my stomach since questioning Jackson earlier that morning had masked my hunger, but as soon as I smelled those biscuits, I realized how hungry I actually was. I hadn't eaten anything since we were there at that restaurant last, early the previous evening.

As we ate, we discussed the case, which we hadn't had a lot of time to do yet in the middle of all the anxious searching we were doing. This was the first time we had really stopped to breathe since we left the station. Even in the car going from destination to destination, we'd sat in tense silence, no one wanting to speak about how quickly the clock was ticking.

"So what did the parents—Curt and Annabelle, I mean—say to you while we were talking to Jackson?" I asked Holm as I blew on my first spoonful of piping hot soup. It was a seafood chowder, and I detected chunks of clams, oysters, crab, and other assorted seafood floating around there with potatoes in the creamy mixture. It tasted as good as it looked and smelled, warming that anxious pit in my stomach and soothing it momentarily.

"More of the same," Holm sighed, shaking his head. "They're a nervous wreck, the both of them, not that I blame them. I'd be the same in their position. Worse, probably."

"They seemed to have changed their tune about Jackson when they first saw him," I pointed out. "Or Annabelle did, at least. Yesterday, she seemed to defend him. Said he wouldn't hurt a fly, didn't she?"

Nina and Holm both nodded to indicate that I remembered correctly.

"Well, yeah, I guess Osborne talked to them some more about these cases and how they usually tend to go," Holm said thoughtfully. "And Curt was always a little suspicious, even more so last night. I guess everything just got her convinced, hopeful even, because, well... you know."

We did know. Things were looking bad for Mikey. It had been more than twenty-four hours since he was taken, and almost twenty-four since he was last seen if the Coast Guard guy was to be believed. And still, there were no new leads if Jackson was to be believed. And no matter how much I wanted it to be otherwise, for Mikey's sake, I believed him. Sure, the guy was a little rough around the edges, but I was inclined to believe Annabelle's first instinct that he wouldn't hurt a fly.

The police had also confirmed since we left the station that his fiancée was actually in Germany, and she was panicked out of her mind when they finally got her on the phone. She hadn't heard anything about any of this, insulated in the bubble of her academic conference. She was on her way to join Jackson now, having hopped on the first flight from Berlin to North Carolina, though she wouldn't land until sometime the following day.

"Anything from the Coast Guard?" I asked Nina, though I knew that she'd checked her phone before we sat down.

She checked it again anyway, looking almost as eager to see if she had any messages as I was. Her face fell, however, when she looked at it.

"No," she said, shaking her head glumly. "Nothing since the last report."

And the last report, we knew, had contained nothing notable, just saying that the only people the Coast Guard had found out on the water today were a lone fisherman who let them search his boat, which was the wrong color anyway, and some swimmers on a private beach not far from there. None of the swimmers had seen anything either, and they were questioned for some time. Just college kids out at someone's parents' beach house for the summer. They hadn't even heard about the abduction yet, not having been into town in a couple of days.

"What's next, then?" Holm asked as he chomped on a biscuit. They were crunchier today.

There was a long period of silence in which no one seemed to have any ideas. We were running shorter and shorter on time—or, rather, Mikey was running short on it. And there hadn't been any new leads since Jackson, and that had obviously gone nowhere fast.

As if on cue, Nina's phone buzzed, and she looked at it so quickly that she nearly toppled her almost full water glass across the whole table when she went to grab it.

"What is it?" Holm asked apprehensively, his whole body suddenly tense. "Is it the station?"

She nodded slowly, her eyes darting across the screen, left to right, and then back to the left again. She didn't answer, though, and just continued to read until her shoulders slumped, and she banged the phone back down on the table with almost enough force to topple the glass for a second time.

I reached out as if to catch it as it wobbled, but it remained in place in the end.

"Nothing new?" I asked, feeling my stomach sink and the food I'd eaten churn inside me as I hoped beyond hope that I was reading her expression wrong.

"No," she said, shaking her head. "Not really. Just that they've mostly cleared Jackson in San Diego. Atlanta police, too. Neither department was able to find anything on him or his fiancée, no guns in the house, not even a can of pepper spray. They've both been at their jobs regularly, where they're supposed to be when they're supposed to be there, and Jackson's custody lawyer doesn't seem to think he's gotten particularly desperate lately. He was only really suing for full custody to try to get summers and some holidays as a last-ditch effort to get Curt and Annabelle to cooperate with him. I guess he figured going for broke made it more likely he'd get what he actually wanted, which was a relationship with his son."

"That sounds like kind of a weird strategy," I remarked.

"It's not that unusual," Nina shrugged. "People get angry, and desperate, and rationalize all kinds of things. He might not actually be wrong, either. Curt and Annabelle did get scared when he filed. Anyway, it looks like that end is all but officially dead."

"What about Curt and Annabelle, then?" Holm asked, almost hopefully. "Do we think they could've done this? Dr. Osborne seemed to think it was a possibility since they did get scared, as you said."

I knew why Holm was hopeful. As wrong as it would be to stage something like this, if Curt and Annabelle were behind it, Mikey was probably unharmed wherever he was.

"It's possible, but I doubt it," Nina murmured. "There's nothing to indicate that it could've been them. And they did come clean about everything else in the end."

"That we know of," Holm pointed out, and she bowed her head to him deferentially.

"That we know of," she agreed, but she met my eyes across the breadbasket, and I knew we were thinking similarly. And if Holm was honest with himself, he probably was, too.

Curt and Annabelle didn't do this. The kid would've turned up by now, or there would've been some other sign of the whole thing. And like the couple said, this was kind of a crazy thing to do in the middle of a custody battle. It didn't reflect well on them, even if they weren't actually to blame for the incident.

"Well, the Coast Guard still hasn't seen anything

new," I said somberly, turning my spoon around in what remained of my soup, my appetite having suddenly vanished after the miniature whirlwind of Nina getting an update and then having it turn out to be nothing. "We might as well go down by the shore and see if we can get anything the police couldn't about the boat. They must've left from somewhere around here if they really are out on the water, which means they either own a boat or took one from someone else here who does."

Holm and Nina both nodded. This was just retreading old ground that the police had already covered, but it was still something to do. And if we were going to retread, it might as well be down by the water instead of just interviewing more residents who knew nothing about this except what they'd heard on the news.

"That sounds like as good a plan as any," Nina said, pursing her lips. Her phone buzzed again on the table, and she picked it up and read it quickly, though she didn't look as hopeful as she had before, her resolve having been used up already.

"What is it?" Holm asked, just a small glimmer of hope still remaining in his voice. I looked down at his bowl and realized that he'd lost his appetite around the same time I had, half a biscuit now discarded and soaking in the broth of the last of his soup.

"It's just Dr. Osborne," she said, her lips set in a

thin line now. "They're going public with the second perp this afternoon, so brace yourselves. There's going to be a lot more press soon. And a lot more panicked people."

"*More* press?" Holm asked. "How could there be *more* press?"

He was right. As soon as the clock had struck nine earlier that morning, there were reporters practically banging on the doors to the police station. And everywhere we went, people asked us questions about what they'd seen on the news. This thing was getting play all over the country—how else would Jackson have seen it all the way in San Diego?

Holm and I were used to working quietly on the sidelines or in foreign countries where cases didn't get much coverage. A very public, sensational crime like this was a whole different ballgame for us.

"Just you wait," Nina sighed. "It's going to get way worse before it gets any better."

14

ETHAN

We drove down to the docks then and took a look around. There weren't many people out, though there were plenty of boats floating in the harbor, unoccupied and abandoned.

We didn't run into any reporters there, thankfully. The part of the case about the sea wasn't public yet, and likely wouldn't be for some time. We didn't want the perps to know we knew about that, and for now, we had a lot of people looking for them officially on the water.

If we didn't find this kid soon, though, the Coast Guard wouldn't be able to devote so much manpower to looking after a certain point. We'd have to enlist the public's help in the search.

Hell, if we didn't find this kid soon, Holm and I might even be pulled off the case. I doubted Nina and

Osborne would be, considering they got here first, but eventually, they, too, would have to pack it up and move on to the next one, only looking into Mikey occasionally in their spare time.

Everyone knew that after a certain point, these cases usually only ended one way if they ended at all. And it wasn't pretty.

We mostly walked in silence, my colleagues no doubt pondering the same as I was how quickly the clock was ticking. At least the gently lapping water in the bay provided some means of calming my thoughts and that now ever-present pit in my stomach.

Eventually, we came upon a man who was cleaning a little gray motorboat off to the corner of the bay, amidst a cacophony of other boats that measured at least in the dozens.

"Hello, friend!" Holm cried out to him, shielding his eyes from the sun as he looked up. "Mind if we talk to you for a minute?"

The man jumped and nearly fell into the shallow water, not having noticed our approach and having had his back turned to us.

He wiped his brow when he turned to see us and chuckled.

"Now hey, there," he said, smiling down at us. "Sorry, I didn't hear you come up. I got pretty lost in my own thoughts, I guess. You looking for something?"

The man hopped down from the boat more

agilely than I would've expected for a man of his age. I would say he was in his late fifties or early sixties, though his hair was dyed blond, and he was carrying a bit of extra weight along his midsection. He was sporting a thorough farmer's tan on his cheeks, neck, and lower arms where his t-shirt cut off, showing that he was probably out here a lot.

"Someone, more like," Holm corrected, and the man's expression grew dark as he wiped his sweaty hands off on his worn jeans and held one out to each of us in turn.

"Ah, I think I've got you," he said, giving a knowing nod. "You're looking for that kid that's all over the news. I'm Marty, by the way, Marty Knox."

"Hello, Mr. Knox, I'm agent Robbie Holm with MBLIS, and this is my partner, Ethan Marston, and our colleague, Nina Gosse, with the FBI," Holm said as he shook the man's hand. "And yes, we're looking for Mikey, I'm afraid."

"Well, I'm glad someone's looking," Marty said. "What are you all doing down here, though? I thought this all happened at the mall or whatever."

"Yes, he was," I said quickly, not wanting to reveal too much. "We're just thorough."

"Well, that's good, too, I guess," Marty said with a shrug as he shook my hand and then Nina's, too. "I'm just sorry you have to."

"So are we," I said darkly. "We were wondering if you'd seen anything out of the ordinary."

"You mean other than everyone being gone?" he asked, scratching the thin layer of hair on his head. "That's been pretty unusual."

"Yeah, I would imagine," I chuckled, glancing back over at all the empty boats. "They all clear out yesterday morning?"

"About half of them," Marty said, scrunching up his face as he considered this. "The rest a few hours after that, when all the shooting happened at the mall."

Holm and I both glanced over at Nina.

"It was just one shot," she corrected with the hint of a smirk. "People have a way of exaggerating things like that."

"Well, that's good to hear," Marty said with a weak smile to match hers.

"Why are you still out here?" Holm asked. "Why didn't you pack up with the rest of them?"

"Ah, I don't know," he shrugged. "It's all a little beyond me, to be honest. I like coming out here, do it every day since I retired early. Plus, I figured that no kidnappers are going to want anything to do with me, so I'm probably safe."

He gave a low, nervous chuckle like he was laughing so he wouldn't yell or worse, to cover the worry we all had for this kid we didn't even know.

"Fair enough," Nina said. "So you haven't noticed anyone else out today?"

"Oh, no, not today," he said. "Not a soul 'till you all showed up. That's why I jumped so high when you did."

We all chuckled again at the memory.

"Do you own this boat?" I asked, gesturing at the small gray motorboat.

"Oh, no, sir," he said, shaking his head quickly. "These are Mr. Samuels's boats. He just lets me borrow this one whenever I'd like, take it out for a spin every morning, as long as I clean it up when I'm finished. I'd love to buy it off him someday, but it would be a bad financial decision for me, I'm afraid."

"It's good of him to let you use it, then," I said, giving him a small smile.

"Sure is," Marty said with a nod. "He's an old friend. He owns the shop not far down from here. Old fellow, and he should've retired a long time ago. His nephew does the books and runs things most of the time, but Mr. Samuels likes to go in everyday anyway and talk to the customers. I'm not sure he'd know what to do with himself otherwise."

I shielded my eyes from the sun and looked down at where Marty was pointing. Sure enough, it looked like there was a one-story building down there somewhere, with a small sign with a boat on it hanging out above the front doors.

"Boat sales place?" Nina asked, wincing as she said the words since she didn't know much about such things, hence why Holm and I were there.

"Oh no, ma'am," Marty chuckled, shaking his head. "You think old Samuels would let me take a brand new boat every day? Hell no. It's a rental place. This one's pretty old, so he lets me take her, but she sure is a beauty, isn't she?"

He reached up and patted the boat gently, and I smiled.

"Sure is," I agreed. Sure enough, the boat was in remarkably good shape for its age, but more than that, she'd served Marty well when he needed her. I had a similar affection for my houseboat at that point.

"Is this Samuels fellow in?" I asked, and he shook his head again.

"Nope, they packed up for lunch about a half-hour ago," he explained. "Talked to him and Danny—that's his nephew—then. They do that every day. Should be back in an hour or so, I'd reckon, but without any business, who knows?"

"Did they mention anything unusual when you talked to them?" I asked. "Other than how quiet it is today, I mean."

"Not much," Marty said, scratching his head again. "Though I guess Danny did say something about a boat gone missing. He kept asking old Samuels who he lent it out to, but the poor old guy couldn't remember. That's not too out of the ordinary, though."

Holm and I exchanged a look, and I could make out the glint of excitement in his eyes that was no doubt in mine, too. *A missing boat.* That could be something. It could be nothing, but it could be something.

"What kind of boat?" I asked, trying not to sound too eager about this.

"Ah, just a motorboat like this one, except more white than gray," Marty said with a shrug. "Nothing too special. As I said, it's not too unusual, though. Mr. Samuels is loaning these things out all the time as he does with me. It drives Danny totally nuts, I know, 'cause it makes it so hard for him to keep all the books. Usually, when push comes to shove, the old man will remember who he gave 'em to, though. That was the unusual part. I'm starting to think the poor guy's losing it, and by the look on his face, Danny does, too. It's too bad. He's a local legend just about. He's been here longer than anyone, and nicer than anybody, too."

"You said the nephew's name is Danny?" I asked, pulling a notepad and pen out of my jacket and beginning to scribble this all down. "Last name?"

"Samuels, just like his uncle," Marty said. "And the uncle's first name is Danny, too, everybody just calls him Samuels, or Old Samuels, or something like that. Hey now, you don't think either of them had anything to do with all this, do you? Those guys wouldn't hurt a fly. A fish, maybe, if it was giving them trouble, but not a fly."

"We're just covering all our bases," I assured him, giving him a smile. "And if a boat's missing, maybe we can help them find it."

"Isn't that a little below the FBI and... uh... em-bell-what's-you-call-it, anyway?" Marty asked, stumbling over the name of Holm's and my agency.

"A little," I relented. "Though we can help someone else by pointing them in the right direction if need be."

"Is there anything else you can think of?" Holm asked. "Anything that might help us? Anyone you've seen on the water today, or maybe yesterday, that looked out of place to you?"

"Haven't seen anybody doing anything in a day," Marty reiterated. "Even out on the water. Except the Coast Guard, if you count them. In fact, there were more of those ships than usual today."

I let that slide, not explaining why that might be, though I was glad to know that the Coast Guard was still looking fervently as ever for Mikey.

"Do you know the name of the ship that's missing?" I asked him, glancing back over at the one he'd borrowed himself and seeing that the name "Annette" was coated across its sternum in calligraphy.

"Uh, let's see," Marty said, swiveling on his feet to gaze out at all the docked boats. "Mr. Samuels named all these old models after ex-girlfriends of his, believe it or not. There's Marcy, and Becca, and Caroline. I do not see Lucy anywhere, and she's one of the white ones, I know that. Don't think anyone rented her out, either, since I remember seeing her when I got back yesterday around this time, and almost everybody was cleared out by then."

"Thank you," I said again, nodding to him in thanks as I scribbled this down. "We appreciate you talking to us, and if you think of or see anything else, just give me a call, okay?"

I replaced the notebook and pen in my jacket and pulled one of my business cards out instead, handing it to him.

He squinted down at it.

"Marston," he muttered as if committing my name to memory. "Will do, Agent Marston. I appreciate what you're doing here."

15

ETHAN

Marty left the docks not long after that, having finished cleaning the boat for the most part. He saluted us and headed up to where he must have been parked in a lot not far from there, where Nina had left her rental car from the airport.

"We might as well stick around until this Samuels guy and his nephew come back," Holm suggested. "Take a look around. Maybe this missing boat is the one we're looking for."

"Hold on, I should send that description to the Coast Guard," Nina said, pulling out her phone and giving Marty's rental boat a penetrating stare as if she were trying to determine how best to describe it properly.

"Give it here," I chuckled, holding out my hand for her phone. "I'll write one."

"Thank you," she said as she passed the phone over to me, looking relieved.

I quickly described the boat and gave the name Marty had deduced, and snapped a quick picture of the witness's boat for good measure, sending it along to Nina's contact with the addendum that "Lucy" was white, not gray.

When I handed the phone back to Nina, we all started instinctively walking toward the boat rental place without really discussing it. I felt like we didn't have an hour to waste, but we didn't have much else to do, and in the meantime, we could keep exploring the bay and hope we ran into another Marty along the way.

We didn't run into another Marty. We walked all the way to the store, just to see that it was closed with an old, worn handwritten sign denoting that the owners were away without a set return time, taped to the inside of the front door's window.

After that, we continued to walk up and down the pier for some time, our steps and my stomach a little lighter now that we might actually have a lead until Nina's phone buzzed.

"It's the Coast Guard guy," she said apprehensively as she looked at it before her shoulders deflated. "They got the message and got the word out to everyone, but nothing new yet."

"Well, that's something at least," Holm sighed,

though his tone revealed he'd gotten his hopes up again when her phone went off.

My own phone vibrated in my pocket just then, as we were walking past the boat rental place for the second time. I pulled it out to see that Diane had messaged me. I had sent her a text earlier about the boat, as well.

"It's Diane," I told them. "She's informed all our international contacts on nearby islands of the boat's name and description."

"I hope some poor bloke didn't borrow it from this Samuels fellow," Holm remarked, chuckling at the thought. "Otherwise, he's in for a scare the second someone sees him."

"Yeah," I sighed, shaking my head. "If the shop owners don't have anything concrete for us or can say for sure that it was stolen, we should probably release this to the media. As much as I don't want to give away this lead, I also don't want the boat to go unnoticed just because we didn't want to do that."

"Fair point," Nina said, biting her lip. "I'll tell Osborne to prepare for that if push comes to shove."

She began typing away on her phone again at this.

"Alright, what's next?" Holm asked, coming to a halt in front of the shop's doors and putting his hands on his hips as he gazed out at the path behind us, which was just an asphalt bike path around the shore.

The parking lot was up above us a bit, on a hill that began right at the edge of the asphalt.

"There's no phone number on the door," Nina remarked, gazing at the shop's doors. "I guess we could try to get an address for one of the owners from the police."

"Maybe we should just head back then," I suggested. "I don't want to miss anything else waiting around here."

I checked my watch. It had been more than an hour now, and Samuels and his nephew weren't back from lunch yet.

"I'll message the police about them, too," Nina said, continuing to type. "There's no use heading back if we'll just have to turn right around."

"There might be news, though," Holm said hopefully.

"If there was news, we'd be the first to know about it," I pointed out, though I was sure my partner knew this already.

We were all getting more than frustrated with the lack of progress, and the summer heat wasn't exactly helping matters.

"We have a lead, though," I said with a vigorous nod, more to convince myself than anyone else. "That's something. We have some movement we can report back to the parents. No specifics, though, unfortunately. We still can't rule them out entirely."

The more we worked this case, though, the less of a suspicion I had about any of the three parents being involved with all this. There was just too much going on, and they all seemed genuine to me, if a bit flawed, though who wasn't, really.

"Let's go," Holm suggested again. "There's no one out here, and I don't really want to be here anymore."

There was sweat glistening on his brow, and I couldn't help but notice that my own clothes were growing heavier by the second. He wasn't wrong. We weren't good to anyone in a puddle on the ground.

"Alright, we can go drive around a bit," I said. "Nina, you said there were private beaches around here, right? Like the one we found those college kids at? Maybe someone's on one of those."

"Ugh, we're knocking on doors again?" Holm sighed, though even he knew there wasn't much else to be done. "Fine."

"Sure," Nina said with a shrug, not sounding too enthusiastic about this, either.

We were all facing the hill bearing the parking lot by then, with our backs to the rental shop doors.

Then, I heard a rustle back over my shoulder, off to the side or even behind the shop.

The noise was too loud to be an animal, and we hadn't seen any animals while in the bay. We also hadn't seen any other people, and the lights in the shop were dark, with no sign of life inside.

I exchanged a look with Holm and then with Nina. Judging by the way they had each tensed up, they heard the same thing that I did.

"Is anyone there?" Nina asked in a loud voice, instinctively reaching to her side where her gun was holstered. "FBI! Put your hands up and step out from behind the building immediately."

There was a long period of silence, to the point where I was beginning to think that I imagined things or that the three of us had some kind of collective hallucination in the heat.

Then, just as I was starting to think that it was really nothing, after all, the noise repeated itself, further to my left this time, but still behind me.

I looked at the other two again and saw that they, too, had heard the second noise.

Almost as one, Holm and I whirled around with our guns out while Nina pulled out her own weapon and covered our backs.

"Federal agents, put your hands up!" Holm, who was closest to where the noise had come from, hollered.

Before I even knew what was happening, a shot rang out behind us, then another that came from right next to me. The next thing I knew, Holm was on the ground, and a man was sprinting out away from him, while more rustling sounds came from behind me and to my right now.

"I'll go this way, you go that way," Nina said quickly, nodding in each direction, and with that, I darted off after the running man while Nina turned to inspect whatever that second noise was.

I jumped over Holm, not having time to duck down and make sure he was okay. I heard him groan, signifying that he was still alive, at least, and out of the corner of my eye, I saw blood drifting out to color the asphalt, though I wasn't sure where in my partner's body it was coming from yet.

The man was fast but not as fast as I was. He was bogged down by far too many clothes, I realized as I gained ground on him, and they looked vaguely familiar.

I almost kicked myself when I realized what it was. He was wearing the exact same disguise as the second man from the mall security footage, the one with the gun. He also had a similar ski mask on, though it was more navy than the black I remembered from the video.

"You're not going to last long!" I hollered at the man as I came upon him from behind. I could hear him panting now, dragged down by so many clothes in the hot sun. There wasn't much of a breeze, either, so there was no cool wind from the ocean to cool him, or myself for that matter.

As hot as I was, though, it wasn't nearly as bad as this guy, who was practically dripping onto the asphalt.

He still had a gun, though, and I cursed under my breath. I didn't want to shoot a man in the back, but I wasn't sure that I was going to get any choice in the matter.

I heard screams and more gunshots ringing out behind me, but I didn't dare turn around to see what was happening with Nina. The second I turned my back on him, this guy could end up killing me.

I tried to remember if the screams were female or not, but I'd hardly been paying attention. Nina had a low-ish voice anyway, and the other perp could be a woman, too, though, so it wouldn't really tell me much to remember.

"Stop, or I'll shoot!" I screamed at the man, holding up my gun but not ceasing my sprint. "I mean it, don't test me!"

I wasn't exactly sure if I meant it or not. Sure, the guy had a gun, but he had his back turned to me, and he wasn't shooting at me right now, like that idiot in the Keys who shot at me without even turning to look while I was chasing him. Still, he had a gun... He was probably going to kick it soon, though, the way things were going for him. Maybe I could just wait it out...

The decision was made easy for me when the man whirled around, seemingly realizing that he wasn't going to make it wherever he was going before collapsing, and shot in my direction.

He shot at me before he had the time to aim properly, however, and I was a rapidly moving target to boot. The bullet ricocheted off the asphalt, and I had to leap out of the way to avoid it ripping up and hitting me in the face.

I quickly aimed my gun at him, in turn, gaining the split second necessary to make a better shot than he had when he jumped in surprise at the bullet's odd movements, seeming to have surprised himself with how poor of a shot it was.

I raised my gun and shot him once, twice, three times in the chest. He fell to the ground in a pile of sweat and blood.

I strained my ears to try to hear anything else from behind me as I continued to run forward until I reached the goon, bending down to make sure that he was out. He wasn't just out. He was dead.

The only thing I could hear at that point, no matter how hard I tried, were the shots ringing in my ears and my own pounding heart. I couldn't see anything behind me, either, other than the shop itself, so I fell down to my knees beside the man's corpse, sweaty and exhausted.

16

ETHAN

I lay in the hot sun for a few moments, not quite able to collect myself yet. Everything was in a haze until I felt something hot and sticky against my arm. I looked down to see that the goon's blood was seeping all into my clothing.

Knocked back into reality, I pulled myself up, fumbled for my phone, and called for an ambulance and backup. It was only a moment before I heard sirens, not far from where we were. Police were crawling all over the area, having come in from neighboring towns and cities to help with the search for Mikey.

Eventually, I managed to crawl back to my feet, regain some of my energy, and make it back to the shop, where I found Holm still groaning in a puddle of his own blood.

I knelt down next to him, squeezing his shoulder gently.

"Help is coming, okay, buddy?" I asked him, looking for some sign that he could hear me. "They'll fix you up real soon."

He didn't answer right away, and for a moment, I was afraid he was slipping. But then the trace of a smirk crossed his softly-parted lips.

"Always trying to steal the glory from me, eh, Marston?" he croaked, and I chuckled, glad to see he was alright.

I inspected him more closely, trying to find the source of the blood, but it had pooled all around the right side of his shirt and the surrounding asphalt, so I couldn't quite make it out.

"Do you know where you were hit?" I asked.

"Arm," he managed, wincing as he said the word. "I'll be fine, Marston. Go check on Nina."

Nina. How had I forgotten Nina? I cursed myself internally and shook my head to clear it.

"Where—" I started to ask, but Holm cut me off.

"Around the other side," he rasped, his voice and attention starting to fade as the sirens drew nearer. "Another... another goon..."

And just like that, my partner dropped his head back against the asphalt and slipped into unconsciousness. I reached out to check that he still had a steady pulse. He did.

I leapt up and jogged around to the other side of the boat rental shop to look for Nina and the other perp. I couldn't remember hearing anything else from their scuffle after the screaming, but that didn't mean much considering how out of it I'd gotten.

They weren't behind the shop, but it still didn't take long for me to find them.

"Stay still!" I heard Nina grumble from my left and I whirled around to see her leading a man in handcuffs dressed much like the one I had killed, except his ski mask was darker, like the one in the security video. Both of them looked unharmed, to my relief.

"Are you okay?" I asked breathlessly as I ran up to meet them.

"Yeah, yeah, I'm fine," Nina said, waving me off. "What about Holm?" She gave me an anxious look, and I realized she must've not been able to check up on him yet.

"He'll be okay, I think," I said, reaching up to run a hand through my sweaty hair and then realizing that it was still covered in the first goon's blood. "Just a shot in the arm. I called an ambulance."

The sirens were growing even closer then, and I realized they must be pulling into the parking lot up above as we spoke.

"Are *you* okay?" she asked, arching an eyebrow at me and looking me up and down. I then realized that I must've been a sight to behold, all sweating and covered in blood as I was.

"I'm fine," I said quickly, shaking my head and dropping my arms to my sides. "The other guy is dead. It's his blood."

"Rudy?" the other goon gulped, almost yelping at this news.

Nina glared at him.

"We can talk about you and your friend later," she snarled at him, as the lights from the police cars and ambulances up in the parking lot reflected down off the water in the bay. "Come on."

She jerked the goon unceremoniously in the direction of the cars and then led him up the steps to the police. I walked back over to Holm and stayed with him until two paramedics with a gurney arrived shortly thereafter, bending down to inspect my partner just as I had moments before. He was still unconscious now, though.

"How long has he been like this?" one of the paramedics asked me.

"Just a couple of minutes," I assured him. "He was awake and pretty lucid a minute ago. Weak, but lucid."

The paramedic nodded like this was a good thing.

"We'll take good care of him," he assured me.

"He's going to be okay?" I asked, taking a hesitant step toward them.

The man squinted back down at Holm's arm, inspecting the wound.

"I'd say so," he said. "Doesn't look like the bullet hit any major arteries. He's lost a lot of blood, though, so he'll probably need a transfusion."

I pulled two of my business cards out of my jacket and handed them to the paramedic, leaving a bloody thumbprint on the white paper.

"Call me when you know anything, okay? Give one to the doctor, too, if you don't mind," I instructed, and he nodded, squinting down at my name.

"Will do, Agent Marston," he said. Then, narrowing his eyes at my bloody clothing, "You alright, yourself? You want to come and get checked out?"

"No, I'm fine," I said, shaking my head. "This isn't my blood."

"Alright, then," he said with a shrug as he and the other paramedic began to load Holm onto the gurney. "You look pretty dehydrated, though, so make sure you have something to drink."

I thought back to lunch, and how after a certain point, I'd been too worried about the case to eat or drink anything and realized that he was probably right, and that was why I had nearly fainted before.

"Thanks, I'll make sure to do that," I told him, wiping some more sweat off my brow with my non-bloodied hand as I followed the paramedics up the set of stairs not far from there to the parking lot.

I looked back one last time at the boat rental shop, though there was still no sign of the owner or his nephew. I made a mental note not to forget to check back in with them when all was said and done. We still needed to know about that boat, and whether Mr. Samuels had really lent it out to someone and forgotten about it, or whether it had been stolen. Maybe the surviving perp would be able to answer that question if Mr. Samuels couldn't, at least.

Up in the parking lot, there were several police cars and two ambulances. The two paramedics hauled Holm into one of the ambulances, groaning and rolling his head as he began to drift back into consciousness.

"It's alright, Agent Holm," the second paramedic, a woman, murmured to him. "You're safe now. We're going to take good care of you."

Before I had a chance to say any parting words to my partner, the ambulance doors closed behind him, and the ambulance itself sped off, sirens blazing again.

A second set of paramedics hauled a black body bag, no doubt carrying the goon with them toward the other ambulance.

"Make sure the forensics team gets to examine him," I said, approaching them quickly before they had a chance to speed off like the ambulance carrying Holm.

"Of course, sir," one of the paramedics said, nodding to me deferentially. "We've already spoken to them about that. They're going to meet us at the morgue."

"Great, good, that's great," I said, nodding to him weakly in turn.

"You okay?" the other paramedic asked me, his brow furrowed in concern.

"Yeah," I managed, not entirely honestly. "Actually, do you have some water or something I could drink?"

"Sure thing," the young man said, leaping up on the ambulance, swinging open the doors, and returning shortly with two tall water bottles, cold and glistening with condensation.

"Thanks," I said, eagerly accepting the bottles and downing one without stopping to breathe, then the other in short succession as the second ambulance sped away, though this one didn't put its sirens back on. Their cargo was already gone.

As the water flowed through me, the life came back to me, as well, and though I was still sweaty and covered with the dead man's blood, I felt infinitely better anyway.

I turned my attention to the rest of the parking lot then, which was crawling with police officers. No forensics guys yet, but hopefully, they would be there soon, and others would meet the body at the morgue.

I looked around for Nina, but it took me a moment to find her. She was by her car, talking with Officer Hollister, the young man who had picked Holm and me up from the airport. The surviving goon was stuffed in the backseat of her rental, his eyes gloomy beneath his dark ski mask.

Nina had a water bottle of her own dangling in her hand at her side, half-empty, and she looked reinvigorated herself.

Hollister turned to watch as I approached, and he winced at the sight of me.

"Damn," he cursed, shaking his head. "Tell me you're not as bad as you look, man."

"I'm not," I assured him with a chuckle. "You should see the other guy."

"He the dead one?" Hollister asked.

"Yep," I confirmed with a nod.

"I'll pass, then," he said, flashing me a wide grin. "Would've loved to see you in action, though. Both of you." He looked from me to Nina and back again.

"I'm sure you would," Nina said, returning the sly gesture.

"We think this is the one who was in the security footage?" I asked, jerking my chin in the direction of the man in the backseat. We were standing a few paces enough away that I was confident he couldn't hear us, and the windows were rolled up. Nina had at least left the air conditioner on for him, though.

"Oh, he is," Nina said with a knowing nod. "Told me himself when I caught him. The other guy was standing lookout outside at the mall, I guess. We don't have any footage of him. I don't know much else. There wasn't a lot of time to talk to him before everyone showed up."

I breathed a sigh of relief as a lot of the tension I hadn't even realized I'd been holding left my body, and that sinking feeling in the pit of my stomach ebbed some. Finally, we were getting somewhere. Now we could work on getting to the bottom of whatever this mess was and getting Mikey back to his parents. All three of them.

"Good," I murmured. "That's really, really good."

"Let's hope so," Nina said, pursing her lips, and I could tell that she was still thinking the worst.

I supposed that one of us had to, but I was going to try to stay hopeful now that we had a real, honest to goodness lead. I wanted to believe that Mikey was still out there somewhere, alive and well. I had to if I was going to keep working this thing. Part of me was afraid to interview the surviving goon, should he dash away these hopes and confirm my worst fears about the boy's wellbeing.

"Do you two need to wash up before heading back to the station?" Hollister asked, looking me up and down again, and I realized that I really must have been a sight to behold. "I can take the guy in if you want."

"No," I said quickly, shaking my head. "There's no time left to waste. We need to talk to this guy, now."

17

ETHAN

When Nina and I walked into the police station, flanking the handcuffed, masked goon on either side, every eye in the room turned straight to us. I got the sense that everyone there had been waiting for us with bated breath, watching the door for our return.

There were gasps when they saw us, however, confirming my suspicion that I looked even worse than I felt, though some of those gasps could've been at the sight of the goon who looked like he was pulled straight out of that security footage.

"Agent Gosse, Agent Marston," Chief Raskin huffed as he moved over to us as quickly as he could manage. "Are you both alright?"

His eyes lingered on my right side, the one that was covered in the dead perp's blood.

"We're fine," I said, waving him away. "We'll just need an interrogation room."

"Sure thing," Raskin said, sounding a little surprised. "Take any one you'd like."

We settled on the one closest to the front room of the station, not wanting the perp to be too close to where Curt, Annabelle, Jackson, and Dr. Osborne were no doubt still waiting in the lounge area at the end of the hall. Not only were Curt and Annabelle witnesses who may need to pick our perp out of a lineup, even though they barely saw him at the mall, but sticking a suspect in a room with not only two but three parents whose child he was accused of stealing out from under their noses sounded like a recipe for disaster to me.

Once inside the interrogation room, Nina roughly deposited the goon in a chair and handcuffed him to the table as I took a seat across from him. This was an impressive feat, considering how large he was and how petite she was in comparison.

Once he was all locked up, she pulled the ski mask off his face, dragging some of his hair along with it and causing him to cry out in pain. She smirked at this.

"Thanks for finally letting me take that off," the man grumbled, giving her a sour look, and I realized that the reason she probably hadn't taken it off before was that she wanted him to stew some in the summer heat.

"No problem," Nina sneered as she sat down next to me. "Now, how about we have a little chat? As I said when I arrested you, I'm Agent Gosse with the FBI. This is my colleague, Agent Marston with MBLIS. And you are?"

"Embell-a-what?" the man asked, scrunching his face up in confusion as he gazed at me.

"M-B-L-I-S," I spelled out for him. "It stands for the Military Border Liaison Investigative Services."

"Ooh," the man breathed, his eyes widening at this in alarm. "Did—did you say military?"

"Sure did," I said, giving him a small smile, and I heard Nina huff with a combination of humor and satisfaction at this reaction beside me.

"You still haven't given us your name," Nina said simply, staring straight at him.

The man was almost exactly as I'd imagined, bulky and with an almost swollen face. He had a small dent of a scar above his right eye, right near the temple, with a mat of dark brown hair and an indent on his chin. He looked like a typical goon. Or a linebacker. An old linebacker, as he looked to be in his early to mid-forties.

He looked from Nina to me and back again, as if trying to work out a way out of this. I could almost smell the fumes from the gears in his head working on overdrive, though he didn't seem to find a solution and continued to just sit there, staring at us dumbly.

"You're not going to find a way out of this one, my friend," I said coolly, gazing into his eyes.

There was another period of silence. He didn't seem to be working a way out of this anymore, however, and his broad shoulders slumped in resignation as he stayed silent.

"Alright, let's start with your friend's name, then," Nina suggested. "You called him Rudy before?"

The guy stared at Nina, then nodded weakly before averting his eyes.

"What about a last name?" she asked.

"He's not my friend," was all he said in response.

"Colleague, then?" I asked, searching for an answer in his body language.

"I guess that's one way to put it," he said, shifting uncomfortably in his seat.

I glanced over at Nina, and the darkness that was washing over me at that moment was mirrored back at me in her eyes. This was organized, then. An organized crime ring of some kind. Human trafficking, even. Things were not looking good for little Mikey.

"Colleagues in what?" I asked, a little harsher than I'd intended, and the man flinched. I didn't particularly care.

"I... uh..." he stammered, looking around the room wildly as if searching for an escape, though he found none.

"Look, bub, you're stuck with us," Nina said,

leaning forward on the table and peering over at him with a piercing expression. "So you might as well cooperate. Let's be honest, you're going to have everything in the book thrown at you anyway, but you might as well not hurt yourself anymore in the process."

The man's eyes widened again at this, but he still didn't say anything.

"Look, she's right, you know," I said with a shrug as if to say that I would help if I could, but there was nothing to be done. "You can only make things worse for yourself at this point, and who wants that? You're smarter than that, right? I can tell you are."

This couldn't be further than the truth, but he seemed to relax a little at this, thinking that I may not hate him quite as much as Nina did.

"I... I... my name's Justin Harper," he stammered at long last.

"Hi, Justin," I said, nodding to him in thanks. "Thank you. Now, why don't you tell us what happened today down at the bay?"

The man hesitated one last time but then launched into a retelling, having worked out that the only way out of this thing was through.

"Well, Rudy and I were waiting for you guys," he explained. "Looking around to see what you knew, if anything. Then, when we found out that you knew about the boat, well... well, Rudy kind of panicked, you see, and then you heard us, and then he shot at you. I didn't shoot at you, I swear..."

He looked between us again, appearing to be rather panicked himself. It wasn't lost on me that he blamed pretty much everything that had gone wrong on his dead companion, who could no longer defend himself. I knew it wasn't lost on Nina either.

Sure enough, she said, "You sure shot at me a few times. Bad shot, though, if I do say so myself. Didn't leave a scratch on me, even scared yourself when you did it."

I realized that this must've been the screaming I'd heard as I chased the other goon, Rudy. Nina and I hadn't had much time to debrief about what had happened away from Justin's earshot.

"Yeah, yeah, yeah," Justin muttered, starting down at the table and not even attempting to get himself out of this one. "But I didn't start it. You get that I didn't start it, right?"

"Sure," I relented with a curt nod. "We'll make sure that the record reflects that."

Not that it would make much of a difference. This guy was going away for a long, long time, and probably for a good while after that.

"Good, good," Justin murmured, more to himself than anyone else by my estimation, staring back down at the table after glancing briefly up at me.

"So how about we talk about what happened at the

mall?" Nina suggested. "Let's go back to the beginning, shall we? Why'd you take the kid?"

"It—it wasn't my idea," Justin said quickly, looking wildly between us yet again. "It was Charlie's. It was all Charlie's, I swear. You have to believe me."

"Charlie?" I asked, arching an eyebrow at him. "Was that the other man at the mall?"

"Yes, yes, that was him," Justin said eagerly. "In the brown jacket. His name's Charlie Black. You can look him up. He's got a long record in Durham."

"Durham?" Nina repeated. "You're from Durham?"

"Yes, all three of us," Justin said, nodding anxiously. "Charlie's the only one with a record, though. Well, Rudy was arrested for petty theft a couple of times, and I was in a bar fight once, but other than that."

"What's in Durham?" I asked. "What do you three do there? You said before that you're colleagues."

"I... uh..." Justin stammered, clamming up at this question and shifting uncomfortably some more, which proved difficult because of the handcuffs.

"What is it?" Nina asked suspiciously, narrowing her eyes at him. "Whatever it is, it's going to come out. You can minimize the damage by coming clean now."

Justin groaned audibly and threw his head back, staring straight up at the fluorescent lights in the ceiling as if he hoped they would sear his eyes away. But they didn't, and he finally returned his attention to the tabletop, blinking as if he saw dark spots where his vision should be.

Whatever it was, it had to be bad. And he knew it, too.

Finally, he took a deep breath and looked back up at me, though he continued to avoid Nina's piercing, no doubt intimidating, gaze.

"Well, the thing is, we, uh... work for this... I guess you could call it a gang," he said, wincing as he said the words.

Dread was filling me from my toes to my forehead again, even worse than before. It sounded like our worst fears were being realized.

"A human trafficking organization," I said simply, my tone as flat as my stomach. "You work for a human trafficking organization."

Justin nodded, and I could hear him gulp all the way across the table.

"You have to understand, we never really dealt with kids until recently," he said quickly. "Not until the boss man realized there was a market for it."

"Just women then," Nina said dryly, her eyes filled with fire now. "You just 'dealt' with women."

Justin hung his head, though I couldn't tell whether it was in shame or because he was mad he'd been caught. I didn't particularly care. Clearly, he wasn't ashamed enough to stop him from doing it in the first place.

I practically had to swallow my lunch to keep from losing it.

"When did they start taking kids?" Nina growled when Justin offered up no more explanation.

"About a year ago, I'd say," he sighed. "I never took one, though, I swear. I didn't have any part in it until now."

"You just didn't say anything and let it go on," I said flatly, and the man hung his head again.

"Look, you don't know what it's like," he muttered.

"No, you're right," I told him, abandoning all pretense of being the good cop in this scenario. "I wouldn't know what it's like to make my way in the world exploiting innocent women and children."

There was a period of silence so tense that you could cut it with a knife before Nina stepped in to try to get some more of the facts straight.

"So this organization in Durham, what are they doing stealing tourist kids from little towns like this?" she asked him.

"We're not," Justin said, heaving a long sigh. "Or at least we weren't supposed to, anyway. Well, we've been —or rather, they've been. Like I said, I had nothing to do with this part of the business till yesterday—well, we've been taking street kids in Durham. Nobody really misses them much, you see."

My blood boiled. I wanted to beat this guy to a pulp right then and there, and with all the rage that was flowing inside me, I probably could've despite his size. Even so, I had to contain my anger. Where would our case be if I did that? So I just clenched my fists beneath the table so hard that it hurt.

Nina's face was ashen white, and I could tell she was feeling similarly. In all her career, in all the things she'd seen and been through, all the cases she'd worked, even this must be a lot for her to handle. Usually, these cases were a one-off, a lone wolf. Horrible, to be sure, but isolated. This? This was a whole other level of sickness. And that was what it was—sickness.

Justin seemed to notice that his words hadn't gone over well.

"I mean... it's just... I mean..." he stammered, trying to find a way to recover from this and failing because there was no way to recover.

"It's alright," Nina said coolly, glaring at him. "We appreciate your honesty. Now, why didn't you take those kids in Durham?"

"Well, we realized the police were starting to get onto us," Justin said, fidgeting in his handcuffs and avoiding both of our gazes now. "We were taking too many kids too often, and they were starting to notice, even though... Well, I won't say it again, I guess."

We knew what he was going to say, anyway. That those kids weren't worth much, so they never expected the police to notice that they were gone or even care if they did.

But it was our job to protect everyone, no matter who they were or where they came from. Especially kids.

"So, uh, anyway..." Justin continued when we both just continued to glare at him. "On our last grab—that's, uh, what Charlie calls it."

Nina let out a low growling sound because this angered her so much, and I wouldn't have been surprised if I drew blood by how hard I was clenching my fists then under the table. Justin just carried on when we didn't say anything, not knowing what else to do.

"So, uh, anyway..." he repeated, looking at us each warily in turn. "The police showed up, tried to catch us, and we ran. Just hopped right on the interstate and panicked, Charlie did. He didn't get off 'till we got here, and the mall was the first thing we saw. Charlie's going on and on about how we need a kid, and if we don't get one, the boss is gonna have our heads. But we can't take one from Durham 'cause the police are onto us there. So the next thing I know, he's running into the mall and grabbing that kid, telling Rudy to wait outside this game store place for us since it didn't look like anybody was in there and we could go in through the back. Some employee must've left it open the night before, so no one noticed, I don't think. Turned the cameras off while we were in there."

There was a flicker of realization in Nina's eyes then, and I realized that this information filled in some gaps that had been eating at her, surrounding the incidents at the mall. This explained how easily the kidnappers had gotten away both times, without being seen by any cameras other than the one from the shoe store or by any witnesses on the other side of the mall from the food court, where the second public exit was. We'd have to confirm with this game store, but the whole thing did line up.

"So you just... took Mikey," I said flatly, not quite sure what to do with this information. "You just grabbed him in a panic in broad daylight because you didn't want to piss off your boss and because you were afraid the police would find you."

Justin bit his lip and nodded weakly.

"Not me, though. I was just an accessory," he added quickly. "Same with Rudy. This was all Charlie's idea, remember?"

"And this all... made sense to you?" Nina asked, shaking her head in wonder. "Seriously?"

"Hey, I never said it was a good plan, just that it was a plan," Justin shrugged. "Well, sort of a plan. More of an impulse after the first plan fell apart, anyway."

Nina and I stared at each other. This was an insane story, though it did explain some eccentricities of the case: why it seemed both planned and unplanned, organized and lone-wolf, spur of the moment yet in some way professional.

"You must've realized what you'd done," I said, still trying to wrap my head around all this. "You must've realized that we would find you eventually, that the whole country would latch onto this case."

"Well, I don't know about the whole country," Justin said defensively. "I don't know if anyone could've predicted that. And, well, to be honest, we weren't really thinking much at all when we did it."

"That much is clear," Nina said, her voice dripping with her customary sarcasm.

"Tell me this, why were you and Rudy in this getup?" I asked, gesturing at Justin's heavy clothing and the ski cap that Nina had discarded atop the table. "While Charlie was just in regular old street clothes?"

"Well, that was from the Durham operation," Justin mumbled as if he was afraid to answer the question. "We had to be disguised to avoid detection, but, uh... one of us had to look normal to, uh, you know..."

He didn't finish his sentence, but Nina did it for him.

"To lure the children in," she said curtly, her mouth set in a thin line. "One of you needed to look normal to get them to come with you without making a fuss."

My stomach churned again as the image of the man in the brown jacket from the security footage luring innocent children into a parked van, away from where they played in the streets and into a life of unspeakable violence and exploitation, seared itself into my brain.

"Alright, so you go into the mall, and you take Mikey, stupid as that was," Nina continued. "What's next? You know I ran back into your friend at the mall again later, I'm sure, so what happened in the meantime?"

"He's not my friend," Justin protested again, and Nina rolled her eyes.

"Your *colleague*, then," she corrected, lingering on the word with some disdain, as if she thought of this man as anything but Justin's colleague, because that would insinuate that they were in some kind of legitimate business venture together, instead of trafficking women and children.

"Right, so I wasn't involved in that whole thing at the mall," Justin said quickly. "The second time, I mean. I wasn't even there. Neither was Rudy."

"Where were you, then?" I asked, almost dreading the answer.

"We were, uh... with the kid," Justin said, averting his eyes from mine. I felt my blood boiling some more.

"And where was that?" I asked, swallowing hard and trying not to picture the worst-case scenario. Justin seemed to realize what I was thinking.

"Hey, we never touched him. We're not like that,"

he said, wagging a finger at me through the handcuffs as if he was insulted that I would ever deign to think such a thing. "None of us are, not even Charlie."

"What do you mean, 'not even Charlie?'" Nina asked, narrowing her eyes at him.

"Well, you know, Charlie's kind of an odd duck," Justin said with a nervous laugh and a haphazard shrug. "But I've never seen him do any of that stuff, he just takes the kids, he doesn't... well, you know."

I wanted to vomit. I couldn't even find my voice to say anything.

"So you and Rudy were with Mikey when Charlie went back to the mall?" Nina pressed again. "Where were you?"

"We were hiding out in the van," he said. Then, before either of us had a chance to ask, "It's parked down by the water now. We drove it there to look for you. Before that, we were in the next town over, hiding out in an abandoned parking lot. Went there straight after we took him."

"So how did Charlie get back to the mall?" I asked, finding my voice again. "And why? Why did he go back?"

"Well, he wanted to see what was going on, didn't he?" Justin asked as if this should be obvious. "We all did. We got a bit on the radio, enough to know there was a crowd at the mall. Then, Charlie, he got it in his head that he could blend in. Rudy and me both offered to go instead since he was so set on somebody going anyway, and nobody saw our faces. But he insisted on doing it himself. Charlie, he's one of those, 'if you want it done right, you have to do it yourself' folks."

Nina and I exchanged a look. There were a lot of words I could think of for the stunt this Charlie fellow pulled at the mall with Nina, but "right" or "smart" weren't any of them.

"Yeah, yeah, I know it didn't go so well," Justin said quickly, reading our faces. "But that's just Charlie, you see. I told you he was weird."

He shrugged as if that was that, settling everything.

"Right, so what happened after the mall incident?" I asked, skipping right over the part where this idiot thought it was a good idea to shoot at an FBI agent in broad daylight when half the country was already looking for him.

"Well, Charlie kind of panicked after that," Justin admitted, wincing as he said the words. "We came back to pick him up, and the next thing we knew, he was stealing a boat!"

Nina and I exchanged another look.

"What boat?" I asked.

"Oh, I don't know, I'd reckon you're probably right that it was that one from the shop we were at, but Rudy and me, we weren't there when it happened," he sighed. "One minute we were in the van, and the next Charlie was grabbing the kid and stuffing him on that damned boat, saying he had to make a run for it, and every police officer in the country would know his face on sight now. Told us to keep watch on shore and make sure nothing else happened."

"He just left you?" Nina asked, incredulous. "Did you have any way to contact him?"

"No, he just ran for it with the kid," Justin said, shaking his head. "Didn't make much sense to Rudy and me, but he said he'd be back in touch somehow, so we kept watch as he asked. The alternative was going back to Durham, and that didn't sound good to either of us. They'd kill us after what happened. Then we ran into you, and well, you know the rest. We didn't want to shoot you, I swear, and that was all Rudy at the start. I was just defending myself. You get that, right?"

And here we were, back to square one, with Justin jumping to his own defense, throwing his dead friend —or colleague, or whatever—under the bus in the process.

"Did Charlie say anything about how or when he would contact you again?" Nina asked.

"No," Justin said, shaking his head. "Just that he would, somehow. I don't know if I believed him or not, but I didn't really want to risk it. Charlie's weird, but he can be mean, too. Not so mean as the bosses back in Durham, but pretty bad. Rudy and me, we just planned to bide our time for a few days, and if Charlie didn't show back up again, we were gonna make a run for it and start a new life somewhere else."

He hung his head, then, as if he actually felt some remorse for what had happened to the other goon.

"You sure he's dead?" he asked in a low whisper, as if he was afraid to hear the answer.

"One hundred percent," I assured him, looking down at my blood-soaked shirt.

Justin winced and looked away from me as if he had just now realized where all that blood had come from.

"Alright, then, Justin, I think that's enough for now," Nina said, standing up and nodding to him while motioning for me to do the same. "Others will be in shortly, I assume, to get more details about this operation in Durham."

Justin winced.

"If I tell on them, they'll kill me," he said, looking up at us with pleading in his eyes. "Even in jail, they'll find a way to kill me."

"You just let the police worry about that," I said, sighing again at the thought of this asshole ending up in witness protection instead of rotting in prison. "I'm sure they'll find a way to protect you."

18

ETHAN

NINA and I huddled together when we were back out in the hall, speaking in low voices so that Justin couldn't hear us where he still sat inside the interrogation room. Dr. Osborne and the three parents wouldn't be able to hear either from where they probably still congregated in the lounge area at the end of the hall, which was too distant for me to see clearly from where we stood.

"So we know it wasn't the parents now, at least," Nina said with a low huff, shaking her head and glaring through the one-way window behind which Justin was fidgeting in his handcuffs.

In a way, I thought he looked kind of relieved to have been caught, to have everything out on the table. Still nervous, though. Who wouldn't be?

"That's one thing, at least," I said, letting out a long breath. "Good news for them, not so much for Mikey."

"We can only hope that Justin's right that this Charlie character isn't weird in 'that way,'" Nina said, giving voice to my own worst fears. "That he just panicked and took him but didn't do anything to him."

"I guess so," I murmured. "He could still kill him, though. What else is he going to do? He can't haul a kid around wherever he's going to start a new life. I assume that's what he's doing. He might just drop him in the middle of the ocean and sail away."

Nina's face darkened at this, and I was sorry to give voice to such a horrible possibility, but we had to be prepared for it if it did happen.

"I guess we just have to find him, then," she said quietly. "We have to find him, and we have to find him fast."

"Someone should call the Durham Police Department and update the detectives," I said. "And the other should update the family."

Nina gave me a pointed look, and she didn't have to say who was going to take which role. Nina was great at her job, but she wasn't exactly as great at the softer parts like this.

"I'll meet you back out front when you're done," she said when she detected acceptance of this in my eyes. "Good luck."

I nodded and gulped, knowing that I would need it.

The parents weren't going to be happy about this, and they weren't exactly happy already. Not with me, not with the investigation, and not with each other.

The trek back down the hallway to the lounge area felt like it took a lifetime, each step heavier than the last.

"Is there news?" Annabelle asked the moment she saw me, her head whipping up from where it had been resting on her husband's shoulder where they still sat on the couch. "There has to be news."

I surveyed the whole room. Dr. Osborne was still sitting in the chair across from Curt and Annabelle, while Jackson was huddled in a far less comfortable looking chair in the left-hand corner of the room. He was pressed up against the wall like he was trying to be as far away from the other two as humanly possible while remaining in the same room.

"Yes, there is," I said with a curt nod, pulling up a folding chair from against the wall and taking a seat next to Dr. Osborne.

"No," Curt said, shaking his head at the expression on my face, his voice breaking. "No, don't say it, don't tell us that."

"Don't worry, Mikey's still alive, as far as we know," I said quickly, knowing even as I said it how ridiculous it was to tell parents in this situation not to worry. "We do have some new information, though. The good news is that all three of you have been cleared."

"Cleared?" Annabelle repeated, shaking her head in confusion. "What do you mean by cleared? Cleared of what?"

"Cleared of doing this," Jackson said darkly from the corner. "It's not just me who was a suspect, then, was it?"

"Suspect!" Curt roared, looking over at his wife. "Us? How dare you think—"

"Curt, Curt, please," Dr. Osborne said, holding out her hands to silence him. "You have to understand how these investigations usually go. Just like Agent Marston told you before, ninety-nine percent of the time, it's the parents who are behind this kind of thing. And failing that, it's someone known to the v—I mean Mikey."

I was sure that no one failed to notice how Osborne stumbled over the word "victim," but at least she caught herself before she said the whole thing.

"I thought you thought it was *him*, though!" Curt cried, pointing almost violently in Jackson's direction, though he made a point of not looking at the other man.

"That was what we thought," I said, nodding slowly. "But we couldn't rule anyone out as a suspect until now. It was nothing personal, I assure you."

"Nothing personal?" Curt repeated, his anger clearly unabated. "You seriously expect us not to take it personally that you thought we could do this to our own son!"

I glanced over at Dr. Osborne, who reached out and placed her hand lightly on Curt's knee to silence him.

"Curt," she said quietly. "You have to understand—this is our work. We see these things every day. People lie to us every day. We don't really know you the way that a close friend or family member would or how you know each other. Our priority isn't you. It's Mikey. We couldn't close the door on any possibilities for his sake."

For a moment, I thought that this was a little too honest, that Curt would push Osborne's hand away and react even more poorly to her words than he had to mine.

But Osborne was excellent at her job, excellent at reading people, and she knew Curt and Annabelle well enough by then, despite what she said, to know what would work on them. And it turned out, the truth worked just fine, to the couple's own credit.

Curt opened his mouth as if to respond but then closed it again, his shoulders slumping slightly as if he was giving in to something.

"Yes, of course," he said, running a hand across his face and practically wiping away his anger. "Of course, that's your priority. And we appreciate that. We do. I just... I don't like the idea of you wasting any time looking for Mikey where he isn't."

"We know you're not, though," Annabelle said

quickly, her eyes wide with fear that we would misunderstand her husband. "Wasting time, I mean. We know you're doing everything you can for Mikey and that you have to pursue the most obvious leads first. It's just that *we* know we didn't take him, so we don't want you spending time on that when you could be looking for him elsewhere."

"That's what Jackson said earlier, just about," I said, smiling at the man in the corner. "And we understand. This is the most difficult thing that any parent can go through. You don't have to apologize to us."

Jackson nodded to me in thanks. I doubted, based on all three parents' body language, that they'd done much to mend fences even though they'd been cooped up here together all day.

"So?" Osborne asked, leaning into me. "You said there's news?"

I closed my eyes, took a deep breath, and then launched into as delicate a retelling of what Nina and I had learned from Justin as I could manage. There was no way to deliver this news well, though. Throughout the whole story, Jackson, Curt, and Annabelle took turns gasping, yelling, and crying. Eventually, we made it to the end, though.

"That's it?" Curt asked when I had finished, throwing his hands up in the air. "You don't have anything else for us?"

I knew how he felt, in a way. I didn't like that we

didn't have anything else yet, either. The story didn't exactly end on a happy note, with Mikey adrift out at sea with a madman who may or may not harm him in some way as the best-case scenario, the worst case being that the boy was already dead.

"I'm sorry we don't have more for you at this time," I said honestly. "I didn't want to keep this from you until we did, though. We'll let you know as soon as we have anything else."

"We... we appreciate that," Annabelle managed through her tears, which had been falling for some time then. "We're glad you told us."

She winced as she said this and bit her lip like she wasn't quite sure this was true. That maybe she would've preferred it if she still didn't know what might be happening to Mikey, that her blissful ignorance from moments before seemed a lot better than what she had to think about now.

It was better that they knew, though. It was always better to know.

"So... so this man..." Curt stammered, swallowing hard. "This man has Mikey all alone in the middle of the ocean? They haven't been seen in a day, so they could be anywhere by now, right?"

I took a deep breath and nodded slowly.

"That depends," I said. "They could be waiting somewhere while he figures out what to do next, or they could be on an island somewhere."

"An island?" Jackson asked from where he was still crouched in the corner, practically constricted into a fetal position in that chair now with his anxiety. "What island?"

"Well, there are a number of possibilities," I said carefully. "This is why I told you before that MBLIS has contacted our international contacts, just in case he shows up on a coastal island."

"He, you said he," Curt said, pointing at me. "What about Mikey? Do you think… Do you think…"

He was unable to finish the thought, though he didn't really need to do so. Dr. Osborne closed her eyes tightly at the thought.

"We're operating under the assumption that Mikey is still alive and well at this hour," I assured them, careful not to give them any false hope in case this turned out to be incorrect. "I'm not going to lie to you, though. This is a very dangerous and potentially volatile situation on all ends."

"Th-thank you," Annabelle sputtered before collapsing into a sea of tears as her husband wrapped both of his arms around her.

"I'm sorry," I murmured, not knowing what else to say. "We're doing everything that we can."

"I promise you that both the FBI and MBLIS have their absolute best agents on this case," Dr. Osborne said quietly, reaching out to place a soothing hand on

Annabelle's knee. "If anyone is going to find your son, it's them."

I figured that this was true enough. If anyone was going to be able to track down this poor boy, it was Nina. And Holm and I were the best agents that MBLIS had.

Jackson practically read my mind, and not in a good way.

"You said that other agent, the other man, he got shot, though," he pointed out. "So he's not going to be able to help find Mikey anymore, is he? You said he's in the hospital and probably has to stay the night."

"As soon as Agent Holm is cleared by his doctor, he'll be back on this case," I assured them all quickly. "Sooner, if he has his way, I'm sure. He's not off the case."

"How can he get back on if he's not off?" Jackson asked, catching me up in my turn of phrase. "That's not how that works. So are they going to send someone in to replace him, or what?"

"I... not at this time," I said, not having expected this to be an issue that any of the parents would even pay attention to, let alone care about, given how much else they had going on right then. "Agent Gosse and I are perfectly capable—"

But Jackson wasn't having it, and he cut me off.

"So you don't have your best agents on it, do you?" he challenged angrily. "If he's one of your best, and you're not going to replace him, you're down a whole man! One of the best men, too. How's that supposed to help you find my son?!"

This was, by all accounts, the wrong thing for Jackson to say at that moment, given how tense things already were in the room, given the recent news, and how tense things were between himself and Curt and Annabelle, given their history.

"Your son?" Annabelle cried, aghast at him. "*Your* son! Where were you the first seven years of his life, then? Where were you when we needed you? Nowhere, that's where. Running away. Curt was there, though. Curt's his father, so get out of here with all your proclamations about how this agent needs to be helping *your* son."

I had to stop myself from groaning out loud and dropping my head into my hands. So we were back to this—full circle, yet again, just like with Justin.

"Alright, alright," I said instead of groaning, holding both my hands up to silence Jackson before he had a chance to respond, and Curt and Annabelle before either of them had a chance to add anything else. "We've been over this before. The past isn't what matters now. It's Mikey. Going over old wounds isn't going to help find him any faster, and if you want to talk about wasting any time, well, this is a case in point right here."

"Agent Marston is correct," Dr. Osborne added

quickly, also before any of the parents could say anything else. "We need to focus on the task at hand, all of us, and keeping in as good of spirits as possible is important for everyone, including Mikey. We're going to need to do another press conference about all this soon, I'd imagine, and having all three of you there could help."

"All three of us?" Curt gaped as if he couldn't believe his ears. "You can't be serious! We're not going out there with him!"

I really did groan this time, running a hand over my eyes.

"Guys, who is this helping?" I snapped, unable to stop myself. "Now I get that you all have legitimate concerns about each other surrounding this custody case, but there's not going to be a custody case if you don't get Mikey back, do you understand?"

They all looked around at each other like they were expecting someone else to say something, but no one did. There was nothing else to be said.

"I think Agent Marston summed that up nicely," Dr. Osborne quipped when Curt and Annabelle looked to her for guidance.

"Look, the important thing is that Mikey has three people who really care about him and want him home," I said, adopting a kinder tone than the one I had used before now. "How can that possibly be a bad thing? Some kids don't even have two, let alone three."

I thought back to Nina and my interview with Justin and how he'd talked about those street kids in Durham who nobody would really miss if they disappeared, taken by the traffickers. Perhaps Mikey really was lucky in that regard, after all.

The parents all looked at each other almost sheepishly. Finally, Annabelle gestured toward a more comfortable chair on the other side of both of us.

"You can sit here, Jackson," she suggested kindly, though I could see that it still pained her. "There's no reason for you to be all huddled up over there any longer."

"Th-thank you," Jackson stammered after blinking at her for several moments as if he thought this was too good to be true. "I appreciate it."

Slowly, he stood and crossed over to sit in the chair almost gingerly, like he was afraid it might break beneath him or that the invitation would disappear as quickly as Annabelle's more welcoming attitude had appeared.

"Good," I said, nodding to each of them in turn. "And as for Agent Holm, I assure you that he will be back to work as quickly as possible and that if we need anyone else, we'll call for them in a New York second. Until then, Agent Gosse and I have this covered. Alright?"

I met each of the parents' eyes and then Dr. Osborne's. The tension in the lounge area had dissipated somewhat, though it still hummed with everyone's anxiety and probably would for some time.

"We have this covered here, Agent Marston," Osborne assured me with a small smile. "We appreciate the update, but we'll be fine. You just go find Mikey for us."

19

ETHAN

From the lounge area, I headed straight back out to the main area of the station to find Nina, just like I said I would.

I didn't see her at first, just some detectives and officers. This was the same set that had been there when I arrived the previous day, so they must've traded off again so the second group could get some sleep.

"She's in there," a guy in a half-tucked-in suit said when he saw me, jutting his thumb in the direction of a desk in the corner.

Then I realized that she'd been there all along, hunched over that desk with a laptop and several files in one hand and her phone in the other. Her dark clothes and hair blended her into the wall behind her, which was a navy color.

"Hey," I called, waving and crossing over to her.

She nearly jumped in surprise when she saw me, then reached over and cleared some more files off a chair that sat at the side of the desk adjacent to her. I gratefully took the seat.

"That bad, huh?" she asked, no doubt seeing the weariness on my face.

"Well, we had to have another chat about who's really Mikey's parent, and who cares more about him, and then why Jackson wasn't there until now, so yeah, it was pretty bad," I sighed, allowing myself to drop my head into my hands at long last.

"Ugh," Nina groaned, wincing out of empathy. "See, this is why I let Osborne handle all this stuff. I'd just mess it up."

"Well, we all have our strong suits," I chuckled, trying to imagine Nina having a go at diffusing that situation back in the lounge. She probably would've just rolled her eyes and rage quit on them, not that I would have blamed her if she did. I certainly wanted to do that at the moment.

"I've been busy, too, it turns out," Nina said, gesturing at the laptop screen.

I leaned in to get a better look at it. She was on what looked like some kind of true crime blog, with blood-red calligraphy as a logo at the top, and I suddenly remembered what she had said earlier about that blogger she ran into at the mall.

"That guy from the mall?" I asked, unable to

disguise my surprise. "That turned out to be something after all?"

"Well, he didn't have anything to do with it, obviously, but he knows about those street kids in Durham," Nina explained. "He's from there, remember? Anyway, I talked to him a bit on the phone—and man, can he talk—but he started noticing a while back that there were a lot of missing kids turning up in the area with a lot of similarities in the cases."

"This is the guy with the blog all about missing kids, right?" I asked, cocking an eyebrow at this.

"Yes, it is, and before you say it, I thought he probably saw what he wanted to see at first, too," Nina said, pointing at me before I had a chance to say anything else. "But then I talked to the Durham police, and well... it all lines up with what Justin told us. All of it. So I'm going to send a Durham detective back to talk to him about it all. He's on his way now. He was shocked the blog guy was onto something, but he's glad he knows now."

"So he'd talked to the blog guy about this before?" I asked.

"Yep," Nina confirmed with a nod. "And the detective did just what you or I probably would've at first and dismissed him as a crackpot with an obsession with these kinds of cases looking for his fifteen minutes of fame. Turns out every once in a while, these guys actually have something valuable to give us, after all."

I thought back to that supposed reclusive hermit of a fisherman in Scotland who Interpol ignored when he said he'd seen the Hollands.

"Yes, I think that might be important for us all to remember," I agreed, nodding slowly. "So these children in Durham, Justin called them street kids? Were they really?"

"A mixed bag, really," Nina sighed, pulling open one of the files to reveal a set of pictures of children ranging the gamut in age, though I noticed that most of the older ones were girls. "There's a handful of runaways, a lot of foster kids—man, do those kids go through it, I'm telling you—and some who just look homeless or like vagabonds of some kind. I don't even know. Anyway, yeah, street kids would be an all-encompassing term for it, I guess."

She looked sadly down at the photographs, and I thought that it must be hard to work these kinds of cases all the time. I was secretly glad that they only came up once in a blue moon for me. And I'd thought it was bad when those goons grabbed that nosy kid in Virginia and held him hostage for just a few minutes before Tessa and I managed to rescue him. This was about a million times worse than that.

"Damn," I said, shaking my head in a combination of incredulity and horror. "And no one but a blogger thought to link all these cases together until now? How many of these kids are there? How long has it been since they were taken?"

"There's about twelve documented cases, all in the past year," Nina said, pursing her lips as she said this, in a skeptical way. "But who knows what the real number is? These are just the ones where someone noticed they were gone, eventually. They were taken at different places and times, but they all just vanished into thin air. Given who these kids are and where they came from, it wouldn't surprise me if the real number were three or even four or more times that."

"You're probably right," I said darkly, pursing my lips.

"I have a feeling I'm going to be working on this one for a long while," Nina said, peering down at the file and shaking her head. "Mikey or no Mikey—at the end of the day, this whole operation is going to have to be brought down, and the FBI is going to want to oversee it themselves."

"I can't think of anyone better for the job," I pointed out, and she gave me a small smile.

"I don't know about that," she said. "Though with Osborne, I guess we make up for each other's weaknesses. As for you and Holm, I imagine this is a one and done thing for you once Mikey is found, or..."

Her voice trailed off as she failed to finish her sentence, though she didn't have to. I knew what she was going to say. That Mikey might not be found, or at least not found alive. There was no reason to say it, though. It was important even—or perhaps especially—for the ones working cases like this to stay positive, not just the parents.

"I suppose so," I sighed. "Diane will want us back in Miami to keep working on the Holland case as quickly as possible, I'm sure. Though I imagine we're both in that boat, so to speak."

I glanced over at her, hoping to catch anything resembling a hint about what she was working on before she came here to find Mikey. But her face was blank, though I caught the shadow of a smirk on her lips as she made herself indecipherable.

"Have you heard anything from Holm?" she asked.

"No, let me text him," I said, sorry I hadn't thought of this myself as I pulled out my phone to send him a quick text. A message from Diane was waiting for me there.

Heard about your scuffle with the traffickers, she wrote. *Stay safe and update me when you can. I'm sure I don't have to remind you how fast the clock is ticking on a case like this.*

I sighed as I read this. I knew already, of course, but there was something about seeing it in writing that added even more of a sense of urgency to the whole thing. That was probably why Diane sent it. That and checking to make sure I was okay without directly asking me.

I texted Holm before I messaged her back, knowing that Diane would want an update on him, too. No doubt she'd heard he'd been shot.

Are you okay? I messaged him. *Need anything? Someone to pick you up? How long are you going to be there?*

To my relief, he texted back quickly, and I realized he'd probably been waiting for a message from Nina or me, hoping to hear how the case was going.

Fine, they're making me stay here overnight, though, he wrote. *I tried to get out of it, but I had to have a second blood transfusion thing. I'll be out in the morning, or I'll leave anyway. Word on the kid?*

I pursed my lips again. For Holm to agree to stay overnight, even begrudgingly, he must not be feeling very well. He lost more blood than we'd realized. Even so, he was alive and seemingly lucid, which was good enough for me given the circumstances.

Of course, Holm didn't care about any of this. He just wanted to know about the case.

A few new leads, as well as some on other kids who've been taken, I shot back quickly. *It turns out it's a trafficking gang in Durham. No time to explain the rest now. Kid on the ocean with other perp in stolen boat after all. Still working on finding them. I'll tell you when we know more*

Holm didn't respond to this, though the message displayed as read, and I knew that he was probably sitting in his hospital bed with that sinking feeling I got when I first found out what was really going on with this case, realizing how much danger Mikey was truly in right now, if he was even still alive.

I flipped back over to Diane's contact information to message her.

Yes, I am hoping to find him before tomorrow. Clock is running out. Talked to Holm. Doing good but being held overnight. All okay with us. Check back in soon.

I then relayed all this over to Nina, who cursed under her breath when she heard the news about Holm.

"Damn, I was really hoping we would have him if this comes to some whole affair on the ocean," she muttered.

"So was Jackson," I reminded her.

"Yeah, maybe it's best if we keep this one to ourselves for now," she said. "They can be kept in the loop on a need to know basis. We don't want them complicating things for us."

"Complicating things?" I repeated, shaking my head in confusion. "The parents? What do you mean? We know none of them had anything to do with this."

"Yes, but when it gets to this late hour in an investigation like this, families sometimes get desperate and lash out, lose faith in the investigation," she explained. "They can take important details on the case to the media, hire private investigators, just all around make a whole fuss and inadvertently make it harder for us to do our jobs. And with this case, we're dealing with even more parents than usual."

"Ah," I said, nodding my head at this, my eyes wide at the thought of this happening. "Well, I can't say I would blame them for getting desperate, but we definitely don't want any of that. Not yet anyway. But if we can't find this kid in another twenty-four hours, or at least get a better idea as to what might've happened to him, well, maybe we should be thrown off the case."

"I don't disagree," Nina sighed, standing up and motioning for me to follow her. "Though if we can't find him, I doubt anyone can. Come on. We have work to do."

20

ETHAN

We headed straight back to the boat shop from the station after I borrowed some clean clothes from one of the detectives. We were hoping to catch either the younger or elder Daniel Samuels before he went home for the day.

The area around the boat shop had been excavated as a crime scene for a couple of hours, but then the police quickly left the area, not wanting to draw any more crowds like the one at the mall on the previous day.

We weren't sure if the boat shop would've reopened when we approached, though as we drew closer, I realized that the lights were on when they hadn't been before.

The closed sign was still flipped, however, and I

pressed my forehead against the front door in an attempt to see if there was anyone inside.

All I saw was a bunch of fishing poles lined up for sale, a front desk donning an ancient cash register, and a fridge off to the side containing live bait for fishing, with some life jackets hanging on the wall next to it for good measure.

"Alright, let's just knock and see if anyone hears us," I suggested, banging my fist against the door. "Maybe they came back, saw the police, and packed up for the day. They could've forgotten to turn off the light on their way out."

This was a likely enough story, but thankfully, a man who looked to be in his late forties or early fifties, with mousy brown hair and a thinly receding hairline, appeared from a back room behind the cash register and peered at us questioningly.

I pulled out my MBLIS badge and flashed it at him, and Nina did the same with hers from the FBI, indicating that we were law enforcement.

A look of realization dawned across the man's sharp features, and he nodded and crossed over to open the door for us.

"Must be the nephew," Nina murmured before he arrived, and I nodded curtly. This was good, considering how the first witness didn't make out the uncle to be all that lucid, though we would need to talk to him, too, in good time.

The man unlocked the door and ushered us through, locking it straightaway behind us.

"Are you Mr. Samuels?" I asked, holding out my hand to him.

"Just call me Danny," he said, taking it. "Mr. Samuels is my uncle. And you are?"

"I'm Agent Ethan Marston with MBLIS, and this is my colleague Agent Nina Gosse with the FBI," I said, gesturing between myself and Nina. "We're here about the missing boy."

"Well, I figured that much," Danny said, scratching the back of his head as he gazed at me. "I heard there was a fight earlier, and when I came back from lunch, some people in uniforms were washing a bunch of blood off the sidewalk right out there. You guys involved in that? Everybody okay?"

"Yes, my partner was shot, but he's being treated at the hospital now and will be just fine," I assured him. "Thanks for your concern."

"That was his blood, then?" Danny asked, raising his eyebrows as he gestured out the window on the front door leading to the spot where Holm was shot. "Damn, I was hoping it was one of the bad guys."

I hadn't even noticed that the blood had been washed away since I'd been so intent on getting inside the shop. I probably would've noticed it if it was still there, though.

"Well, one of them was shot, too, and it didn't turn

out so well for him," Nina chuckled. "That was down a bit, though." She gestured to the right, where I'd shot the perp named Rudy.

"Ah, I came in the other way," Danny said, glancing in that direction. "Must've missed it. I'm glad he didn't get away, though. Now, what can I do for you?"

"Did you talk to the police when you got back at all?" I asked him, and he shook his head right away.

"No, there weren't any police around when I got here, just those guys in those weird jackets or whatever," he explained.

"The forensics team," Nina interjected, and he nodded.

"Yeah, I think that's what they said they were," he said. "Anyway, they wouldn't tell me what was going on. I just assumed it was something to do with the kid 'cause... well, what else would it be? We hardly even have so much as a traffic violation 'round here."

This didn't surprise me.

"You assumed correctly," I confirmed, nodding to him. "So, would you mind us asking you some questions about one of your shop's boats?"

Danny looked taken aback at this, so much so that he took a literal step away from us.

"You can't... you can't seriously think that we had anything to do with this?" he asked. His expression was one of bewilderment more than anything else.

"No, nothing like that," I quickly assured him. "It's

just that we believe one of your boats has been stolen, is that correct?"

"S-stolen?" Danny stammered. "I don't remember anything ever being stolen. Well, a kid took a candy bar from the cash register once, but his mama made him give it back and apologize to Uncle Dan."

"Well, we talked to a customer of yours earlier, and he told us that you were missing a boat," Nina explained. "That you were talking to your uncle about it while he was in the store?"

"Oh, that must've been Marty," Danny said, relief washing over him as he realized what we were talking about. "He was the only one in this morning. All day, really. Everyone cleared out after that whole shooting thing at the mall. Were you all involved in that, too? I heard a bunch of people got shot."

"Yes, that was his name," Nina confirmed with a low laugh. "And yes, I was the agent on the scene for that incident, but no one was shot. It seems like there's been some exaggeration through the grapevine. You're not the first one to say something like that."

"Oh, yeah, you'll find that's how it works 'round here sometimes," Danny said, to his credit also looking relieved to hear that things weren't as bad as the gossip mill made them out to be at the mall. In my experience, a lot of people loved for there to be *more* crazy things to talk about, not less, though they'd be hard-pressed to admit as much.

"I imagine so," I chuckled. "So what can you tell us about this missing boat Marty was talking about?"

"Now, I don't know about stolen," Danny said, looking skeptical about all this. "My uncle, he's always loaning out boats to old friends, or acquaintances, or anyone who wants one, really, and can't afford it. It's been our one real argument over the years since I started keeping the books. And he's getting up there in age. He probably just lent old Lucy out just like the others and forgot. That's what Marty heard."

"Well, we're looking into it anyway," I said, not wanting to ask any leading questions.

"Now, everyone in town would know that they could just ask Uncle Dan for a boat, and he'd give it to 'em, as long as they could catch him when I wasn't around," Danny continued. "There wouldn't be any point in stealing one. He even let a couple of those college kids take one once, a couple of summers back. We had a real fight about that one, I'll tell you—"

"That's alright, I think you've painted the picture," I said, holding up a hand to stop him. "The thing is, we have it on good authority that one of the men who took Mikey—that's the boy's name—took him out on the water in a stolen boat from your shop yesterday and might be en route to one of the foreign coastal islands with him right now."

Danny's eyes widened again, and for a moment, I worried that he was going to tumble right over. Nina, for her part, reached out to steady him in case he did, but he waved her off and leaned against a nearby table that donned some t-shirts with the shop's name and logo on them.

"S-s-seriously?" he stammered, clutching his free hand to his chest. "Lucy? You think they took Lucy?"

"We're pretty sure," I confirmed with a nod. "We have a witness willing to testify to that effect."

Well, referring to Justin as *willing* seemed a bit of a stretch, but he'd do it anyway when push came to shove.

"Danny, could you maybe take us out to see where Lucy was before she went missing?" I asked him.

"And then it'd be a real help if we could talk to your uncle, too," Nina added. "Just to make sure that he didn't lend the boat out to someone after all. We don't want to go off looking for the wrong boat."

"I... uh, yeah, he's just in the back," Danny murmured, wiping his brow and looking vaguely overwhelmed by all this. "I'll, uh... I'll just go grab him if you don't mind."

"Of course," Nina said, nodding to him deferentially, and we exchanged a look. It was good news if the elder Mr. Samuels was actually here, too. Kill two birds with one stone.

"We'd better find this kid tonight," Nina muttered as Danny disappeared into the back of the shop once more to retrieve his uncle. "Or at least get a lead on what island they could be on."

I checked my watch almost instinctively at this. Soon it would be nearly two days since Mikey was taken. That was not a good timeframe. Not good at all.

Danny returned quickly with a slightly shorter, hunched, and very much older version of himself. In addition to sharing the same name, it looked like the uncle and nephew bore a striking physical resemblance to each other, as well, with the elder Mr. Samuels bearing a receding hairline so far back that his hair was really just a collection of white wisps atop his head. He had a long, thin face much like his nephew's, too, with sharp angles to match.

"Hello, Mr. Samuels?" I asked, holding out my hand to the older man as they approached.

"Huh?" he asked, craning his neck to try to hear me better.

"Hello, Mr. Samuels, my name is Agent Ethan Marston, and I'm with the Military Border Liaison Investigative services, MBLIS for short," I repeated, practically yelling now so that the old man would hear me and explaining the acronym preemptively as I was sure he would think he misheard a word if I just said the acronym alone. "I'm here to ask you some questions about your missing boat, Lucy."

The old man shook my hand loosely, his veins

sticking out in his wrinkled skin. I would have put him in his mid-eighties, at the very least.

"Hi, I'm Agent Nina Gosse with the FBI," Nina added, shaking Mr. Samuels's hand in turn. "I'm with Agent Marston."

"Lucy!" Mr. Samuels exclaimed when he realized what we were asking about before swiveling to his nephew with a decidedly aggravated look on his face. "You went and reported me to the FBI over a missing motorboat, you ungrateful little brat!"

The old man swatted his nephew on the shoulder with his limp hand, though the interaction didn't seem to me to be entirely mean-spirited. I had a feeling that these two just had this kind of teasing rapport, though I thought that Mr. Samuels was probably serious when he assumed we were here just because a boat was missing.

"Oh, no, sir, we're not here about that directly," I said quickly, suppressing a laugh, a feat made even more difficult by Nina's failed attempt to hide a snicker next to me. "We think that someone stole your boat and used it to transport a missing child into international waters."

"Hah!" Mr. Samuels cried, pointing wildly at his nephew. "I told you it wasn't my fault! I told you!"

Danny chuckled and gave me a weak, apologetic smile.

"I'm sorry," he said. "My uncle and I go round and

round on this issue, so I suppose he has to take this as sort of a win for him."

"Don't talk about me like I'm not standing right here, boy!" Mr. Samuels cried, though he was smiling at the younger man. "Anyway, it's me you should be apologizing to, not them."

"Yes, uncle, I suppose you're right," Danny said, rolling his eyes. "I'm sorry for not believing you before."

"Now was that so hard?" Mr. Samuels challenged.

"Yes, yes it was," Danny told him.

I had to suppress another laugh, and Nina passed one of her own off as a cough.

"Do you need some water, my dear?" Mr. Samuels asked her.

"No. No, I'm fine," she said, her voice coming out raspy as she waved him off and covered yet another laugh into her arm. "Thank you, though."

I cleared my throat to wipe away my own laughter and turned back to Mr. Samuels.

"So, Mr. Samuels—" I started, but the old man cut me off.

"Please, son, I don't know why everyone insists on calling me that, you just call me Dan, alright?" he instructed, and Danny let out a guffaw.

"You don't know why?" he repeated incredulously. "You can't be serious, uncle. You've made everyone call you that for as long as I can remember."

"Yes, well, they're with the FBI and that embell-a-what's-it, so they can call me whatever they like," Mr. Samuels snapped back, and Nina and I both had to suppress yet another storm of laughter. We really did meet some characters in this line of work of ours.

"Alright, yes, well, Mr... I mean, Dan, are you absolutely certain that you didn't loan the white motorboat you call Lucy out to anyone else yesterday?" I asked. Then, to the nephew, "It was yesterday you noticed that the boat was missing, is that correct?"

"Yes, it was yesterday around ten in the morning," Danny confirmed with a nod. "She was there the previous evening when I closed up shop."

"And around what time was that?" Nina asked. "When you last saw this boat, I mean?"

"Around six in the evening, that's when we tend to lock things up for the day," Danny said. "And she was there, I know it for sure."

"Alright, Mr... I mean, Dan, so are you sure that you didn't give it to someone?" I asked, narrowing my eyes at the old man to indicate that this was serious. "Your nephew and one of your customers—Marty—said that you do this fairly often. So I'm wondering if there's any chance at all that you loaned Lucy out without remembering, or maybe someone thought you were giving permission, but they misunderstood you? Is anything like that possible at all?"

"No," Mr. Samuels said definitively, shaking his

head with some emphasis. "I don't forget these types of things. You ask anyone, now I know I'm old, and I forget what I had for breakfast sometimes, but I never forget anything about my boats. Never."

Nina and I both turned to look at Danny to confirm this, and he nodded begrudgingly, giving a shrug.

"It's true enough," he said. "Drives me bonkers, I'll tell you that. He won't remember the most basic bookkeeping practices or to *tell* me when he loans out one of the boats, but he never forgets that he actually did it."

"You seemed quick to assume that he'd forgotten before," Nina pointed out, arching an eyebrow at him.

"That's because he *wants* me to be losing my mind, the ungrateful bonehead," Mr. Samuels spat, swatting at his nephew's shoulder again almost good-naturedly despite his words. "That would mean he could stop me from helping people so much."

"Helping people!" Danny cried, throwing his arms up in the air in exasperation. "Uncle Dan, you're going to drive us out of business if you keep just handing boats out to people. And I bet at least two-thirds of them could pay full price if they really wanted to. Maybe not Marty, and he's a good guy, and I don't mind that much, but the rest of them? Come on."

"There's no shame in being neighborly," Mr. Samuels said, gesturing wildly in Danny's direction again. "I thought your parents raised you better than that. I sure taught you better than that!"

"Okay, okay, I think this is kind of getting into the family dispute territory and no offense, but that's not exactly what we're here for," Nina said, holding out a hand each to stop Mr. Samuels and his nephew from continuing with this.

Neither man seemed to be *angry* with the other, exactly. I got the sense that this was just the family dynamic they had going, and they seemed to kind of enjoy it to a degree. Like some families played board games together, this family argued about small stuff like this. Well, it sounded like it might not be too small if the store was actually going to go out of business, but Nina was right that that was none of our concern, really.

"Look, Mr. Samuels... er, Dan, and Danny, if you're both absolutely certain that this boat wasn't lent out to someone you know, then that means that it's likely the boat we're looking for," I continued. "So could we see where it was taken from?"

"Sure, sure, follow me," Danny said, beckoning for us to follow him back out the shop doors.

"I did not lend it out!" Mr. Samuels cried from behind us, and it became clear quickly that he was tagging along. "I would remember something like that. I remember everything about my boats. Everything!"

"I'm sure you're right, sir," Nina said, a little wearily,

as she helped him follow us out toward the bay and all the collected boats where we had talked to Marty earlier that day.

Danny led us to an empty slot amidst all the boats, close to where Marty's boat was.

"Here she is," he said, gesturing at the space right next to the shore. "Or was, I guess."

"I don't see a lot of blank spaces," I said, glancing out across the area. "No other ones, actually. Do you not have a lot of boats out right now?"

"Nope, not a one," Danny confirmed, shaking his head. "All of 'em got returned in the last day or so when people started clearing out of town. Marty's was the last one back today. I hope things pick up again soon. Erm, I mean, I mostly hope you find that poor boy, of course."

"I get what you mean," I chuckled, placing a reassuring hand on his shoulder. "I hope business picks back up for you again soon. And in the meantime, we'll see what we can do about finding Mikey."

"You're sure it was the boat named Lucy?" Nina asked the men. "A lot of these look the same to me. It couldn't have been one of the other ones?"

"Nope, I always make sure the boats go back in the right spaces," Danny said, gazing out across the docked boats almost proudly. "Never switch 'em up, not a single time since I started here."

"He was always anal-retentive, ever since he was a

boy," Mr. Samuels added, and Nina and I both had to suppress another round of laughter.

"Well, without my anal retentiveness, this place wouldn't run," Danny snapped back. "You remember how bad it was before I moved back here. The place was practically in shambles."

"Ah, the good old days," Mr. Samuels lamented, gazing wistfully out across the sea. Nina let out a real chuckle then, but neither of the men seemed to notice or care.

"Alright, so can you describe Lucy for us?" I asked the man.

Both men went on to describe the motorboat in almost excruciating detail, all the way down to little dents, scratches, and general wear and tear from the years it had been in use. It seemed like Danny wasn't the only one who was anal retentive, in a way. I decided it must run in the family.

As they spoke, I pulled out my notebook and began scribbling down all these details to pass on to the Coast Guard later on. Nina just looked mystified by the whole thing, like she wondered how anyone could pay that much attention to the little details on an old motorboat, especially in an area absolutely full of them, almost identical to one another.

"Thank you. This is all really helpful, guys," I said quietly when they were finished, scribbling down the last detail that Mr. Samuels mentioned, a large dent on the back left bumper of the boat from a run-in with a cruise ship during a storm many years ago.

"You really think this could all help find that little boy?" Danny asked hopefully.

"It definitely could," I said, nodding to them as I returned my notebook and pencil to my jacket pocket. "You never know what details will end up being important in these kinds of cases, and we're as certain as we can be that Mikey is out there somewhere on this boat."

"What little boy?" Mr. Samuels croaked, looking between us in confusion. "Who the hell's Mikey, and why's he on my boat?"

"Uncle Dan, don't you remember what we saw on the news at dinner last night?" Danny asked gently. "That little tourist boy who was taken at the mall? That's why we haven't had any customers all day and why those people were cleaning up that blood earlier. One of the kidnappers was shot."

"Oh, right," Mr. Samuels said, though he didn't really seem to remember. "Wait, you're tellin' me that some creepy kidnapper's on my boat?"

"Way to miss the point, Uncle Dan," Danny sighed, looking at Nina and me apologetically again, but we both just laughed.

"It's alright," I chuckled. "We'll do our best to get Lucy back to you, Dan. I know how important the relationship is between a man and his boat."

"I like this one," Mr. Samuels said, pointing at me. "Don't you like this one, Danny?"

"You have a million boats, Uncle Dan. Why is this one so special?" the nephew sighed.

"All of my boats are special!" Mr. Samuels cried. "Why do you think I named 'em after my exes!"

"You barely remember your exes," Danny pointed out.

"Well, I remember my boats," Mr. Samuels shot back stubbornly, and I didn't even try to stop myself from laughing this time.

"Well, thank you again for your time, guys," Nina said, nodding to both men in thanks.

"Hold on. You're saying that some guy is taking this kid to another country or something?" Mr. Samuels asked.

"You remember what you heard pressing your ear against the wall when I was talking to them before I went back to get you, but you don't remember seeing all that blood when we came back from lunch?" Danny asked his uncle with characteristic exasperation.

"I remember anything that has to do with my boats!" Mr. Samuels reiterated before turning his attention back to me. "I'm telling you, Lucy's a good old boat, but she's still old. There's no way that guy's gonna get to the next island over in her in one piece. He'd have to stop in a cave somewhere or travel along the shore if he doesn't want to drown."

"Really?" I asked, raising my eyebrows at this and exchanging an excited look with Nina. "Would he know this just by riding in it for a while?"

"If he knows anything about boats, yeah, which he should," Mr. Samuels said. "Everybody should know about boats if you ask me. And you should ask me."

"I don't disagree," I chuckled.

21

ETHAN

As Nina and I headed back up to the parking lot and her rental car, I checked my watch. It was getting to be around dinner time.

As eventful as the day had been, I was worried that we were running short on time. Mikey could be anywhere on this great big ocean, and while we knew a lot more about what had happened to him after he was taken from the mall, I couldn't help but feel like we still weren't doing enough to figure out where he was now.

"I should call my contact with the Coast Guard," Nina said, pulling out her phone as we stopped in front of her car, and I leaned back against its side.

"Agreed," I said with a nod, pulling out my notebook and handing the description of Lucy over to her. "And ask them... ask them if they'd be willing to pick us up in a little while."

"Pick us up?" she repeated, arching an eyebrow at me.

"I think it's time we go straight out there and look for Mikey ourselves," I explained. To her credit, she didn't miss a beat with this.

"Alright, then," she said, stepping off to the side as her phone rang.

I didn't try to listen in on the conversation. She'd tell me what it was about. I just took a moment to lean back and breathe in the ocean air, enjoying the sun beating down on me for once.

"They'll be here in an hour," Nina's voice said, cutting into my brief reprieve in not too long. "They'll have a boat for us to take out, and they could send one guy with us if we want. Otherwise, they'll let us branch off so we can cover more ground faster."

"Yeah, that'll work," I said, nodding and squinting at her in the sun. "We can grab a bite to eat in the meantime, so we don't have to worry about it later."

The owner of the restaurant we'd been going to didn't look surprised to see us.

"Hey, where is your friend?" he asked when we walked in. "Everything alright, I hope?"

"Yes, he's just... elsewhere," I said, not wanting to say that Holm had gotten shot. The rumor mill in this town was running wild enough as it was.

"We'll take whatever you have on hand," Nina told the man. "We're in a hurry."

"Coming right up!" he cried, disappearing right into the back.

There were only two other occupied tables in the restaurant, at the height of dinnertime.

Before Nina and I could even get settled at our usual table, the man returned with two heaping plates full of seafood pasta to keep us both full, along with some of those biscuits for good measure.

It was delicious, and my pasta was full of garlic and butter, and crab and lobster bits. I hadn't realized how hungry I was after that gunfight until all the food was right in front of me.

"What do we think about this boat?" Nina asked me when we were both about halfway through our plates, working quickly to try to get done before the Coast Guard arrived.

"I'm thinking that either Mikey and this Charlie guy are hiding out somewhere, or they drowned trying to make it to one of the islands on such a small, old boat," I said darkly, wiping some cheese sauce off of my upper lip.

"Do we think that he would know enough about the boat to get it back somewhere in time to avoid drowning?" Nina asked. "The Coast Guard said they originally spotted them in international waters."

"I know," I said, as I had been turning this around in my head ever since our conversation with Mr. Samuels and his nephew. "It wasn't far out, though, and the witness didn't give an exact location since he didn't realize this Charlie guy was a wanted man until he got back to shore. They could've turned back around."

"You didn't answer my question," Nina pointed out. "Do we think this guy would have enough knowledge to do that, even?"

"I don't know," I said honestly, pursing my lips. "We just don't know enough about this guy, just that he works for a human trafficking organization and that he's a little strange. And honestly, even if he had the knowledge, I'm not really sure that he would have the presence of mind to turn around anyway, given the situation."

"I was afraid you were going to say that," Nina sighed, setting down her fork and peering out the window toward the ocean in the distance.

"I mean, he was panicked enough to take this kid in the first place and then steal the boat," I continued. "We don't even know if he knows a thing about boats! Does he know how to refuel? Does he even have enough fuel to make it very far? Would he even know?"

"So basically, for all we know, he could already have killed Mikey, or they could both already have drowned, or they could be hiding out in a cave somewhere biding their time, or they could've come back to shore without us realizing it yet," Nina summarized, her mouth set in a thin line.

"Yeah," I said, letting out a long breath. "Not sounding so great, is it?"

"No," she agreed. "We can only hope it's the cave thing."

"It looks like that's our best option," I agreed. "Did you talk to the Coast Guard about that?"

"Yes," she confirmed with a nod. "When that boat comes into shore for us, they're going to send a guy to debrief us on the area and the caves and other possible hideout places around here that they could be using. Then we'll go from there."

"They already got guys looking through those places?" I asked.

"They're starting now," Nina said. "They looked through some of them already, but their focus since Mikey was taken has been on spotting the boat out at sea, mostly in international waters. That's where we assumed we would find them based on the little information we had at the time."

"These cases can change at the drop of a hat," I sighed, shaking my head. "One comment at the end of our conversation with that old man, and our whole tactic changes."

"That's the thing about these," Nina said, meeting my eyes. "You never know what little detail is going to end up being important. Take that guy's blog, for example. I only talked to him for a minute and put it at the bottom of my pile of things to look into. And he turned out to be the only one who had put two and two together correctly."

Her brow furrowed like she was angry with herself for not seeing this connection any earlier. I reached out and placed my hand over hers across the table.

"Look, it's not your fault," I assured her. "It's not any of our faults. We're doing the best we can, and for all we know, someone else wouldn't have even put that random guy's blog in their to-do pile at all, even at the bottom. Same with talking to that old man. Most people would've just dismissed him as a crackpot, too. We've said it before, and it's true. If anyone's going to find Mikey, it's us."

"And if we don't find him?" she asked, meeting my eyes again, and I could see the worry there—the same worry which had been threatening to overtake me all day.

"Then we'll know we did everything we could," I assured her, applying some gentle pressure to my hand over hers. "Us, and the police here, and the police in Atlanta and San Diego, and the Coast Guard. We're all doing what we can for this kid. This is a really bad situation, though. The odds were never in his favor from the start, knowing what we know now."

This was true enough. If Mikey turned out to still be alive at this hour, it would be no small miracle. It was a needed miracle, though, for the boy and for all three of his parents.

Nina gave me a small smile, then shook her head as if she was coming back to herself and pulled her hand out from under mine gently, giving it a squeeze on her way out.

"You're right, Ethan, of course, but we have to keep hope up," she said, all uncertainty now gone from her face. "If we don't, well, who will? We're more likely to find him if we think he's still alive out there, and as far as I'm concerned, he is."

I nodded and smiled at this.

"Yes, me too," I assured her. "We need to set an example for everyone else. I have a feeling we'll find him tonight when we go out on the water. We have to. The clock is ticking, and he's waiting for us to get there."

"I hope you're right," she said, looking anxiously at the time stamp on her phone.

"Did the Coast Guard say anything else?" I asked. "About another sighting, or about the boat's description, or anything?"

Of course, I knew that if anything this major had come up, she would've told me already. But still, I had to ask. It was part of keeping that hope alive, in some small way.

"Only that they were grateful for such a detailed description," she said, shaking her head. "They were only looking for a generic white boat before, and now they have a better idea of what they're dealing with."

"I guess all that time spent looking on other islands, and with Diane contacting foreign countries to tell them to be on the lookout of this guy wasn't good for much in the end," I reasoned. "In all likelihood, they're back in American waters, or... well, we don't need to talk about the worst-case scenarios again."

"The Coast Guard did say that if we don't find them in the next day or so, they're going to start looking for shipwrecks on the ocean floor," Nina added. "I know we're trying to stay positive, but that's an important thing to mention for our timeline."

I pursed my lips at this new information. I didn't like it. I didn't like it at all, really. If the Coast Guard started doing that, it was a signal that they assumed Mikey was dead. The other agencies would follow suit, then.

Sure, Holm and I would be allowed to stick around for a few more days just in case before heading back to Miami to pick things back up on the Holland case, but that would just be a formality, so it didn't look like we were giving up. Nina and Dr. Osborne would probably stick around for a little longer, a couple of weeks maybe, but most of their focus would be turned to taking down the whole criminal trafficking organization in Durham, not on finding Mikey anymore.

The police would keep the case open, and they'd keep looking for a while. Maybe locals would start organizing their own search parties, and the media would stay on the story for another month at least. But eventually, everyone but the parents would move on, leaving them with no choice but to hire those private investigators and make the rounds on any news station that would still take them, begging for someone to keep looking for their son.

No, we needed to find Mikey, so that didn't happen. Too many broken families had to suffer that fate of uncertainty. If we didn't find him alive, we had to at least find a body to give his family some closure. They deserved that much, at least, and so did he.

One way or another, we would have to bring this boy home. There simply wasn't any alternative. Not one that I could live with, anyway.

22

ETHAN

We finished eating earlier than we expected, our appetites killed by the talk of what may have happened to Mikey already, and even further dampened by unspoken thoughts of what he might be going through now. Wherever the boy was, he was no doubt terrified and wishing he was anywhere else in the world.

"Looks like the ship's going to be an hour late," Nina sighed when she checked her phone as we walked out of the restaurant. "They want to look at some caves on the way in, check and see if they might be there."

"That's good, that's good," I said, covering up my mutual disappointment that our trek out to look for Mikey ourselves would be delayed. "Whether we're there or not, the point is that we find them."

"True, but I'm itching to get out there," Nina said,

flashing me a grin. "I've only been out on the water on a case once, and that was in New Orleans with you. Good times."

"If you're talking about when we all almost got killed by nearly a dozen goons who ambushed us in the dark, uh, yeah, good times," I chuckled, though I did look back on that case fondly since it was the first time I'd met Nina. The case was now colored in my mind by the knowledge that the Hollands were orchestrating things behind the scenes, unbeknownst to us at the time.

"So what do we do now?" Nina asked, throwing her hands up in the air weakly. "We've turned this whole town up and down, and there are still police and detectives out looking. Neighboring towns, too. I don't want to just sit around until the Coast Guard shows up."

"Agreed," I said, just as my phone buzzed in my pocket. Pulling it out to squint at the tiny screen in the waning daylight, "It's Holm. He wants an update."

"We could go see him," Nina suggested. "Can't hurt to throw around a few ideas, see what he thinks."

"And we'll be able to tell the parents that there are still three agents working on the case," I added. "Not a bad idea. The hospital's not far from here, I remember. I'll tell him we're on our way."

The first thing I noticed when we got to the hospital was just how small it was. There were barely any cars in the parking lot of the one-story, boxy white building, and the ones that were all seemed to be in staff parking lots.

When we walked through the front door, the woman sitting behind the front desk seemed to know who we were immediately, even though I'd never seen her before in my life.

"You must be the other agents," she said quickly, practically jumping out of her chair to greet us. "Are you here to see Agent Holm?"

"Sure are," Nina said. "Can you give us his room number?"

The woman directed us down a nearby hallway to the third door on the right, where the door was standing open to reveal Holm lying in bed, his arm all bandaged up where he had gotten shot, and some nasty bags under his eyes. Even so, he grinned with his whole face the second he saw us.

"I was beginning to worry that you guys forgot all about me," he scolded in a tone of mock disappointment. "Like I get one bullet lodged in me, and I'm not even important anymore."

"Did they get it out, then?" I asked, narrowing my eyes at the covered wound.

"Yeah, didn't take much," he said, shrugging it off. "Doc says the real problem was all that blood I lost lying there. They fixed that up too, though."

He gestured up to an empty bag hanging above his

IV, traces of red remaining in the clear packet from his last blood transfusion.

"How many of those did you have to have?" Nina asked, furrowing her brow at it.

"Just two," he said dismissively, and Nina and I exchanged a look. Two was one more than he probably should've had to have, which meant that his condition was likely more serious than he'd led us to believe. He looked better now, though.

"Well, we're just glad you're going to be okay," I said, reaching out and squeezing his good shoulder gently.

"The real question is what's been going on with you," Holm said quickly. "You haven't texted in a while, 'till you said you were coming here."

Nina and I quickly caught Holm up on everything we'd learned from both the elder and younger Daniel Samuels and the Coast Guard.

"Whoa," he sighed when we finished, giving a low whistle. "That's a lot for a couple of hours. So now we don't even think this guy could've fled to an island somewhere?"

"Not unless he picked up another boat along the way," I said with a nod.

"So either he doubled back when he realized he couldn't make it and found his way to shore undetected, or he's hiding in one of these caves somewhere along the coast, or..." Holm surmised, his voice trailing off before he got to the worst-case scenario.

"Yes," I said curtly. "Those are the three options as we see them. Unless, as I said, he somehow got ahold of another boat."

"That would mean that he would have to get back to shore, and then find another boat somehow, then head right back out on the water without anybody seeing him," Holm said, shaking his head. "Seems like a lot of work for a guy in a state of panic and who doesn't seem to be in the right headspace to make a lot of sound decisions. Do they even have any food or anything? When's the last time he ate or drank?"

"Well, most of those boats come stashed with some food and water in case of emergencies," I pointed out. "And the younger Daniel Samuels doesn't seem like the type to forget to restock."

"So it seems like they have to still be out there somewhere, hiding out and biding their time until this Charlie fellow can figure out what to do next," Holm said, setting his jaw hard as he made this decision. "That has to be it. The other scenario is just too unlikely, or..."

We all knew what he was going to say but didn't. That the most likely scenario was probably that Mikey was dead, and Charlie was probably dead, too. But we weren't there yet. As Nina said, it was important to keep faith at this hour, believe that the search could still yield something. We all knew that, too, including Holm.

"Yes, that's what we're thinking, too," I agreed, nodding to him as I leaned back against the nearby windowsill. Nina had taken a seat in the lone chair by the door.

"We're going out on the water as soon as a Coast Guard ship comes back into the bay," Nina explained. "We're just biding our time until then. They're a little late because they have a set of caves they want to check out on their way in."

Holm's eyes widened at this, and I groaned internally. There was a reason I hadn't brought this up myself. I knew my partner far too well at that point in our careers. Come hell or high water, he was going to want to come with us.

"You're going out to look on the water!" he cried, predictably and true to form. "Hold on, let me just get this crap off me, and I'll come with you. Why didn't you say anything sooner?"

My partner moved to begin taking off his IV and other monitors, but I noticed how he winced as he sat up in the bed. There was no way this was happening. Clearly, the doctors thought he needed to be watched overnight in case he needed a third blood transfusion or had some kind of reaction to the first two. I'd been in this business long enough to know when doctors were just being overcautious or not, too, and Holm looked fragile enough compared to his normal state to convince me that he needed to be right where he was for the time being.

"Whoa, there, hold on," I said, reaching out and gently pressing on Holm's sternum to push him back into bed. "You're not going anywhere until a doctor clears you to, understand?"

"Oh, come on, Marston, I've seen you walk out of situations like these all kinds of times!" he exclaimed, though he didn't push against my effort to return him to his original position, possibly because he was too weak to do so. "You were running around down in Haiti after a bullet went into your arm with nothing but a field medic's bandage to cover it up! And you had a concussion on top of that!"

This was all true enough, though I hadn't technically seen a doctor who could've told me not to do any of this. I also didn't sustain the concussion until Holm and I were already in the middle of tracking down our adversaries far away from where I could've gotten any medical assistance.

"That bullet barely grazed my skin," I corrected him. "And the concussion came later, though not much later, I'll give you that. And this is an entirely different situation. I know for a fact that if I looked anything like you do now that day, you would've sent me straight back to the Dominican Republic in a second flat."

Holm bit his lip and narrowed his eyes as he

considered this, trying to find a way to argue. But he came up short and settled deeper into his bed.

"Alright, alright," he sighed, closing his eyes tightly. "But if you break this case without me, I'm never letting you live it down."

"Noted," I chuckled, knowing that if Holm gave up the good fight this fast, he really wasn't feeling all that well. "You can yell at me as much as you want when you get better, but for now, I just want you to rest up and make sure you can crack the *next* case with me."

"If you think I'm letting you get anywhere near the Hollands without me, you've got another think coming, buddy," he said, reopening one of his eyes to peer at me with some disdain.

I glanced over at Nina despite myself, who was staring down at the floor and suddenly seemed very interested in her shoelaces.

We hadn't talked much about the Holland case and Lafitte's ship, given how much we'd been focused on Mikey the past two days, and rightly so. But I was still itching to figure out what Nina was working on for the FBI before she was put on this case, and perhaps more importantly, why she was so cagey about the whole thing. And I knew that as much as I was dying to find out, Holm was even more so.

"Come on, Gosse, you ever gonna tell us what you know?" Holm asked, peering with that one eye over at Nina now. "You can't hold out on us forever."

I didn't mention that, technically, I was sure that Nina could hold out on us for however long she liked, especially if she had the full force of the FBI behind her. I did get the sense by her aversive body language whenever we discussed this, however, that she wished she could tell us what we wanted to know.

Nina just pursed her lips and peered back at him as if he hadn't asked her a question at all. He just sighed and shrugged.

"In all seriousness, though," he continued, reopening both of his eyes now. "You guys had better go out and find this kid tonight, with or without me. Don't worry anymore about the Hollands or me or anything else. All that matters is that boy. He's waiting for you."

23

ETHAN

We assured Holm that we would do everything we could to find the boy tonight, but his words brought that sinking feeling back to my stomach in full force. It'd been abating some now that we had some actual solid information about the case, but dread was starting to fill me all over again, though it was of a slightly different kind this time.

Before, I'd been most worried about all the endless possibilities of what might be happening to Mikey, who could've taken him, where he could be now. Now, it was the lack of possibilities that created that pit in my stomach. Our options were dwindling, as were Mikey's right along with them. Either they were hiding out there somewhere, or they were dead at the bottom of the ocean floor. Those were the only truly plausible options at this stage in our investigation.

From the hospital, Nina and I drove back to the bay area, parking in a lot about a half-mile down from the boat rental shop. I wondered if Mr. Samuels and his nephew were still there. I doubted it.

It was dark out now, as the sun had set while we were talking to Holm. This was just yet another reminder of how fast time was passing and how little we had left before people started to give up on that little boy. I resolved not to be one of them.

Together, Nina and I walked down to the bay where a Coast Guard boat was coming into shore. Two men greeted us there in their uniforms.

"Are you Agent Gosse?" one of them asked Nina, and she nodded, holding out her hand to them each in turn.

"Nina Gosse," she said. "And this is my colleague, Ethan Marston with MBLIS."

I nodded to them and then shook their hands.

"Good to meet you, Agent Marston. We're glad you're here," the second man said as I greeted him.

"You going to let us come out on your boat with you?" I asked, squinting at it in the dark. It wasn't large, but it would do. Four would be a crowd aboard, though, so we might have to take them up on their offer to take it ourselves and let them wait for another one to arrive. We'd cover more ground that way, too.

"You can do whatever you want, Agent Marston,"

the first man told me. "You're in charge here, as far as we're concerned."

"I appreciate that," I said, giving them each a grim smile. "Now, what are your names?"

"I'm Luke Prior, and this is Matt Andrews," the first man said. Prior was blond, and Andrews had brown hair. Other than that, they could be brothers, with the same sleek, muscular swimmer's build and broad shoulders. They looked to be in their late twenties or early thirties, the both of them.

"Hi, Luke, Matt," Nina said. "Good to meet you. Find anything in those caves along the shore?"

Prior and Andrews exchanged a look.

"Well, actually," Andrews said. "We did find something that we thought you might be interested in. Not the kid, obviously, but there were some food and wrappers and stuff."

"Food and wrappers?" I asked, shaking my head in confusion. "You mean someone was there? I imagine a lot of people visit these caves. We ran into some college kids earlier who said as much."

"Yeah, but the thing is, Luke recognized some wrappers," Andrews said, pointing to his companion and waiting for him to finish the story.

"Yeah, so basically, I've lived in this town for a while now, and old Mr. Samuels has let me take one of his boats out now and then for a solo fishing trip on my days off," Prior explained. "And this one time, one of the first times I did that, I got a little lost and didn't have any food. So I had to dig into the emergency supplies on the boat."

"You think the food was from one of Mr. Samuels's boats?" I asked, jumping on this new piece of information. "What makes you think so? Is the food different from what you could buy in any supermarket around here somehow?"

"Yeah, well, Danny, Mr. Samuels's nephew, he's really on top of this sort of thing," Prior said. "So he orders this stuff in bulk on the Internet, and it all comes in these little white packages without anything but the name of the food and basic ingredients in boldface black type. Not like anything you'd pick up at a supermarket. And that's what we found in the cave."

I exchanged a look with Nina.

"But you didn't find this Charlie guy or Mikey?" Nina asked them, and they both shook their heads.

"We scoured every corner of those caves, I swear," Andrews assured us. "And we sent another team in after us just to get another set of eyes on it. But there wasn't anything else there."

"Did you take the wrappers from the cave? Do you have them?" I asked, and they both shook their heads for a second time.

"We didn't want to mess with the scene," Prior explained almost apologetically. "We're not trained in doing that kind of stuff, like preserving it right or whatever. We didn't want to make things harder on you guys."

"But we left the second team there at the scene," Andrews added quickly before I had a chance to say anything else. "We didn't want someone else to come along and tamper with it accidentally, either, so we left them there until you can get a forensics team out to look at it or whatever. We also wanted someone there in case they came back. The guy and the kid, I mean."

"Do you have any idea how long that stuff might've been sitting there?" Nina asked, her brow furrowed in deep thought. "Was there any food left over? How old was it?"

"No, nothing left over," Prior said, shaking his head.

"I suppose if they're on the run, they're not going to want to waste any food," I added. "They wouldn't open anything they weren't going to eat entirely."

"That's assuming this guy's thinking straight, which he doesn't seem to have been this whole time," Nina pointed out.

"Fair enough," I relented, though I certainly hoped that Charlie was thinking straighter now than he was before. Otherwise, what did that mean for Mikey?

"As for how old it was, I'm sorry, but I couldn't tell you," Andrews said apologetically. "Maybe the forensics guys will be more help, but it was all dry food and water, and all that was left were a couple of crumbs. The wrappers were kind of wet from the ocean spray coming into the cave, but that could mean anything. Minutes or hours, who knows?"

"We understand. Thank you for telling us all this," I said, giving them each a strained but grateful smile. "And you did well calling in another team and leaving someone there to look after the scene and not messing with it yourselves. We're going to have to call that forensics team in to excavate it right away."

I looked to Nina at this, and she nodded and pulled out her phone.

"I'll just be a minute," she told us. "I'll go call the station and get someone down here." And with that, she walked several paces away so that we could continue talking without obstructing her call.

"How about you tell me where you've already covered and where you think we should look next?" I asked Prior and Andrews when she was out of earshot. "Are you two done for the night?"

"Oh, no, sir, none of us are stopping until this boy is found," Prior assured me, his tone and expression very serious. "We were going to wait here for the forensics team and lead them out to the caves. Another boat is coming in soon."

"Alright, that's good, that's good," I said, nodding slowly. "Thank you guys for dedicating yourselves to this. How long have you been going?"

"In the search?" Andrews asked, and I nodded again. "Since late last night, around midnight, I'd say.

But we took a couple of hours off this afternoon, and we're good to go through the night again."

"Lots of energy drinks, too," Prior added for good measure, and we all chuckled.

"Well, we appreciate it," I told them. "We know that everyone's running on fumes here, ourselves included, but time is of the essence in cases like this one."

They both nodded gravely, and all humor was wiped off their faces.

"As for your question, there are a few possibilities we think are pretty good," Andrews said, pulling a folded map of the ocean out of his pocket. I looked over his shoulder at it to see that there were bright red markings along the coast in several places. A couple were crossed out.

"These are the caves that we were going to search through," Prior explained, pointing at the red parts. "The crossed-out ones are the one's we've already searched. See this star? Those are the ones where we found the wrappers."

I followed his hand and saw that one of the markings I'd taken for a poorly-written "x" was actually a star.

"Now these are the caves nearest to there," Andrews said, pointing to a few red spots to the right of the starred area. "The ones on the other side have already been searched. If they're still in the area, I'd bet anything that they're in one of these caves."

I squinted closer at the map. It looked like there were four or five possibilities along the ocean.

"We've got three teams, including yours looking for them," Prior explained, following my gaze. "But we're both here, and the third is waiting for the forensics team. We tried to call another boat in, but they're too far out. We've also got some ships looking for them further out in the ocean. We can call them back in if you'd like."

"No, we should be able to cover this ourselves once we get a forensics team out there," I said, shaking my head. "And we don't want to put all our eggs in one basket. That could've been someone else's rescue supplies, or they could've gone back out into the open water. We just don't know for sure."

"Understood," Andrews said, standing very straight. "That's what we thought, sir."

"You've done well," I assured them both again. "If Mikey's to be found, we'll find him tonight. Let's make sure of that. We all know how short on time we're running, here."

"Is it true?" Prior asked, leaning in close to me like he was afraid that someone else might hear. "Are we going to start looking for a body if we don't find him tonight? That's what people are whispering."

"Let's not go there yet," I said, offering just the sort of non-answer that confirmed the men's suspicions.

"It's important to stay positive, for Mikey's sake and for our own."

Both men nodded and hung their heads, showing that they knew exactly what I wasn't saying. That if Mikey wasn't found soon, he was probably dead, and even if he wasn't, everyone would start assuming that he was.

It had to be tonight. It had to be.

Nina walked back over to us then, her face cloaked with worry.

"What's going on?" I asked, taking a step toward her and furrowing up my own brow. "What's wrong?"

"I... I don't know," she said, shaking her head in confusion and staring down at her phone. "I can't get ahold of anyone."

"No one?" I asked, raising my eyebrows.

"No one," she confirmed. "Not a soul is answering at the station."

24

NINA

Nina and Marston left the two Coast Guard men at the dock to watch the boat as they rushed back to the police station to see what was going on. There was never any question that that was what they had to do. It didn't make sense that no one was answering. Chief Raskin, one of the detectives or officers, Dr. Osborne—one of them should be answering their phones. But not a single one did.

Marston drove the rental car while Nina continued to call, hoping that she'd just had a bad signal by the water and that someone would answer her soon. But she knew that wasn't it. The call would've dropped if she'd had a bad signal instead of going to voicemail every single time.

"Anything?" Marston asked her, glancing over as he

rounded a corner to plow through the now deserted downtown area toward the station.

"No," she said, shaking her head and pursing her lips. "Something must've happened."

"We don't know that for sure," Marston said, glancing at the time on the car's dashboard. "It's getting late. They could've been transitioning in another team like they did last night. It's around the same time."

"What about Osborne?" Nina asked. "She would've answered."

"She could have her phone off while she's talking to the parents," Marston mused, though his tone was slightly panicked like he was trying to rationalize away the silence. "There's no rule that says they all have to stay in the station, either. It would do them all some good to get some fresh air, maybe check into a hotel and sleep in a real bed for a change."

Nina supposed that this was all possible. But Osborne always answered her phone. So did the lead detective on the case. This was all too important to go silent over nothing.

When they arrived at the station, there were no other cars in the parking lot.

Nina and Marston looked at each other.

"I... I don't know how to explain this one away," Marston said as he parked, aghast at the sight of the empty lot. "At least we know they probably aren't inside, I guess?"

Nina couldn't make sense of it. Why would the station be abandoned at any time, let alone in the middle of a major case like this? Something must've happened. Something she and Marston didn't know about yet.

She tried Osborne yet again before they went inside, but the psychologist didn't pick up.

At the front doors, the two of them peered inside, trying to see. The front room's lights were still on, but no one was there. Nina couldn't detect any movement inside.

Marston opened the door. It was unlocked. Nina stared at it, and he followed her gaze.

"Something happened," he said, shaking his head. "Something to make them clear out of here fast."

Just like that, both of their weapons were drawn. The whole thing was eerie, and a chill ran up and down Nina's spine.

They scoped out the whole front room, then Raskin's office. No one was there, but there were files and donuts and whiteboards and cups of coffee abandoned as if right in the middle of everything.

"It's like they just picked up and left in the middle of whatever they were doing," Marston remarked in a low whisper as the two of them crept as silently as they could manage around the front room, not wanting to alert anyone who may be lurking where they shouldn't be to the agents' presence. The MBLIS agent examined a half-eaten donut, jelly squirting out onto the napkin on which it rested.

"I know," Nina whispered as she considered the whiteboard in the center of the room. It looked like someone had stopped writing mid-word and dropped the marker onto the ground. She picked it up and placed it on the ledger.

There was a half-drunk cup of coffee on Raskin's desk and a file open to a page in the middle. He was just gone. Everyone was.

"What about Dr. Osborne and the parents?" Marston asked as they surveyed the front room, their guns still held ready at their sides.

"I guess we can check, but I doubt they're here if everybody else is gone," Nina whispered with a shrug, and she covered Marston as he began to creep down the long hallway past the interrogation rooms.

The lounge area was predictably empty as well, nothing to indicate that anyone had been there at all except an empty chip bag sitting on the coffee table in front of the couch.

"Where could they be?" Marston asked, shaking his head in wonder as he made sure no one was hiding back by the vending machines off to the side. But there wasn't a soul there. There wasn't a soul in the whole station that they could find.

"What about the perp?" Nina asked, suddenly remembering Justin. "Someone from Durham was interrogating him when we left, so he must still be in the interrogation room unless someone grabbed him before they left."

Marston perked up at this, seemingly having forgotten the gangbanger, as well. But then he narrowed his eyes.

"I don't remember seeing him when we passed through the hallway," he murmured. "All the interrogation rooms have one-way windows, remember? We would've seen him."

Nina deflated at this. It was true. If Justin had still been there, handcuffed to that chair, they would've noticed them, as high on alert as they had been.

"Let's check anyway," she whispered. "It can't hurt. Hell, let's check all the rooms, make sure nobody's hiding in there away from the window."

And so they both trekked back through the hallway, peeking one by one into the interrogation rooms. They each took turns going in to look while the other stood guard at the door in case anyone came up behind them. But they came up empty-handed time and again, one room after another.

When they reached the room where they had interrogated Justin what felt like a lifetime ago, Marston pushed the door open and pressed his back against the wall, inching inside while Nina waited in the doorway facing the hallway, her gun held at the ready in case anyone tried to sneak up on them.

"What do you see?" she hissed back at the MBLIS agent when he didn't say anything.

"Nothing," he breathed. "Well, nothing except a pair of broken handcuffs. He's gone."

Nina froze as that chill in her spine spread throughout her whole body.

"Broken handcuffs?" she repeated, all the worst possibilities running through her head. "What do you mean broken?"

"Come and see for yourself," he suggested. "I'll cover you."

And just like that, they switched places, Marston taking her place at the door as she turned to take in what lay behind her.

There they were. Justin's handcuffs, dangling from the table where he'd been chained for most of the day. Well, not quite. Half of them were dangling from the table. The other half lay on the ground, broken off in the middle, and halfway through the circle where it had lain on his wrist. There was some blood there like he'd been scratched in the process of removing them.

"But... how..." Nina stammered, trying to work through how he could've done that on his own.

"He must've had help," Marston called darkly from the doorway, reading her mind. "Someone was here. Someone came to get him."

"Well, I don't see any bodies," Nina said, turning to stand next to him then. "So no one must've been hurt when it happened. Whoever it was must've scared them enough to clear out of here, though."

She pulled out her phone and stared at it, willing it to explain to her how this happened and why, especially why no one had called to warn them about what had happened, to tell them that the others were alright or that the station had been attacked.

Together, she and Marston surveyed the entire station again, just to be sure that they were alone inside. It didn't take long, given how small it was. Then they locked the doors. There were security tapes, but they didn't have the codes to access them and see what had happened.

Once she was sure that they were alone and speaking in a normal voice wouldn't alert anyone unsavory to their presence, Nina pulled her phone out yet again and called for Osborne. Almost predictably, she heard it ringing from the lounge area down the hall and winced.

"Well, I guess that explains that one, at least," Marston muttered, shaking his head. "She must've left it here when she left. I don't suppose she knows your number by heart?"

"I doubt it," Nina said, pursing her lips. "Nobody memorizes those things anymore."

"Too bad," Marston sighed, his eyes misty as if they were longing for a simpler time.

As if on cue, Nina's phone rang. She glanced at it.

She didn't recognize the number, but it was from a local area code.

"Hello?" she answered.

"Agent Gosse, it's Osborne," the psychologist's voice called from the other line, and Nina breathed a sigh of relief. "I got your number from the director's office. I left my phone at the station. There's been a problem—"

"I know," Nina said, cutting her off. "We're in the station now, and the perp, Justin, is gone. What happened? Where is everyone?"

"You're in the station?" Osborne asked, her voice suddenly panicked. "Are you alone? Are you alright?"

"Yes, we're fine," Nina said, suddenly growing nervous again as she scanned the front room where they were standing. "What do you mean?"

"Well, there were just so many of them!" Osborne cried. "Are any of them still there?"

"Who?" Nina asked quickly, glancing over at Marston as he stepped toward her, his brow furrowed in concern. "What do you mean there were so many of them?"

"The goons, the ones who broke out the other one," Osborne explained. "They acted like they were going to kill him for talking to you, but then they just hauled him away. There weren't many people here when it happened. It's like they chose the moment the detectives and officers were going to change shifts. Raskin was practically on his way out. There were too many of them. There was nothing we could do."

"I... I understand," Nina said, glancing back over at Marston, telling him with her eyes that something was wrong. "How long ago was this? Was anyone hurt? Where are you all now?"

"About forty-five minutes ago. I'm sorry I couldn't reach you 'till now, there was a lot to take care of, and I thought you were going out on the water. We all went to the hotel where we're staying," Osborne explained quickly. "Checked all the parents in. They needed a good night's sleep, anyway. We're trying to run things from here for now, and a SWAT team is coming in soon to take back the station from the city, but if you're already there, and everything's clear..."

"The station's clear," Nina said with certitude. "We surveyed it twice, some parts three or four times. You should send some cars over, and we'll check and make sure everything's clear outside, too."

"Alright, I'll do that," Osborne said, and Nina could hear her barking orders to someone near her. "They'll be there in a few minutes. Stay safe."

And with that, Osborne was gone. Nina turned to Marston and told him everything she'd learned. When she finished, he cast a weary hand over his face.

"Well, that is something, isn't it?" he asked, shaking his head. "They must've really not wanted him to testify, to take a risk like that. Someone had to have watched them, to know when they were switching shifts."

Another chill ran up and down Nina's spine at this. She didn't like that. She didn't like that at all.

"Well, we should go check outside," she said, wanting to do something instead of just standing there. "We don't want anyone to jump the officers when they get here."

25

ETHAN

Together, Nina and I headed outside to scope out the outside of the station. I doubted anyone was out there. If they were, wouldn't they have attacked us when we first arrived? Even so, someone could be hiding from us instead of looking to kill us, so we checked anyway.

The station was a small boxy building, standing alone in front of the parking lot. There was a laundromat across the street, in a building next to a gas station and a pharmacy. It was late, though, and none of those businesses appeared to be open.

Together, the two of us crept around the brick building, looking every which way for any would-be attackers.

We were toward the back of the building when I saw it. The edge of a boot, sticking out around the nearest corner. I elbowed Nina and jerked my chin in that direction.

Her eyes grew wide as she saw it, and she pressed a finger to her lips. I nodded and crept out further in front of her, my gun at the ready. Nina followed close behind me.

We were able to see well enough then to know that the boot was connected to a foot, which was connected to a leg. We didn't dare look any further than that since he would likely see us then.

"Hands up, or I'll shoot!" I cried, and the leg shot out around the corner in surprise, as if the man attached to it had nearly jumped out of his skin.

"FBI, come out here with your hands up and weapons on the ground where we can see them, now!" Nina hollered, stepping out next to me with her own weapon held high in front of her.

The leg disappeared behind the wall, then, but I didn't hear any footsteps. He was still cowering back there.

"If you cooperate, whoever you are, nothing will happen to you," I assured him, in a bit gentler of a tone now. "If you don't cooperate, there will be problems."

A shot rang out, catching me off guard. I instinctively dropped to the ground, pulling Nina along with me. We crouched there, our weapons out in front of us, as we tried to catch our bearings.

It took me a split second to realize that it had been

a warning shot. The man had shot into the air to distract us and ran, and after the blaring sound of the gunshot, I was barely able to make out his footsteps as he made his getaway.

Barely.

I jumped to my feet and ran after him as soon as I realized what was happening, and Nina caught on fast, too, only a step behind me as we chased after him.

"Stop!" I cried. "Hold up, or I'll shoot!"

Two times in one day, I'd been faced with this exact scenario, having to shoot a man in the back as he ran away from me, carrying a deadly weapon he'd already proven he had no qualms about using. I didn't like it. I didn't like it one bit.

It was dark, and the man was dressed in dark clothing from head to foot, much like the others from earlier that day and Justin in the security footage from the mall. It must have been some kind of uniform for this gang.

I barely made it out as the man turned around to shoot me. But I made it out in the nick of time.

I shot once, then twice, and the man fell to the ground, his gun stretched out in front of him without having made a shot.

Nina and I stopped briefly, but then she rushed forward, and I followed her. I confiscated the gun quickly as she knelt down to speak to him. He was still alive, though his breath was ragged.

"Are you alright?" she asked him. "Are you alright? What's your name? What were you doing here?"

He didn't answer as I quickly called for an ambulance and then knelt down on his other side.

"Are there any others?" I asked, a little harsher than I intended. "Are you the last one?"

He gave a short shake of his head, though the motion was clearly difficult for him. Blood spilled out of the right side of his chest and onto the sidewalk, though the pace was slow. I didn't think I hit any major arteries.

"No, there aren't any others, or no, you aren't the last one?" I asked him.

"No others," he managed to croak as I heard sirens ring out in the distance. Either the ambulance was already close, or the policemen had heard there was a problem and put on their sirens on the way to the station.

"Why did you break him out?" Nina asked.

"J... just lookout," the man stammered. "Not a part..."

"You were a part of it, and you damned well know it," I snapped, having no patience for these goons leaping to their own defense at this hour in the investigation. "Now stop it with that and just tell us what happened, now!"

The man gulped and nodded, and some more blood spilled out of him and onto the sidewalk.

"Came to get him..." he murmured. "No... testi..."

But he couldn't get the word out, no matter how hard he tried.

"Your bosses didn't want him to testify, okay," I said, nodding along. "We get that. Anything else? Does he know where Mikey is, and he didn't tell us? Where's the boy? Come on."

I motioned for him to continue, but the man's eyes just grew wide as he tried to shake his head again.

"We... nothing to do..." he tried to say, but then he just gave up and kept shaking his head.

"I don't think he knows anything," Nina said, shaking her head and looking up from the man. "I really don't. The gang probably figured out we had this guy when the Durham police got involved, and they came down to bust their guy out and stop him from testifying."

"We can only hope they didn't kill him," I muttered. "He was worried that might happen."

"I need to call my supervisor," Nina said, standing up, wiping some blood off her arms on her jeans, and pulling out her phone. "He's going to need to hear about this. The Durham police will need our help to track this guy down."

"What about Mikey?" I asked, my blood suddenly running cold. Holm was stuck in the hospital already, and now if Nina left me to go look for Justin, what did that mean for the missing boy? Had everybody given up on him already?

"Don't worry," Nina said quickly, seeing my expression and reaching out to place a steadying hand on my arm. "I'm still all yours tonight. We need to go back and help the Coast Guard look through those caves. But after that…"

Her voice trailed off, but she didn't have to finish. I just nodded.

"I understand," I told her. "You have those other kids to think about. And the kids who might be taken next if you don't stop these guys. They're just as important."

I hated how fast Mikey's clock was running out. There just wasn't enough manpower to keep up this investigation for much longer without sacrificing other dimensions of the case. This whole thing was suddenly way bigger than just one little boy who was taken from his family.

Finding Justin was so important because, without him, the whole case against this gang fell apart. He had all the details about where and when all this stuff was happening and who was involved. Sure, he'd told the Durham police some of that already. But without his testimony in court, would any of it matter in the end? Without that, how many kids other than Mikey would be hurt?

But I was still going to find that one little boy. I was

still in his corner, and he was still my priority. And for tonight, at least, the same was true of Nina.

The sirens were growing closer now, and shortly, three police cars full of officers and detectives, and one ambulance arrived in the parking lot. Nina went around to greet them while I stayed with the perp.

I glanced down at him. He was unconscious now. I almost felt sorry for him—almost. The other guys had all abandoned him to take Justin wherever they were going and left him behind to update them on what was going on here. They probably wanted him to scope out the place for a while and tell them what we were doing, and who was there, and when. It hadn't gone well for him.

Soon, two paramedics came to retrieve the man, and I went out to rejoin Nina and the detectives. When I got there, she was just finishing up explaining to them everything that had happened, including our plan to go out on the water that night and look for Mikey with the Coast Guard.

"Marston, this is Detective Lance with the Durham police," Nina explained, introducing the man she was speaking with. "This is Agent Ethan Marston with MBLIS, the man I was telling you about."

There were several other uniformed officers behind the man. I recognized some of them from the delegation of Durham police that had arrived that afternoon to speak with Justin about the gang.

"We hear you're going back out to look for the missing boy," Lance said, and I could tell that he didn't seem exactly happy about this. "You understand it's been nearly two days since he was taken."

"Yes, but remember what I told you," Nina said, jumping in quickly before I had a chance to respond. "The wrappers were found in that cave from the stolen boat."

"Those could be from anyone," the stern-looking man said, cocking an eyebrow at her. "And our star witness was just abducted from under our noses. Surely our manpower is better spent…"

"Finding a gangbanger instead of a little boy?" I challenged, taking a step closer to him.

"That not what I…" he started to say, his voice trailing off as he tried to find the right words.

"Then what do you mean?" I asked, though he predictably offered no response. "Look, I get that it's important for you to find Justin and to try this case in court. Those other kids are depending on you to find them, too. But this one depends on me, and I'm not giving up on him. Not yet. We can reevaluate if we still haven't found him tomorrow."

I knew that I really didn't want to reevaluate if it came to it. But what other choice did we have? The Coast Guard was going to start looking for a body tomorrow, anyway.

I did know one thing. Holm and I were going to be

here for a while if we didn't find Mikey soon. The problem was that we were the only ones solely devoted to finding him. Everyone else had other priorities when it came to this case, even Nina now.

"I understand," Lance said, though he clearly still wasn't happy about it.

I knew he had no beef with me still looking for Mikey. That was why I was here, after all. MBLIS was on this case because Charlie took the boy into international waters. But Nina? He clearly wanted her working with him on taking down the whole gang, and I couldn't say I blamed him.

"Well, do you have everything under control here, then?" Nina asked him, signifying that she was with me for now, and that was final.

He nodded.

"Alright, then," I said, turning to her. "Let's go find Mikey."

26

ETHAN

Together, Nina and I drove back out to the water, where we met Prior and Andrews back by their docked boat, along with several other men in similar uniforms who I didn't recognize. There was also a forensics team and a second, larger boat next to the first one.

"Those must be the guys they were waiting for earlier, so they could take the forensics team back out to those caves," Nina said as we parked and began to walk down to them.

"Got here pretty quick," I said, nodding.

"Well, I told Osborne about the wrappers and everything, and she got a team down here pretty quickly," Nina explained. "She wants to find Mikey as much as we do."

"I imagine after spending so much time with the parents, probably even more," I remarked. Osborne struck me as a stern enough woman, but she seemed to have a good heart.

"Yeah, I know she's a bit icy, but she got in this line of work for a reason," Nina said. "She really does care."

Prior and Andrews waved to us as we approached, looking more than excited to see us.

"Good, you're back," Prior said when we joined the group. "We heard one of the perps broke out at the police station?"

"More like he was broken out," I said darkly, noting that though the young Coast Guard men looked concerned, they also appeared a little excited by the whole thing. This was probably the most action they'd seen in their careers, at least while stationed in this sleepy little corner of the country.

The men's eyes widened at this.

"That's enough about that for now, though," Nina said quickly before they could ask any more questions. "We're running short on time, and we need to find Mikey. Do you have any more news for us?"

"Well, we were just about to take this team out to that cave and see if they can get any DNA or whatever off of those wrappers and stuff," Andrews explained, gesturing to the forensics team.

"You have the details for our lab techs at MBLIS?" I asked them. "They'll want to see this data."

Yeah, Bonnie and Clyde, as we called our lab techs, would want to be all over this. With things being so slow with the Holland case lately, I knew they were itching for something more concrete to do.

"Agent Marston, I assure you that we're more than capable—" the nearest forensics tech, a man who looked to be in his mid-forties, began to say, but I held up my hand to stop him.

"I'm sure that you are," I said, forcing a smile. "We just like to be thorough, is all. You'll understand."

Bonnie and Clyde were the best in the business. No matter how capable these guys were, or any forensics team for that matter, the two of them had a knack for pulling things out of data that no one else had a chance of finding.

"Of course," the man said, nodding to me, though he didn't exactly look ecstatic about the whole thing.

"Alright, so where do you want us?" Nina asked Prior and Andrews, who exchanged a look.

"Well, while you were gone, we sent another team out to some of the caves on that map," Andrews said, pulling it back out and illustrating for us. Sure enough, more of the red circles were crossed out now, indicating that they were already searched and deemed dead ends.

I felt my stomach sink as I saw that they were the caves closest to the ones where the wrappers had been found. The ones where we had most hoped we could find Charlie and Mikey. Of course, they still could've been there, without leaving a sign, if they already moved on down the shore by the time the Coast Guard arrived.

"Alright, then," I said, gritting my teeth together and attempting to swallow my discomfort. "What's next, then?"

"Well, there are two larger sets of caves left," Prior explained. "We've already got our guys heading to the ones farthest away from here since it'll take you longer to get out there. If you two can go to the remaining set, we should be able to finish them all tonight while still letting us take these guys out to the first scene."

"Got it," I said, nodding and exchanging a look with Nina. Somehow, it was all feeling even more real with our only two remaining options staring us right in the face.

"Are there any more?" Nina asked hopefully, though I was sure she knew as well as I did that if there were, the Coast Guard men would've told us by then. "Any other options after these caves?"

Prior and Andrews looked at each other again, and then to an older man in a Coast Guard uniform standing to their left.

"I'm afraid after this, our main option is to start looking on the ocean floor," the man said, his mouth set in a grim, firm line.

I nodded, that pit in my stomach making a raging comeback for the third time that day.

"We understand," I assured them. "And we really appreciate all of your help on this case."

"Hey, we couldn't have done any of this without you," the older man said, reaching out and shaking my hand. "We're always glad to lend a hand to MBLIS."

Nina and I took Prior and Andrews's boat then, waving farewell to the others as they sped off across the water in the opposite direction, toward the first set of caves where all those wrappers had been found.

It was a calm night, and we could see the stars as clear as day in the sky above us, next to a sliver of a moon.

Nina interlinked her arm with mine as the boat whirred along.

"Whatever happens, I'm glad we got to meet up again," she told me, and I smiled down at her.

"Me too," I murmured, pressing my lips to her temple. "Even if you are still holding out on me about Lafitte's ship."

She chuckled into my shoulder as if she knew that I couldn't let that opportunity pass me by.

"Don't worry, Marston," she said, pulling away from me just a bit. "All in good time."

I wanted to press her further but thought better of it, just enjoying the calm of the water after a hectic two days in which I barely found a moment to rest.

When I'd wished for a case or a bit of action amidst all the paperwork, this wasn't exactly what I'd had in mind. But either way, I was glad to have gotten the opportunity to work with Nina again. I just hoped something would come of it for Mikey's sake.

We chugged on like that for the better part of an hour, and then two, barely talking and just enjoying one another's presence. We didn't discuss the case. There was a lot to talk about, but for some reason, we just let the words rest in the air between us, sitting there as the minutes ticked by, an ever-present reminder of the race against the clock.

I thought back on everything that had happened the past few days, wondering if we could've done anything differently. Did we waste too much time looking into Jackson and the other parents? No, I knew that I would do the same thing all over again with the information we had. It was just the most logical thing to do at the time.

Still, hindsight was twenty-twenty, and I wished that we hadn't spent so much precious time chasing down leads that turned out to go nowhere.

"We'll keep looking, you know," Nina murmured into the night, breaking past my thoughts. "I know what that Durham detective said, and the Coast Guard, too, but if we don't find him tonight, we'll keep looking. You and Holm aren't planning on going anywhere, are you?"

I could hear the grin in her voice as I stared down at the boat's motor, softly whirring in the night.

"No, not for a while, at least, if we don't find him," I promised. "Though at a certain point..."

"I know," she said, finishing my thought for me when I didn't. "At a certain point, your boss will need you back in Miami, and it'll be time to move on. I know."

"You've worked cases like this before," I said, and she nodded. "Does it always feel like this? Like everyone's just going to give up on the kid before it's time?"

"Yeah, it does," she sighed, hanging her head over the edge of the boat and peering down at the water as if she didn't want to look at me anymore. "Every single time. It always feels too early, even when it isn't. You get invested in these kids, you know? Every good agent does. It's impossible not to."

"So you've been on cases where you didn't find the child before?" I asked, and there was a period of silence before I heard her sigh.

"A few," she said. "More times than not, we find them, though."

She didn't offer up more details, but I pressed her anyway. I couldn't help it, as my anxiety was starting to get the better of me.

"Even at this hour?" I asked. There was more silence.

"Not usually," she finally relented.

"How many times has it gone on this long where

you found the kid?" I asked, bracing myself for the answer.

"I..." she started to say, but she didn't finish. Her non-answer was an answer in and of itself, I supposed.

"I see," I muttered, staring down at the motor again.

"That doesn't necessarily mean anything," Nina said quickly. "This is an odd case, so it wouldn't be out of the question to have an odd result, as well."

I knew as well as she did that she was straining here, though. The oddities of this case made it less likely that we would find Mikey, not more. Charlie took him out of desperation, and he could dispose of him out of desperation, as well.

"Anything from the forensics team?" I asked her. We'd been waiting on results for some time now, and since we were traveling farther than them, the hope was that they would have some preliminary results before we even reached our own destination.

More than anything, we were hoping for proof that Mikey had been in that cave. That he had been alive sometime today, and that Charlie hadn't just disposed of him the second they got on the water.

Nina checked her phone. There was nothing there. But as if on cue, my own phone began to buzz. I looked at the caller ID and shook my head in surprise.

"It's Clyde, one of our lab techs," I explained, glancing up at Nina.

She raised her eyebrows.

"Come on, answer it, then," she said eagerly, motioning for me to do so.

"Clyde? Hey, Clyde, this is Marston," I said, putting a finger in my other ear so that I could hear him speaking over the whir of the boat's motor.

"Marston? Marston, good, I'm glad I caught you," Clyde said, his voice coming in a bit muffled from the bad connection out on the water. We were close enough to shore that I still had one, though.

"What is it, Clyde?" I asked hurriedly. "Did the forensics team get you their results?"

"Yep, and Bonnie and I found something they didn't," he said. "Some trace DNA from your kid. They just found saliva from your perp, which was pretty obvious, but I can see how they missed the trace DNA."

"Trace DNA from Mikey," I repeated, glancing up at Nina excitedly. "You found trace DNA from Mikey. Now, what does that mean, Clyde?"

"Well, it could mean a few things," Clyde said, equivocating like a true scientist. "It could mean that he was there, eating the granola bar we found it on. That's the best-case scenario for his sake, obviously."

"Well, yes, but what else could it mean?" I asked, scrunching up my face in confusion. I remembered one of the lab techs maybe explaining trace DNA or something to me before, but I'd forgotten what any of it meant, if I'd ever understood it in the first place.

Nina was standing and practically hopping in front of me now, wanting to hear what was going on for herself. She was waving her hands in between us wildly.

"Hold on, Clyde, before you answer, I'm going to put you on speakerphone so that Agent Gosse can hear you, too, okay?"

"Oh, uh, okay," Clyde said, sounding a bit surprised at this as I removed my phone from my ear and pressed the button so that his voice came out tinny and even more muffled, though both myself and Nina could hear him now. "Hello, Agent Gosse, pleased to meet you... er, hear you, anyway."

"You too," Nina called into the receiver. "What were you saying about trace DNA?"

"Right, well, like I was just telling Marston, the forensics team in North Carolina found your perp's DNA on one of the wrappers—pretty straight forward, saliva. They didn't find the other evidence. When they sent it to us, Bonnie and I found the trace DNA on one of the other wrappers. That belongs to your missing kid."

"So that means he was there, right?" Nina asked excitedly. "He was there in the cave with Charlie. He wasn't dead yet. Do you know how long ago that was? Can you tell?"

"Well, hold on, not so fast," Clyde said, chuckling nervously, the sound crackling over the poor connection. "That's possible, sure, but there are some other possibilities, as well. There's a reason the first forensics team didn't find this evidence. It's slight and might not mean what we want it to."

I could see Nina's face fall in real-time.

"Oh, okay," she said, clearly deflated. "What else could it mean, then?"

"Well, the only thing we know for sure is that Mikey came into contact with that wrapper somehow," Clyde explained. "He touched it, brushed against it, something like that. We don't know when or why. There's no saliva or anything like that."

"So basically, Mikey could've touched the wrapper sometime when they were out on the water, and then Charlie could've taken it into the cave and eaten it later," I surmised, my stomach sinking slightly again at this.

"Yes, that's what I'm saying," Clyde agreed. "But it could also mean that Mikey ate the granola bar in that cave. I mean, you said that the food was all locked away with rescue supplies, right? So why would Mikey come into contact with it if your perp didn't intend to give it to him to eat?"

As Clyde spoke, the line began to crackle more as the reception grew weaker.

"Clyde, is there anything else?" I asked him. "You're starting to break up a bit."

"No, that's pretty much it," he said. "We're still

sorting through the rest of the data, but I wanted to try to catch you before you got to those caves. That's what the forensics team told me you were doing. I hope this helps you some."

"Yes, it does, thank you, Clyde, and thank Bonnie for us, too," I assured him.

"Will do, Marston," he said. "Good luck." And with one more crackle, he clicked away.

Nina and I stood there in silence for a few moments as I maneuvered the boat around a corner, creeping us closer to our destination.

"Well, that's something, at least," she murmured after some time, sinking back into a sitting position along the side of the boat.

It was, at the very least, a glimmer of hope.

"Odds are, that was Mikey's granola bar," I said, nodding slowly as I thought this over. "Clyde hinted as much. He didn't want to say for sure, of course, but I could tell he was leaning that way."

"Yes, I thought that, too," Nina said, the hint of a smile tucked behind the corners of her lips. "Why would he have touched it if he didn't eat it? I just wish we knew when."

"I doubt that it was before they were first spotted on the water," I reasoned. "Prior and Andrews said there are some waves and stuff in the cave where they found the stuff. I bet it would've washed away back then. Also, Charlie seemed to want to get out of there quickly. He was panicking yesterday. He probably wouldn't have thought about eating for hours, at least."

"Yeah, I think you're right," Nina said, some, but not all, of the excitement returning to her sharp, pixie-like features now. "They wouldn't have thought about having to eat for a while, at least. It wouldn't make sense to hide in a cave right away, either, especially since they were seen out on the water later that day. I bet they were there sometime today, which means that he didn't kill Mikey right away. He could still be alive."

"Yes, yes, he could," I said, meeting her eyes and smiling despite myself.

Mikey was still out there somewhere. I had never been more sure of it. We were going to find him tonight. We *had* to find him tonight. He'd fought this long to stay alive. The least that we could do was not give up on him yet.

I glanced up ahead of us and then down again at the map Prior and Andrews had given us. We were coming upon what looked like some caves along the shore ahead on our right.

"I think this is it," I said, glancing back over at Nina to find a familiar glint waiting for me there in her eyes.

"Alright, then," she said. "Let's go in and get him."

27

NINA

Nina's whole body was thrumming with nervous energy as Marston led their boat into the first cave in the set of several. The boat was small, and the hum of the engine low, but it wasn't so small or unobtrusive that they wouldn't be noticed if someone was in the cave.

Nina pulled out her gun the second they turned inside, just in case. She noticed Marston doing the same, though he was mostly occupied with maneuvering the boat around the narrow corners of the cave and the channel leading up to it.

She pulled out a flashlight from a kit Prior had pointed out to her and shined it around the whole area, scanning the small cave with her eyes and ears.

The cave was a mostly open area, with water flowing all around. There didn't look to be any natural resting spots on rocks or anything. It was just like a small lake with no beach around it. If they wanted to hide out in here, it would have to be on their boat, and she didn't see one anywhere.

While the cave was deep, it wasn't all that wide, and Marston took them in further until they could tell for certain that no one was there.

"Onto the next, I guess," he murmured, turning the boat around quickly and heading back outside.

Nina agreed, though she remained on alert the whole time until they got back out into the open water. She didn't want to be caught off guard just in case something was lurking beneath the surface of the water.

Nothing came, however, and the two of them churned on to the next cave, a far narrower one full of twists and turns.

Marston had to work not to crash the boat here, and Nina was sure that if she had been tasked with running it, they would've been dead already.

She craned her neck as he worked to see around each dank corner of the cave, but nothing came of it. It took them some time to reach the back, and still, there was nothing and no one to be found except for some moss and the occasional clump of algae.

When they reached the back of the cave, Marston shook his head and stood up straight.

"Let's wait here for a moment," he said, leaning

back against the side of the boat and pulling out the map again. "It looks like there's one more cave in this configuration."

"Does it say anything about what it's like?" Nina asked, briefly peering over his shoulder at the map as she kept most of her attention trained on anything that might lie in front of them.

"No, nothing," he said, shaking his head and folding it back up as quickly as he'd taken it out. "It's not very detailed. Like I had no idea that this one was going to be so..."

"Hall of mirrors?" Nina finished for him when he couldn't seem to find the right phrase, and they both laughed.

"That's one way to describe it, I guess," he chuckled, glancing around at all the twists and turns in the area. The way the light reflected back up at them in odd angles around the cave made it seem kind of like a hall of mirrors to Nina.

"Well, let's hope the third one's the charm," Nina said, and Marston began to press the boat forward some more.

Nina still stood at the ready in the front of the boat with her gun, though she doubted anyone was in there with them. They'd searched the whole place, and even if they hadn't, she doubted many people other than Marston could maneuver through here without crashing, and this Charlie character surely wasn't one of them.

As they went back through the place, she also looked for any signs that they might've been there before and that someone had tried to get through the winding rocks and failed in the process.

She'd looked on the way in, and she knew Marston had, too, but they were looking at it from a different angle, now.

And that's right when she saw it—the paint, grazing off a nearby rock near the mouth of the cave. So faint that she could tell it had been left not too long ago and nearly washed away by the water flowing in and out of the cave.

"Marston, do you see this?" she hissed, pointing at it roughly.

"Sure do," he said, squinting in that direction in the light from her flashlight. "Looks fresh."

As they passed the area slowly, Marston reached up and grazed his hand lightly across it so that a fleck of the paint came off on his finger. He looked down at it as if studying it carefully.

"It's hard to say for sure, but it is white, and it seems like the same old shade of white as a lot of Mr. Samuels's boats," he said finally, seeing the confusion written across Nina's face.

"Well, there's only one way to find out for sure," Nina said, glancing over her shoulder at the cave's entrance, which was barely in their line of vision. "And that looks pretty fresh to me. I don't know about you, but I'd estimate that if that paint had been there any longer, it would've washed away."

"I agree," Marston said, nodding to her. "Can you take a picture of it?"

But Nina was already pulling out her phone to do so, the flash blaring through the dark cave several times as she looked to get at the image from every possible angle, just in case the forensics team ended up needing any of this.

"Alright, then, let's go," Marston said when she seemed satisfied with her pictures, and she stood watch as he continued maneuvering the little motorboat around the twists and turns of the cave until they reached its mouth.

Nina's stomach was doing backflips. Mikey had to be in this next cave, or at least near it. He had to be. She was sure of it, or at least she wanted to be sure.

They became very quiet as they whirred toward the third and final cave in the sequence. Nina wiped some sweat off of her hands on her jeans so that she could grip her gun more firmly.

Marston maneuvered the boat into the mouth of the final cave. This one was wider than the last, but still quite small. There were fewer twists and turns here, though unlike the first cave, this one wasn't wide open, so Nina couldn't see it all when she shined her flashlight beam across it.

Marston took them back and then to the left around a corner. Still, they couldn't see the back of the cave. Only what felt like a kind of hallway filled with water, leading to another turn up ahead and to the right.

Before Marston turned the second corner, Nina's flashlight beam landed on something floating in the water. She blinked and stopped for a moment before realizing what it was, holding up a hand behind her to make sure that the MBLIS agent didn't take the boat any further than he already had.

She bent down and picked it up. A plain white wrapper with granola bar ingredients listed on it, a few soggy crumbs remaining in the package.

She turned around and held it up for him, quickly flicking off her flashlight beam as she did so.

It took a few moments for her eyes to adjust to the darkness, but when they did, she saw that Marston had realized what she had. This was one of the wrappers from the rescue kit in Mr. Samuels's boat. Charlie and Mikey were there. They might still be there.

Marston quickly silenced the motor so that they could listen. Nina worried that they'd already given themselves away to anyone who may be waiting there in the cave.

It was some time before they heard anything, and

Nina was starting to think that they were alone, and whoever had been there was long gone.

But they weren't. After a few moments, they heard a soft child's voice ringing through the cave, giving it a natural echoing quality.

"Mister, I'm getting thirsty again," the boy said, and Nina and Marston stared at each other.

It was Mikey. Who else could it be? It was a boy's voice. He was alive. Mikey was alive.

"Shut up," a snide man's voice clapped back at the boy. "I thought I told you to go to sleep."

"I want to go home," the boy whined. "When do I get to go home? You said I get to go home."

"I told you, I'm working on that," the man snapped.

"How are you going to get to Atlanta, though? We can't take this boat to Atlanta, can we? You said you would take me back to Atlanta," the boy complained.

"I told you, I'm working on it!" the man cried. Then, muttering as if to himself, "I just need to figure out a way to leave you there without anyone seeing."

"I promise you, I won't tell anybody about you," the boy assured the man. "If you just take me home, I'll tell them I took a bus or something. That's all."

"Oh, shut up," the man said again. "I can't trust you to do that. But I can't afford to not take you home, either. Oh man, I've done it this time. I should've listened to Justin..."

Nina stared at Marston again, unblinking. Charlie

wanted out, she realized. He knew now how reckless his actions had been, and instead of killing Mikey in another impulsive act, he was biding his time, trying to find a way to return the boy to Atlanta without getting arrested.

Well, good luck with that. That's all she could say about that plan, though she was glad he had realized killing Mikey wasn't going to help him any.

His first plan had probably been to take the boat to one of the foreign islands, sell Mikey to another trafficking gang or even a lone-wolf predator there, or barring that, throw him overboard. But then he realized the boat, Lucy, wasn't going to get him there, and he was stuck creeping along the North Carolina shore. If he killed the boy here, there was no doubt that someone would find the body, and Charlie himself would probably be recognized anywhere he went from all the news reports, local and national.

In short, Charlie was screwed, and now he was literally stuck in the corner of this cave without anything to do.

Nina and Marston looked at each other again. Nina motioned toward the sound of the voices with her gun as if asking a question. Marston nodded. By now, they were in sync. He understood her perfectly.

And with that, Nina tossed him her flashlight, and he turned it on along with the boat's motor while she held up her gun with both hands.

"FBI!" she screamed. "We have you cornered. Come out here with your hands up and your weapons down, and hand over the child at once."

There was a moment of silence, a loud plopping sound as if something dropped into the water, and a curse as Charlie realized what was happening to him.

"We know you want out, Charlie, and this is your way out," Marston called out to him. "We know you want to return the boy, so just hand him over and be done with this, okay? This can all be over if you just give him to us."

"Wh-what's going on, Mister?" the boy's voice stammered. "Are they police?"

"That's right, Mikey, we're the police," Marston said, his tone suddenly kind and warm. "The man's going to give you to us now, and we're going to take you back to your family, okay?"

"Is that—" Mikey started to ask, but Charlie cut him off.

"Shut up!" he cried again.

"Charlie..." Nina began in a tone of warning, motioning for Marston to inch the boat forward. "Don't do anything you might regret. We've already been through that a few times in the past couple of days, and it hasn't worked out so well for you so far, has it?"

They rounded the corner to reveal the edge of the cave with the flashlight beam. Charlie and Mikey had managed to park their boat in a relatively dry area against the back of the cave, away from the open water. It looked like they'd been holed up there for a while, and the whole area stunk of sweat, stale food, and fear.

Mikey sat huddled in the left-hand corner of the cave with his legs scrunched up against his chest, his arms wrapped around his knees, and a blanket covering most of the rest of him. He was dirty and trembling but otherwise looked no worse for wear, with the same clothes on that he had been wearing when he was taken.

Charlie, on the other hand, looked like he was about to combust. His eyebrows were all patchy like he'd been picking at him, and his pock-marked cheeks looked even more hallowed now than they had on the security video. He was wearing that brown jacket that had become his main identifier, and he was almost entirely covered in mud from head to toe. Nina surmised that he'd probably taken a tumble somewhere in the shallow water. He was hunched up in the opposite corner of the cave from Mikey, which meant that he was closer to the agents and their boat than the boy was.

Charlie stared at Nina as if he was trying to figure out a way out of this one and kept coming up empty.

"Come on, Charlie, don't do anything rash—" Marston started to say, just as Charlie reached into his jacket pocket and pulled out a gun.

Nina had to stop herself from groaning.

"Come on, man, we've already killed Rudy, and Justin's told us everything," she told him. "Then your gang got very mad and took him off to God knows where. We'll get him back, though, hopefully in one piece. All this goes to say that we're probably the closest thing to friends you've got left in this world."

"Look, your gang's going down, with or without you," Marston added. "Well, most likely without you, considering that they're prepared to dump you just like they did the others. Do you really think they'll protect you after this? And we'll need a witness of our own against them, so we can help each other out. Just give us the boy."

Charlie was still hesitant, his hands trembling around the gun. Nina and Marston both had their own weapons pointed right back at him.

"You did well not hurting him, and planning to bring him home," Nina continued. "But you can't have really thought you could make it to Atlanta without being arrested? This is all working out the best it could've for you. You just have to go with it."

Charlie's eyes darted around the cave. Though Marston had dropped his flashlight beam to the side so he could hold his gun with both hands, there was a dim light from a lamp on the stolen boat that illuminated the back of the cave. Dim enough so that the agents hadn't been able to see it before, but bright enough that Nina was now able to make out most of what was happening in the cave without squinting now that she was in full view of the light.

Mikey was looking back and forth between his captor and the agents with wide, darting eyes, his knees trembling beneath the blanket.

"Mikey, why don't you come over here with me?" Nina offered, holding out an arm for the boy.

"Don't do that!" Charlie hollered, holding out his own arm to stop the kid.

This wasn't going to happen the easy way, then.

Charlie took a step toward the agents, brandishing his weapon, and Marston quickly jumped down from the boat and moved between him and Mikey.

Nina, for her part, rushed for the boy, holding out her arm to him still while keeping a close eye on what was going on in the other corner of the cave.

A shot rang out, and she dropped down into the shallow water, motioning for Mikey, who remained huddled in the corner, to do the same.

"Get down, Mikey, get down," she urged him, and he hesitantly looked up at Charlie and Marston and then ducked his head down between his knees.

More shots rang out, and Nina looked up to see Charlie falling into the water, blood pooling around him. Marston had shot him in the leg. She internally thanked him not for going for a fatal shot from the outset. If they didn't find Justin, it was true that they would need Charlie to testify. They hadn't been lying about that.

Nina watched with horror as Charlie tried one last-ditch attempt to cripple Marston with another errant shot, but it ended up hitting the stolen boat instead, right in the dent on the back left bumper that old Mr. Samuels had gone to such great pains to describe. Poor old Lucy. She'd been through a lot. Nina couldn't even begin to understand all these guys' obsessions with these boats, but she knew enough to gather that old Dan would not be happy about the state in which Lucy returned to him.

Mikey ran to Nina after Charlie was shot, and he wrapped his little arms around her waist and buried his face in her side as she rose from the water, covered in mud and dripping wet, with more than a few pebbles from the bottom of the water stuck in her shoes.

She looked over at Marston again. He was handcuffing Charlie, having confiscated the gangbanger's gun.

It was all over. They'd found him.

"Everything's going to be okay," Nina whispered to Mikey, and it felt like the weight of the world had been lifted off her shoulders.

28

ETHAN

We were able to send up a flare from the Coast Guard boat at the mouth of the cave since our cell reception was still bad, and two helicopters soon arrived. One to take Nina, myself, and Mikey back to the police station, and the other to transport Charlie to the hospital for treatment.

There was a group of armed officers set to go with him, too. We weren't taking any more risks with our suspects, not when we needed testimony to take the bigger guns down.

When we were flying in the helicopter, Mikey stuck close to Nina while we asked him some questions.

"Mikey, my name is Ethan," I told him, ducking down so that I was eye level with him and holding out my hand to take his if he would let me. He did.

"Mikey," he muttered, looking at me with the same wide, scared eyes he'd had since I first saw him.

"I know," I said, giving him a warm smile. "I know your parents."

"You do?" he asked, his eyes growing wider now, though not with fear this time, but with hope.

"Oh yes," I said, making sure I looked very serious. "They miss you very, very much. They've been looking for you this whole time, and my friend Nina and I have been helping them. So have the police."

I glanced up at Nina, and she nodded down at the boy to confirm. She still had her arms around him. She looked awkward but pleased with the way this had turned out.

"So, Mikey, can we ask you some questions about what happened to you?" Nina asked him, and he craned his neck to look up at her and nodded.

Though there were tear streaks on his muddy face, he hadn't cried once since I'd first seen him. I wasn't sure if he was in shock, or if he was all cried out, or if he was just brave. Probably a combination of the three.

"Alright, Mikey, thank you," I said, flashing him another smile. "Why don't you tell us everything you remember since your parents took you to the mall yesterday."

"Well, I looked at the gum balls..." Mikey started to say, his lip starting to tremble. "And then that man took me. He never told me his name, so I just called him Mister. I didn't want to be rude."

"I'm sure you weren't rude," I said, glancing up at Nina and stifling a laugh at the notion that Mikey wouldn't want to be rude to the man who had just abducted him at gunpoint.

"What happened next, Mikey?" Nina asked. "Were there any other men?"

"Well, they took me through the game store, the two who were in the mall, and then there was a third one outside," Mikey said, his story immediately lining up with Justin's. "Then the men were fighting a lot. I didn't really understand what they were talking about. I think it might've been about me."

The boy almost pouted at this revelation.

"Mikey, I want you to know that none of this was your fault," I told him, squeezing his little hand in my much larger one. "None of it at all. Those men, they did a very bad thing taking you from your parents, and they're going to pay a high price for that if they haven't already. We've already caught the other two men, so none of them are ever going to hurt you again, I promise."

I didn't bother to tell him that one of the men was already dead, and the other might be at the hands of other goons. I figured that might be a little much for him to handle right now.

"Okay," the little boy sniffled, though he still didn't cry.

"Alright, Mikey, what happened next?" Nina asked, giving him a gentle squeeze.

"Well, then there was the boat," Mikey said, taking a deep breath as he moved on to the next part of his story, the one we didn't know much about yet. "I don't know where it came from. They argued about it some more, and then the other two went away. I don't know where they went."

"That's alright, we found them," I reminded him. "And then we found you. What happened when you went out on the water?"

"Well, we went way far out at first, but then Mister got really upset, and the boat started making funny sounds," Mikey said, his lip starting to tremble again. "It was really late, and I couldn't see any land anymore. He said something about going to another country. I didn't want to go to another country. I wanted to go home."

"I know, Mikey, and you aren't going anywhere other than home," I promised him, squeezing his hand again. "What happened after the boat started making the funny noises?"

"Well, then Mister started looking through some stuff on the boat, and that's when he found the food. I was glad about that because I hadn't eaten all day.

Mom said that we couldn't have breakfast until after we got my new swimsuit at the mall, and, well..."

Mikey looked like he understandably might actually cry now at the mention of his mother, and Nina smiled down at him.

"Don't worry, you're going to see your mom really soon," she assured him. "We're going to see her right now, actually. And your dad."

We exchanged a look, knowing that Mikey actually had two dads, but he didn't know that yet. Whatever happened next, or however they chose to tell him, there was no doubt that cat was coming out of the bag very soon if it hadn't already. Even so, it wasn't our place to break that particular news to the boy. The parents were going to have to figure out how to do that themselves, maybe with some help from Dr. Osborne.

"Promise?" Mikey asked, staring back up at her.

"Promise," she said, breaking into a smile and giving him another squeeze around the shoulders.

"So what happened when the man you were with realized there was something wrong with the boat?" I asked the boy.

"Well, he got really angry, and he started stomping around, and I was scared we were going to fall off 'cause the boat was shaking so much," Mikey explained, his eyes wide with fear again at the unpleasant memory.

"Did he ever hurt you?" Nina asked, furrowing her

brow together in concern as she asked the question. "Did he ever touch you at all or make you uncomfortable?"

"No, I don't think so," Mikey said, shaking his head. "He grabbed my shoulder once when he was mad, and the boat was making all those noises. For a minute, I thought he was going to hit me, but he didn't."

Nina and I exchanged a look as relief no doubt washed through us both. If the worst Charlie had done to Mikey was grab his shoulder a little too hard once, I would take that as a big win.

"He gave you something to eat, then?" Nina asked. "I remember you saying in the cave that you were hungry."

"And thirsty," Mikey said, nodding knowingly. "There was some food and water in those weird packets on the boat, and he let me have some of them when we stopped in a cave after the boat stopped making those noises. I wanted more, though, but he wouldn't let me. He ate one and then gave me two, and we shared a water bottle, but he said he didn't want to run out of food in case we were out there for a while. But then you came!"

Mikey smiled at both of us brightly, and another wave of relief crashed over me. Charlie had tried to take care of the kid, at least, even giving him more food than he ate himself. Mikey would surely be traumatized by this experience, but it could've been so, so much worse, even with finding him.

"That's good, Mikey, really good," I told the boy. "And we'll get you some food very soon. We just have to get you back to your parents first."

"I'd like that, thanks," Mikey said, and Nina and I both laughed.

"Did the man ever say anything to you?" Nina asked. "Anything at all that you can remember?"

"We didn't talk much," Mikey said thoughtfully, scrunching up his face as if he was trying to remember. "Whenever I asked any questions, he just told me to shut up. He talked to himself sometimes, though. He kept saying how much trouble he was in or something about that. Is he in trouble?"

"Oh, he's in a lot of trouble," I chuckled. "People aren't supposed to take kids from their parents, and you're not even the only one he's taken. But don't worry, we'll take care of him. We'll make sure that he doesn't hurt any more kids ever again, okay?"

"Okay," Mikey said, almost cheerily, and a paramedic came over to look him over for bumps and bruises, abruptly ending our conversation.

We'd have time for a longer interview later, but for now, Nina and I were satisfied that Mikey would pull through this with a little help from his family and Dr. Osborne.

"Well, that could've gone so much worse in so

many ways," Nina muttered to me as we stepped off to the side to make room for the paramedic. She couldn't keep the smile off of her face, and I was pretty sure that I was the same.

"You could say that again," I chuckled as I watched Mikey cheerfully interact with the paramedic. "Kid's gonna crash soon. He probably hasn't slept in two days. But for now, I'd say things are going way better than I could've expected."

"Hey, you were right not to give up on him," Nina said, nudging me playfully in the ribs.

"Told you he was still out there," I grinned.

"I've never been happier to say you were right," Nina beamed.

The helicopter ended up depositing us in the parking lot of the hotel where we were staying, and where the police officers, Dr. Osborne, and all three of Mikey's parents had evacuated when the police station was attacked. There was a throng of people waiting there for us, even though it was the middle of the night at that point.

The lead detective on the case was the first to get to me, and I gave him a quick rundown of everything that had happened while I watched the relief that I was already feeling wash across his face. Chief Raskin was next, closely followed by the older Coast Guard man I had spoken with earlier, and then the Durham police detective, Lance, who had been so against wasting resources trying to find Mikey since he was probably already dead.

"Uh, good job, agent," he said, holding out a begrudging hand to me.

I took it. Why not?

"Never give up on a case," I warned him. "You never know what might happen."

"Understood, sir," he said, giving me a small smile that might've even reached his eyes.

Dr. Osborne was next, closely followed by Curt and Annabelle, who rushed Nina and Mikey the instant they saw them.

"Oh my God!" Annabelle screamed, clutching her son close to her chest. "You found him! I can't believe you found him."

Mikey buried his face in his mother's stomach as both parents wrapped their arms around him. He didn't say anything. He just let them encase him and tell him he was safe now. His little shoulders were shaking.

Curt shakily reached out to give both myself and Nina a hug, despite the fact that we were covered in gunk and water from the cave, not to mention Charlie's blood.

"Thank you," he said, his voice trembling. "Thank you so much. You have no idea what you've done for us. We'll never forget it."

"We were just doing our job," I told him, shaking

his hand. "And make sure you never forget how lucky you all got today. Most people don't get a mulligan like that."

"We won't," Curt assured me, swallowing hard. "We promise."

I noticed soon that Jackson wasn't out there in the parking lot with us. Quickly, Mikey was cleared by the paramedics to go, and we all went inside to discuss what had happened some more. Jackson was there, practically hiding behind a plant in the hotel lobby and trying to blend in with the mass of policemen and other law enforcement personnel occupying the area.

When he caught sight of Mikey, his relief was unmistakable, though he still didn't approach us as I sat down with Curt, Annabelle, Dr. Osborne, and Mikey to catch them up on the night's events. Nina went off to talk with someone in an FBI jacket who I imagined was her supervisor.

Mikey fell asleep on Annabelle's shoulder almost the second he sat down. She held him tightly to her as if she was afraid he might disappear if she let him go for a single second.

"Alright, catch me up," Dr. Osborne said quickly, glancing over at Mikey with some wariness. "Should you and I step outside?"

I realized that Osborne and the parents didn't know yet what had happened to the boy while he was held captive, so I quickly caught them up, assuring them that he was a bit dirty, tired, and hungry, but otherwise unharmed. Their relief was palpable.

"Thank God," Curt sighed, his whole body practically deflating as he released the tension he'd been holding for so long.

"I'll be," Dr. Osborne said, shaking her head in disbelief. "I never would've guessed this ending, I'll tell you that much."

"I know," I said darkly. "I don't know that I would've either, but I couldn't be happier with the way things went. Now everyone can focus on finding those other kids and taking down the whole gang. This shouldn't happen to any other kid again. Not here, anyway. Not this way."

"We couldn't be more grateful," Annabelle gushed, looking at me with almost pleading eyes. "Anything we can do, just name it."

"No, ma'am, I was just doing my job," I assured her just as I had her husband, holding up a hand to indicate as much. Then, despite myself, I glanced over at Jackson still lurking behind that plant, watching us intently.

Annabelle followed my gaze, and surprisingly, her face softened.

"Come here, Jackson," she called out, waving him over. "Come sit with us."

Mikey didn't move, snoring gently on his mother's shoulder as he got some well-needed rest, but the gesture was what counted. Annabelle was welcoming Jackson into their family, in a way. It probably wouldn't be smooth sailing, but at least it was a start.

Tentatively, Jackson meandered over to us and leaned against the side of the couch that Dr. Osborne and I were sitting on across from Curt, Annabelle, and Mikey. It seemed as if Jackson was afraid to get any closer to them.

"Is he okay?" he asked in a voice so soft I could barely hear it, unable to take his eyes off of Mikey.

"Yes, he's going to be just fine," Dr. Osborne said, reaching up and squeezing Jackson's hand.

We quickly gave Jackson a rundown of everything that had happened and everything that Mikey had told Nina and me about his adventure with Charlie on the water.

"So he really is okay, then?" Jackson asked when we were finished, looking more than a little surprised. "Like, he was just cold and hungry? Nothing else happened to him?"

"No, nothing else," I chuckled. "You've all got a good kid here. Don't lose him again."

"Oh, we won't," Curt assured me, squeezing Mikey's shoulder gently from the boy's other side.

"No," Annabelle said softly, burying her face in her son's wispy light brown hair. "No, we won't."

"It will take some time to get things back to

normal," Dr. Osborne told them, her characteristically stern expression returning to her after a brief reprieve. "In fact, I'd say you need to work toward a new normal, instead of looking back. Mikey got very lucky today, but he's still going to be affected by what happened. He'll probably regress a bit for a while, have some separation anxiety. That's all to be expected. School in the fall might be an ease-in kind of process this year, instead of just going back right away. The good news is that you have a couple of months of summer to prepare."

"We... we understand," Curt stammered. "Or if we don't yet, we will."

"I'll be with you every step of the way," Dr. Osborne assured them. "I'll have other cases, but I'm not far away from you in Virginia, and I'm not going to abandon Mikey. I'll see your family through this."

"Thank you so much," Curt said, looking more than relieved to hear this. "We appreciate that. We know Mikey will need more help, and this is probably just the beginning. We're just so glad to have him back."

"And we'll have other help, too," Annabelle said, smiling up at Jackson.

"I wouldn't dream of making his life more unstable right now," Jackson said quickly.

"We know," Annabelle said. "And thank you. But as they say, it takes a village."

"I, um... thank you," Jackson said, hanging his head as if he couldn't believe that this was all happening.

I glanced over at Dr. Osborne and smiled. Her eyes sparkled.

"When does your fiancée get here?" Curt asked Jackson, looking up at the other man in what I had to assume was their most friendly interaction yet.

"I... uh, she lands early this morning," he sputtered, clearly surprised by this one-eighty, though pleased.

"Well, we look forward to meeting her," Annabelle said. "And to introducing the both of you to Mikey."

Jackson looked like he might just cry for joy.

29

ETHAN

I slept for a few hours after that, though my body ached for more after such a harrowing and physically demanding case.

When I awoke and returned to the hotel lobby, I saw Jackson and a woman I didn't know talking to Mikey while Curt and Annabelle stood off to the side, watching them and drinking coffee. The boy was laughing, and so was the couple. I couldn't help but smile and think that we'd done well on this one. This just might have turned out to be my most rewarding case yet.

The lobby was still crawling with law enforcement, and the clerks standing at the desk looked more than a little uncomfortable with the situation, though they didn't say anything to that effect.

"Hey, thanks for letting us use your space," I told

them, leaning against the front desk. "We really appreciate having such a large area to meet after what happened yesterday."

"Of course," a young woman with a manager's name tag said, forcing a smile. "We're happy to help. And so glad that you found Mikey."

I glanced up at a small television hanging above the breakfast area off to the side of the lobby. Predictably, there was a reporter on there excitedly talking about how the boy had been found the night before.

As I squinted at the screen, I realized that the woman was standing outside this very hotel, making her report.

I slowly made my way toward the front doors, only to be practically assaulted with camera flashes and microphones being jabbed in my face the second I stepped outdoors.

"Are you one of the agents who found Mikey?" a reporter asked.

"Which agency are you with?" another asked. "MBLIS or the FBI?"

"Will you be working on the case to take down the human trafficking ring in Durham?" another cried, practically throwing his microphone over the mass of bodies in front of him to get to me.

I blinked, overwhelmed by this sudden exposure to the media. I was used to working more behind the scenes.

Suddenly, someone was grabbing me from behind and pulling me back into the entryway between the front doors and the lobby.

"Whoa, Marston, sorry. Someone should've briefed you," Nina said, and I turned around to see her standing there, grinning at me.

"It's alright," I said, blinking a few times and running a hand across my face in an attempt to recover from the onslaught.

"They must've seen your badge," she said apologetically, glancing down where it hung at my belt.

"Oh, right," I said, pulling it off and hiding it safely away in my jacket pocket, as I didn't need any more of that today. "So I'm guessing you briefed the media?"

"Yeah, Osborne did a press conference early this morning with the family, once Jackson's fiancée flew in. The whole thing was pretty melodramatic, lots of crying, but I got through it."

"You were in the press conference?" I asked, unable to hide my surprise that Nina would put herself through such a thing willingly.

"Try not to sound so surprised," she said dryly. "But yeah, someone had to brief the press on the law enforcement side of things. I told Osborne not to get used to the company, though. I won't be doing any more of those things if I can help it."

Her eyes flicked involuntarily to the TV screen I

had been looking at before, which we could see through the large glass double doors to the hotel.

Sure enough, there was Nina standing at a podium, looking more uncomfortable than I'd ever seen her. But she was there alright.

"They keep showing it," she grimaced. "I don't know why they keep showing it. Not just locally, either. It's all over the national networks, too."

"Well, it is big news," I chuckled. "And I'm sure you did just fine."

"Ugh," Nina groaned, rolling her eyes and peeling her eyes off of the screen.

"Why didn't you wake me for the conference? I would've been happy to help out," I told her, though I secretly didn't mind not having to deal with any of that mess.

"Yeah, well, I figured one of us should get some sleep, at least," Nina shrugged. "Plus, I'm going to be on this thing for a while yet, dealing with the Durham part of the case. I figure the public might as well get used to me."

"I thought you said you weren't going to be doing any more press briefings," I reminded her, shooting her a sly grin.

"Yeah, well, my supervisor might make me," she grumbled, shooting another scathing look back at the television screen. "He says they liked me or something."

I practically roared with laughter at this.

"Well, I can't say I blamed them," I chuckled, as she turned that glare of hers right on me.

Just then, I heard a familiar voice come roaring out from where the throng of reporters still stood.

"Hold up, hold up, let me through," Holm hollered at them. "Federal agent coming through! No, I will not answer any of your stupid questions."

I laughed again and opened the front door for my partner, pulling him through and into the entryway where Nina and I stood. His clothing and hair were all tousled, and he looked a little tired, but otherwise, he seemed no worse for wear.

"You're back!" I cried, patting him on the shoulder as he smoothed out his rumpled clothes. "How are you feeling?"

"Oh, I'm fine. Those doctors are always overzealous anyway," he said, waving away my concern. "All they're worried about is lawsuits."

"I don't know about that," Nina said skeptically. "You weren't looking too hot when we went to see you yesterday."

"Yeah, well, we all know that was just an excuse so you two could keep all the glory to yourselves," Holm said, winking at her. "I thought I told you not to go breaking this case without me!"

"Well, I thought it was all about finding the kid," I

pointed out, rolling my eyes, though we all knew that Holm was just messing with us.

"Yeah, but you did that already!" he cried. "Now I get to complain about it."

"Oh, okay, is that how that works?" I laughed, shaking my head at him.

"Damned straight," he said, giving me a wink this time.

"Were you actually discharged, or did you run out of there the second you saw the news?" I asked, giving him a stern look.

"Well, I can't say the news didn't speed things up a bit, but I was discharged," he relented. "I'm the proud owner of a clean bill of health! Well, with orders to follow up with someone back in Miami when we get home."

"Make sure he does that," Nina said, giving me a pointed look.

"Oh, I will," I assured her. "And so will Diane. Come on, partner, let's go get you some coffee."

I dragged Holm through the double doors to the lobby and back to the breakfast area, Nina following close behind us.

When we got to the table strewn with cereal, coffee, and pastries, however, I turned around to find that she was gone. I scanned my eyes around the clusters of people all over the lobby until I found her spiky black hair. She was talking to the man I remembered coming up to her the previous night when we got off the helicopter, who I assumed to be her supervisor. They seemed to be deep in conversation.

"Speaking of Diane, I talked to her this morning," Holm said as he filled a cup to the brim with black coffee, not seeming to notice that Nina had gone. "She said you didn't even call her to tell her you broke the case."

His tone was one of mock chastising, and I groaned as I realized that he was right. I pulled out my phone to find a couple of missed texts from Diane congratulating me for finding Mikey and asking when I thought we would be back in Miami to pick up work on the Holland case.

"I forgot," I said, running a hand across my face as I tried to remember everything that had happened the night before. It was all such a blur.

"It's alright, she's not mad," Holm said, handing me a cup of coffee of my own. "She figured you were just tired or got caught up in everything else that was going on. Man is it a relief that you guys found that kid, though. I was starting to get worried the case would go cold, or even worse."

"Yeah, me too," I admitted, grabbing a cinnamon roll from the table and sitting down across from him at a nearby table. "I'm just glad nothing major happened to him while he was gone."

"Is that so? The news was pretty vague about the

details, obviously," Holm said. "So he wasn't abused or anything?"

"No, nothing like that," I assured him, and he relaxed his shoulders as if he'd been carrying some extra tension there on the issue. "Charlie didn't so much as touch his shoulder, it doesn't sound like. The guy just kind of freaked out and then stayed on the water, and then in the caves, trying to figure out what to do next. When we found them, he was even telling Mikey that he was going to find a way to sneak him back to Atlanta without anyone knowing about it."

"That... sounds like a terrible plan," Holm said, scrunching up his face in confusion. "Did he really think he wouldn't get caught?"

"I think he knew that he would probably get caught, but that things would definitely be bad for him if he killed the kid," I sighed, shaking my head. "I think he realized pretty quickly how much of a mistake he'd made, and then he just hid out and tried to work out some scheme to get himself out of it."

"Sounds pretty weird to me," Holm said with a shrug. "The whole thing seems weird to me, but whatever."

"It was a weird case," I laughed. "We have a knack for getting those, though."

"We sure do," Holm sighed, shaking his head.

"Hey," I heard Nina's voice behind me, and I nearly jumped in surprise as I swiveled around in my seat to face her. She was standing behind me with her hands behind her back.

"Hey," I said, glancing back over at where the man she had been talking to now stood, speaking with Detective Lance from Durham. "Is that your supervisor?"

"Sure is," Nina said, giving me a sly smile and pulling out a chair to sit down next to me. Then, she set a small black telescope on the table between us, and a small, yellowed old note on a frayed half-page, guarded up in a protective seal.

"What is this?" I asked, staring down at the items and shaking my head in confusion.

"Something we found on Lafitte's ship," she said. "I just got cleared to give it to you. Read the note. We think it was from the *Dragon's Rogue* originally."

I stared at her, unable to believe my ears. Then I gingerly reached down and pulled the note up so that I could read it.

Thought you might like this, the note read, in all too familiar handwriting. A reminder of old times.

"That's... that's Grendel's handwriting," I stammered, recognizing it instantly from the journal. "This was on Lafitte's ship?"

Nina nodded.

"We don't know if the Hollands put it there or what," she said. "Maybe one of your experts can inquire about its authenticity. I'm sorry I couldn't give it to you until now. Bureaucracy has its drawbacks, as I'm sure you know. As for the ship itself, we're still not through with it, but we're going to invite you out to see it as soon as we can. I need to finish up with this case in Durham first, though."

"I... I understand," I managed, gently picking up the telescope and balancing it in my hands, then. "Nina, this is amazing, thank you."

"No, thank you," she said, grinning and meeting my eyes. "We did it, Marston. We found him."

"Yeah," I said, unable to stop a smile from spreading across my own face then. "Yeah, we did it."

EPILOGUE

"Wow," Charlie breathed when I was finished, for once not complaining that I had ended my tale too soon. "For a minute there, I actually thought you might not find that kid."

"Yeah, me too," I admitted, wincing at the memory as I finished off my third and final drink for the night. "I'd never been more glad to be wrong."

The alcohol settled in my stomach, warming me up. I'd needed a fair amount to get through that story. Just the memory of the race against the clock to find Mikey tied my stomach into knots.

"Man, that's always a nail biter," Mike said, letting out a low whistle. "Couldn't have turned out better, though."

"No. No, it couldn't," I agreed with a chuckle. "We got very, very lucky that night, and so did Mikey."

"Well, what happened next?" Ty asked, characteristically jumping straight to the next thing without taking a moment to enjoy what we'd just finished. "Was Mikey okay? Did his parents start getting along better?"

"Oh, yeah, things turned out alright for them," I assured my audience. "Last I heard, he goes to see Jackson and his stepmom on summers and alternating holidays. The parents didn't even have to litigate after all was said and done. They were just all glad to have their son back safe and sound."

"How was he psychologically, though?" Mac asked, getting at the heart of the issue as she was apt to do. "That's a lot to go through for a little kid, even if he wasn't abused."

"Good question," I said, nodding to her. "Last I heard, he still sees Dr. Osborne sometimes, but he's an otherwise well-adjusted kid. He just has a great story to tell, is all."

Mac nodded thoughtfully, seeming satisfied with this answer.

"Did Mr. Samuels get his boat back?" Jeff asked, grinning at the memory of the old man.

"Oh, yes," I chuckled. "I returned it to him the next day. He was a little chagrined at the damage, but he mainly seemed excited that one of his boats had been through such an exciting adventure. He said it was just proof that Lucy was the best boat he ever had! The nephew just rolled his eyes."

Everyone laughed at this, and I mean everyone. The other customers were all gone by then, and every bar girl was now standing around the booth, listening to the end of my story. I think they'd been there since around when Nina and I figured out that Justin was missing at the station.

"What about Justin?" Charlie asked. "Did you ever find him?"

"Oh, yeah. Holm and I weren't on that part of the case, but Nina and the detectives from Durham found him the night after we found Mikey. The gangbangers had intended to kill him but wanted to know what he'd told us first, and he was smart enough to figure that out and hold out long enough for the police to find him. He was pretty beat up, but he lived."

"And the rest of the gang?" Jeff asked eagerly.

"Well, that took longer, but eventually, everything fell into place," I sighed. "They even managed to rescue some more kids. Not all of them, but I suppose we couldn't get that lucky. Anyway, no kids have been taken in the area since, as far as I know."

"And Holm was okay, too?" Ty asked. I noted that he knew better than to ask where Holm was now, though I could tell that he wanted to know.

"Yeah, he was alright," I said, waving away the kid's concern. "He'd lost a fair amount of blood, but he was okay. I made him follow up with that doctor in Miami, and the guy said he was fine. He had some kind of condition that made him need the extra blood transfusion. I don't remember what they called it. Anyway, everything turned out alright in the end. This is one of my more harrowing stories, but it's also more uplifting than a lot of the other ones, I think."

"You guys did get pretty lucky with this one, didn't you?" Mike remarked, winking at me as he finished off the last of his beer, and Rhoda quickly moved to clear up all our empty glasses.

"Sounds like they get pretty lucky most of the time," she remarked as she took my whiskey glass from me.

"You could say that," I chuckled. "It always drove the other agents nuts. Anyway, we didn't really feel lucky while we were in the thick of it. It was a really tough case. But in the end, yeah, we were on cloud nine."

"What about that telescope, though?" Charlie asked, his eyes drifting up to where it hung above us on the wall. "Did it really come from the *Dragon's Rogue*?"

"Now, you don't think I'm going to answer that tonight, now, do you?" I asked, winking at him in my own turn.

"Come on, it had to have come from the *Dragon's*

Rogue," Ty complained. "It was Grendel's handwriting, wasn't it?"

"Yeah, but remember, the Hollands forged the fake journal," Mac pointed out. "They could've forged the note, too, right?"

Ty opened his mouth as if to argue the point but didn't seem able to find any retort.

"My, you do have them wrapped around your finger, don't you?" Mike asked, raising his eyebrows at me.

"I suppose," I said coolly. "Though I won't be saying any more tonight. *That* will have to be for next time."

As I spoke, I nodded in the direction of an ornate piece of metal hanging on the wall above the telescope. Everyone stared at it, but they knew better than to ask what it was.

I wasn't going to tell them. Not yet, anyway.

AUTHOR'S NOTE

Hey, if you got here, I just want you to know that you're awesome! I wrote this book just for someone like you, and if you want another one, it is super important that you leave a review.

The more reviews this book gets, the more likely it is there will be a sequel to it. After all, I'm only human, and you have no idea how far a simple "your book was great!" goes to brighten my day.

Also, if you want to know when the sequel comes out, you absolutely must join my Facebook group and follow me on Amazon. Doing one won't be enough because it relies on either Facebook or Amazon telling you the book is out, and they might not do it.

You might miss out on all my books forever, if you only do one!

Here's the link to follow me through e-mail.

Here's the link to my Facebook Group.

Made in the USA
Columbia, SC
24 February 2025